PENGUIN CL

## A DEAD MAN'S M

MIKHAIL AFANASIEVICH BULGAKOV was born in Kiev in May 1891. He studied and briefly practised medicine and, after indigent wanderings through revolutionary Russia and the Caucasus, he settled in Moscow in 1921. His sympathetic portrayal of White characters in his stories, in the plays *The Days of the Turbins (The White Guard)*, which enjoyed great success at the Moscow Art Theatre in 1926, and *Flight* (1927), and his satirical treatment of the officials of the New Economic Plan, led to growing criticism, which became violent after the play *The Purple Island*. His later works treat the subject of the artist and the tyrant under the guise of historical characters, with plays such as *Molière*, staged in 1936, *Don Quixote*, staged in 1940, and *Pushkin*, staged in 1943. He also wrote a brilliant biography, highly original in form, of his literary hero, Molière, but *The Master and Margarita*, a fantasy novel about the devil and his henchmen set in modern Moscow, is generally considered his masterpiece. Fame, at home and abroad, was not to come until a quarter of a century after his death at Moscow in 1940.

Originally from Hull in Yorkshire, ANDREW BROMFIELD studied Russian at Beverley Grammar School and then took a degree in Russian studies at Sussex University. After teaching Russian for several years in Ireland, he was variously resident in Glasgow (postgraduate studies), Soviet Armenia (teaching English), Cyprus (editing) and Moscow (translating and interpreting). His work as co-editor of the first editions of *Glas*, a journal of Russian literature, led into a career as a full-time literary translator. He has translated essays, stories and novels by numerous modern Russian authors, including Vladimir Voinovich, Victor Yerofeyev, Leonid Latynin, Dmitry Bakin and Mikhail Kononov, but is best known for his translations of the works of Victor Pelevin and Boris Akunin.

KEITH GESSEN lives in New York. He is a founding editor of the literary and political magazine *n+1* and the author of *All the Sad Young Literary Men* (forthcoming).

MIKHAIL BULGAKOV

# A Dead Man's Memoir
## *A Theatrical Novel*

*Translated and edited with notes by*
ANDREW BROMFIELD
*with an Introduction by* KEITH GESSEN

PENGUIN BOOKS

PENGUIN CLASSICS

Published by the Penguin Group
Penguin Books Ltd, 80 Strand, London WC2R ORL, England
Penguin Group (USA) Inc., 375 Hudson Street, New York, New York 10014, USA
Penguin Group (Canada), 90 Eglinton Avenue East, Suite 700, Toronto, Ontario, Canada M4P 2Y3
(a division of Pearson Penguin Canada Inc.)
Penguin Ireland, 25 St Stephen's Green, Dublin 2, Ireland
(a division of Penguin Books Ltd)
Penguin Group (Australia), 250 Camberwell Road, Camberwell, Victoria 3124, Australia
(a division of Pearson Australia Group Pty Ltd)
Penguin Books India Pvt Ltd, 11 Community Centre, Panchsheel Park, New Delhi – 110 017, India
Penguin Group (NZ), 67 Apollo Drive, Rosedale, North Shore 0632, New Zealand
(a division of Pearson New Zealand Ltd)
Penguin Books (South Africa) (Pty) Ltd, 24 Sturdee Avenue, Rosebank, Johannesburg 2196, South Africa

Penguin Books Ltd, Registered Offices: 80 Strand, London WC2R ORL, England

www.penguin.com

First published as *A Theatrical Novel* in Russia in 1965,
in volume 8 of the journal *Novy mir*
Published in Penguin Classics 2007

020

Translation, notes and editorial matter copyright © Andrew Bromfield, 2007
Introduction copyright © Keith Gessen, 2007
All rights reserved

The moral right of the translator has been asserted

Set in 10.25/12.25 pt PostScript Adobe Sabon
Typeset by Rowland Phototypesetting Ltd, Bury St Edmunds, Suffolk
Printed in England by Clays Ltd, Elcograf S.p.A.

ISBN: 978-0-140-45514-4

www.greenpenguin.co.uk

Penguin Books is committed to a sustainable
future for our business, our readers and our planet.
This book is made from Forest Stewardship
Council™ certified paper.

# Contents

# Chronology

1871–8 Russo-Turkish war.

1881 Alexander II assassinated. Alexander III ascends the throne.

1891 Mikhail Afanasievich Bulgakov born on 15 May to the family of a professor at the Kiev Theological Academy.

1894 Nicholas II ascends the throne.

1898 The Moscow Art Theatre stages Chekhov's *Seagull*. First Congress of the Russian Social-Democratic Party (RSDP).

1901 The Moscow Art Theatre stages Chekhov's *Three Sisters*.

1903 At its Second Congress, the RSDP splits into Bolsheviks and Mensheviks.

1904–5 Russo-Japanese War.

1905 The 1905 Revolution.

1906 The first Duma (Russian Parliament).
   April: Russia's first Constitution enacted.

1907 Bulgakov's family moves to 13 Andreevsky Spusk, which later inspires the setting for his novel *The White Guard* and his play *The Days of the Turbins*.

1909 Bulgakov graduates from the First Alexandrov Gymnasium (i.e. grammar school) and begins his medical studies at Kiev University.

1910 Leo Tolstoy dies.

1913 Bulgakov marries Tatyana Nikolaevna Lappa.

1914 The First World War begins. St Petersburg renamed Petrograd. Bulgakov and his wife work in front-line hospitals.

1916 Bulgakov graduates from the university and works in rural hospitals in Nikolsk and Vyazma in Smolensk Province.

1917 Bulgakov starts writing *A Country Doctor's Notebook*, based on his own experience.

The February Revolution (23 February–8 March). The State Duma is convened in Petrograd.

March: Nicholas II abdicates the throne in favour of Grand Prince Mikhail. Mikhail transfers power to the Provisional Government. Lenin returns from abroad.

June: The election of the Constituent Assembly is set for September.

August: The election is postponed to November.

25 October–7 November: The October Revolution.

December: The Constituent Assembly elections begin. The Cheka (Soviet secret police) is established.

1918 Bulgakov returns to Kiev and establishes his own private medical practice.

January: The Constituent Assembly is dissolved.

March: The Treaty of Brest-Litovsk is signed with Germany.

April: The British land at Murmansk, heralding numerous other attempts at foreign intervention in Russia.

June: Russian industry is nationalized.

November: The First World War ends. Russia repudiates the Treaty of Brest-Litovsk.

1919 Bulgakov moves to Vladikavkaz, where he gives up medicine and devotes himself to journalism and literature.

March: The Comintern is founded. Admiral Kolchak launches his campaign against the Bolsheviks.

October: Allied forces withdraw from Murmansk and Archangel.

1920 March: The Allied blockade is lifted.

November: The civil war ends in Russia.

1921 The Bulgakovs move to Moscow, where they live for several years in the apartment which is the model for the 'evil apartment' in *The Master and Margarita*.

March: The New Economic Policy (NEP) is introduced to replace the rigours of 'War Communism'.

1922 February: The Cheka is replaced by the OGPU.

April: Stalin becomes Secretary General of the Communist Party.

1923 Bulgakov works on the novel *The White Guard* and stories for the cycle *The Diaboliad*.

December: The Treaty of the Creation of the Union of Soviet Socialist Republics is signed.

**1924** Bulgakov is divorced from Tatyana Lappa and marries Lyubov Belozerskaya. He writes the story *The Fatal Eggs*.

January: Lenin dies. The Constitution of the USSR is ratified.

The USSR gains wide international recognition.

**1925** Several chapters from *The White Guard* are published. Bulgakov works on his story *A Dog's Heart* and the plays *The Days of the Turbins* and *Zoyka's Apartment*.

**1926** *The Days of the Turbins* premieres at Stanislavsky and Nemirovich-Danchenko's Moscow Art Theatre and *Zoyka's Apartment* at the Vakhtangov Theatre. Following a search at the Bulgakovs' apartment, the manuscript of *A Dog's Heart* is confiscated.

**1927** The Fifteenth Communist Party Congress is held. Stalin assumes control of the Party.

**1928** Bulgakov's plays *Flight, The Days of the Turbins* and *Zoyka's Apartment* are all banned from performance.

The First Five-Year Plan is adopted.

**1929** Bulgakov starts work on his *Theatrical Novel (A Dead Man's Memoir)* and the play *Molière*. The production of *The Days of the Turbins* at the Moscow Art Theatre is closed down. He meets Elena Shilovskaya, later to be his third wife, the prototype for Margarita in *The Master and Margarita*.

**1930** Bulgakov receives a phone call from Stalin, always an admirer of his talent. Stalin apparently helped him obtain a position with the Moscow Art Theatre. Bulgakov works on a stage adaptation of Gogol's novel *Dead Souls* for the theatre.

The drive for the collectivization of agriculture and industrialization is launched.

**1932** Bulgakov's play *The Days of the Turbins* is revived at the Moscow Art Theatre. Bulgakov is divorced from Lyubov Belozerskaya and marries Elena Shilovskaya. He works on the novel *The Master and Margarita*.

There is famine in Ukraine.

The 'Russian Association of Proletarian Writers' is disbanded.

**1933** The USA recognizes the USSR.

**1934** The Second Five-Year Plan.

The First Congress of Russian Writers.

The Soviet Union joins the League of Nations.

**1935** Bulgakov completes his play *Alexander Pushkin*.

The Stalinist purges begin, following the assassination of Kirov.

**1936** Bulgakov's play *Molière* opens at the Moscow Art Theatre and is banned after seven performances. He leaves the Moscow Art Theatre and works as a librettist at the Bolshoi Theatre.

Gorky dies.

The new 'Stalin' constitution is promulgated.

The show trials of Zinoviev and others begin.

**1938** Bulgakov completes the manuscript of *The Master and Margarita* and his stage adaptation of *Don Quixote*.

The Third Five-Year Plan begins.

**1939** Bulgakov works on the play *Batumi* and reads the entire text of *The Master and Margarita* to friends.

The Nazi–Soviet non-aggression pact is signed.

**1940** Bulgakov dictates the final corrections to *The Master and Margarita*.

The Soviet Union attacks Poland and Finland.

Bulgakov dies of nephrosclerosis on 10 March.

**1941** On 22 June Germany invades the USSR.

# Introduction

Bulgakov began writing this, the story of his literary and theatrical career, in the summer of 1929. It was his 'year of catastrophe', as he called it. A long and brutal campaign against him by Party critics had culminated in the removal of all his plays from the Moscow stage; his prose works had stopped passing the censorship years earlier. 'Everything is banned,' he wrote to Maxim Gorky that summer, 'and I am ruined, slandered, all alone.' A theatre to which he'd sold a play, since pulled from the repertoire because of the censorship, asked for the advance back. Not long after, visitors to a leading avant-garde Moscow theatre could watch a play that included 'Bulgakov' in its 'dictionary of dead words' – alongside 'bureaucracy', 'bohemia' and 'bagels'. The literary semi-autobiography that he started that summer would eventually be called *A Dead Man's Memoir*, not only because its narrator commits suicide at the end but because its author, too, felt dead.

Bulgakov had launched his writing career comparatively late in life, after serving as a doctor in two wars – Russia lost the first to Germany and Austria in 1918, and then Bulgakov's side, the loose conglomeration of anti-Bolshevik forces known as the Whites, lost the second in 1921. Bulgakov gave up medicine and contemplated emigration – his two younger brothers, who had fought for the Whites, had both left the country – but concluded, as much from literary ambition as anything else, that he must stay. He came to Moscow in the autumn of 1921. He was thirty years old.

The scion of a distinguished Kievan family, Bulgakov cut an exceedingly strange figure in the post-revolutionary capital.

Despite his poverty, his grey suit was always neatly pressed; when talking, he insisted on the old forms of address; and, most of all, he made no particular secret of his hatred for the Bolsheviks. It was not so much that the new rulers were splitting up the old estates, looting the churches or arresting their opponents: it was that they had such *bad manners*. Bulgakov was not the only one who thought so, and he wasn't the only one walking around Moscow in cufflinks – despite mass emigration, the old world of the intelligentsia had not simply disappeared overnight. (Bulgakov's friend Yuri Slyozkin, for example, who appears in these pages as Likospastov, was from a family of Russian generals; Alexei Tolstoy, who appears here as the famous writer Izmail Bondarevsky, was also known as Count Alexei Tolstoy.) But Bulgakov may have been the only writer who so openly despised the Bolsheviks in everything he wrote. Perhaps because he had come to literature already grown, he had no time to lose his illusions about it, and he maintained a profound belief – you can sense it in this *Memoir* – in the eventual triumph of literature over politics. In his diary of the early 1920s, he noted with amazement the hypocrisies the old aristocracy was subjecting itself to: one acquaintance, 'a true blue anti-Semite', was singing the praises of the Bolshevik leader Volgogradsky – like many Bolsheviks, a Jew. 'The human mind goes numb,' wrote Bulgakov. He came to the conclusion that such hypocrisy was not only impossible for art but also dangerous to the hypocrite; he thought that it might be possible simply to be a writer, and produce his work honestly, and be left alone.

Bulgakov went about his early literary career accordingly. He had arrived in Moscow at a time of hunger and he fought for his survival. 'I drew my lot and it said "death",' he later wrote of that time. 'That's when I woke up. I developed an unheard-of, monstrous energy. And I did not die.' He worked for an impoverished writers' organization, then for a private newspaper, then for *Gudok*, the surprisingly popular newspaper of the Soviet Railworkers' Union. At night, he worked on his fiction, in particular a novel about the Russian civil war that would come to be called *The White Guard*. This is the novel whose composition and strange publication history is described in *A Dead Man's Memoir*.

The novel is about a family in Kiev, the Turbins, struggling to keep its dignity and honour during the civil war in 1918. Written while the wounds from the war were still fresh, the very title was provocative to the Reds. Nonetheless, Bulgakov's friend Isai Lezhnev, the editor of a new literary journal called *Russia*, undertook to publish it, and the first two instalments appeared in early 1925. Then politics took over. Before the third part of *The White Guard* could appear, *Russia* was shut down and Lezhnev expelled from the Soviet Union (taking with him the corrected galleys of the novel's final part). Bulgakov's own apartment was raided, his manuscripts and diaries seized and he himself called in for questioning. What was worse, or almost worse, in the absence of a complete edition the novel began to be pirated. A publisher in Riga put out a book called *The White Guard*, consisting of the first parts as they appeared in Lezhnev's journal and a conclusion *which they wrote themselves*. A Parisian publisher also produced an unauthorized text.

Despite all this, the novel caught the attention of literary Moscow. In particular, it was seized upon by Konstantin Stanislavsky's famous Moscow Art Theatre. Though the Art Theatre (MKhAT, to Russians) was internationally known for its productions of Chekhov, it had not yet found its footing in the Soviet era – it was still mostly staging the classics. The theatre's literary section immediately recognized in Bulgakov's historically significant but at the same time deeply domestic novel a perfect opportunity for their entry on to the contemporary scene. As it turned out, Bulgakov had had the same idea: he was already working on a draft of a play when he was contacted by the Art Theatre.

Almost immediately there were problems. The older actors, some of whom had performed in the original Chekhov productions, could find no roles for themselves in a play where none of the main characters was older than 28. There were also political considerations: Bulgakov's play was a very sympathetic portrait of an old, relatively privileged family of the Kiev intelligentsia, at a time when it was important for the Bolsheviks to continue asserting that all supporters of the old regime were parasites, criminals and cowards. As a result of this, notwithstanding the stubbornness of the author (to the end of his life, Bulgakov would always be told that he didn't understand how things 'worked'), some compromises had to be made. The title couldn't have 'white' in it, naturally, and they settled on *The Days of the Turbins*. Some stage directions also had significant effect. At one particularly poignant moment, the Turbins, aware that their cause is lost, sit in their warm living room and sing the old Russian national anthem, *God Save the Tsar*. Stanislavsky insisted that in this scene the characters be drunk.

Despite the compromises, or even because of them, the play was a sensation when it premiered in mid 1926. The Soviet public had never seen anything like it: an artwork that depicted the terrible civil war they'd experienced without cant or cries of victory or ideological correctness. Observers reported that audiences sat rapt in their seats, with people openly weeping; there were enough cases of fainting that an ambulance came to be parked outside the Art Theatre; it was noted that during the intermission no one ever left the hall.

The play might have signalled the beginning of a cultural and even ideological reconciliation, a new openness in Soviet life. But it was too early for that, and anyway, as the narrator Maksudov says here about something else, 'You have to be joking!' (p. 13). *The Days of the Turbins* became the flashpoint for an ideological battle between, on one hand, the still rabid revolutionary critics who saw it as an apologia for the old aristocracy and, on the other hand, strangely enough, Josef Stalin. Stalin simply liked the play, and the ideological wars then being fought within the intelligentsia were alien to him. (Lenin had once wanted to close down the Bolshoi Theatre; Stalin merely thought the music of Shostakovich's *Fifth Symphony* hard to follow.) In 1926, in any case, Stalin was on Bulgakov's side, but he was not yet all-powerful; the cultural press was not at his beck and call, and article after article railed against the White apologist Bulgakov. Eventually, it became too much; when Bulgakov's new play, *Flight*, about the emigration of one of the brothers Turbin, reached Stalin in 1929, he admitted it was anti-Soviet. *Flight* was rejected, and *The Days of the Turbins* pulled from the stage.

The year 1929 became a turning point for Bulgakov's subject matter. He had previously written short sketches about the literary life, as a point of general interest, while his main theme was the impingement of politics – in the forms of armies, of course, but also as a mode of thought – on the experience of daily and domestic life. In 1929, however, his main productions were the autobiographical fragment which later became *A Dead Man's Memoir*; a series of increasingly desperate letters to the government about his situation, asking that they let him emigrate; and an extremely angry play, called *The Cabal of Hypocrites*, about a playwright of genius from the distant past (Molière) who was hounded to his death by his critics. From this point on, Bulgakov took the situation of the writer as *the* paradigmatic situation of the individual in Soviet society, and nearly everything he wrote focused on this theme. The year before, he had produced an early draft of *The Master and Margarita* – except that wasn't yet its name because the figure of the Master, the saintly artist hounded into an insane asylum by his critics, was absent. The other absent figure, actually, was Margarita, the Master's true love: she came into being after Bulgakov met Elena Shilovskaya, also in 1929. It was to her that he addressed the autobiographical fragment, which at the time he called 'To a Secret Friend'.

The next spring, a strange miracle occurred: the day after the poet Mayakovsky, author of the 'dictionary of dead words', committed suicide, Bulgakov received a telephone call from Stalin. His letter pleading for some relief from his situation had been received, Stalin told him. 'The comrades and I read it,' he said. Bulgakov had asked that he be allowed, if he could not emigrate, to work in some capacity at the Art Theatre, and Stalin suggested that this would now be possible. Bulgakov said that he would like to meet Stalin and discuss some of these important matters, and Stalin said, 'Of course, of course, we will.'

Bulgakov was never granted an audience with Stalin, though the dictator would continue to display a keen and oddly friendly interest in his favourite anti-Bolshevik writer. Bulgakov did, however, immediately go to work at the Art Theatre as a writer-in-residence, and his new status as the recipient of a Stalin phone call meant that his plays could once again be staged. *The Cabal of Hypocrites* went into rehearsals under the title *Molière*; other projects were discussed; eventually, even *The Days of the Turbins* was ordered back on to the Art Theatre repertoire.

The trouble was Bulgakov would not change. The better and more clearly he wrote, the more every line contained a critique, only slightly veiled, of the existing order. *Molière* went through endless rehearsals and rewrites as Stanislavky tried, in vain, to purge it of its obvious references to the contemporary political situation. In the meantime, Bulgakov wrote yet another play about an artist hounded to death by his critics. *Pushkin*, with its many scenes about the Tsar's secret police and its spies, was an even more pointed attack on the Soviet regime, which had retained almost all the old trappings of Russian tyranny and then added some touches of its own. *Pushkin* did not pass the censorship; *Molière*, incredibly, after years of mind-numbing rehearsals, did pass – and ran for fewer than ten performances in 1936. It seems Bulgakov thought that Stalin's protection was actually an endorsement of his art; in fact it was only an acknowledgement of his talent, and a desire for that talent to be persuaded, somehow or other, to serve the state. Upon the appearance of *Molière* in 1936, Party critics, in their published reviews and also, as we now know, in their reports to the Politburo, clearly and quite accurately explained that it was an anti-Soviet play. It was pulled and, just as in 1929, the rest of Bulgakov's projects followed. (*The Days of the Turbins* was excepted from this by a kind of inertia, or double jeopardy, and would continue to play at the Art Theatre for years to come.) Bulgakov was again in a hopeless situation, and, furious this time too at what he experienced as the Art Theatre's betrayal, he sat down to record the story of his literary and theatrical career. Between November 1936 and September 1937, Bulgakov turned 'To a Secret Friend' into what is now *A Dead Man's Memoir (A Theatrical Novel)* and read it privately, at home, to his friends.

*

The book telescopes the events of a decade into a period of a year and mixes together elements from the actual production of *The Days of the Turbins* and *Molière*. But though it distorts time, it remains a classic *roman-à-clef*, faithful to the characters' prototypes even in their smallest details, and the people who heard Bulgakov read would instantly recognize their friends in the book – and, for the most part, laugh. (The exception was the caricature of the ageing Stanislavsky, which some deemed too much.) What is far more interesting now is Bulgakov's transformation of the materials of his writing life at the two points of his career when he believed he was absolutely finished as a writer – how unexpectedly *gentle* the satire of the people who finished him really is. The distinguishing feature of the *Memoir* as a *roman-à-clef* is Bulgakov's ability to personalize a series of events that in retrospect (even to him, in 1936–7) would seem to have been dictated by large and intractable political considerations.

Because how does oppression work? You can't, in the end, arrest everyone – there would be no one left to write plays, or put them on, or, for that matter, to attend them. The truth is that the authorities need only drop some hints, and some part of the population will always be found to take the hint and put it into action. Isai Lezhnev's magazine was shut down by the secret police in 1925 – and in 1933, Lezhnev recanted, returned to Russia and became a Party-line critic for, among other publications, *Pravda*. *The Days of the Turbins*, for which in 1926 Stanislavsky was ready to risk his entire theatre, was pulled from the stage because of Stalin's reaction to *Flight* – no divisions of the secret police were obliged to march three blocks to the Art Theatre from the basement of Lubyanka. In 1936, *Molière* was cancelled because it had been declared anti-Soviet – and the Art Theatre didn't need to be asked twice. None of this appears in *A Dead Man's Memoir*. Instead we see only frailty and vanity and thwarted ambition, for *these* are always and everywhere the true levers of power. Lezhnev, in the character of Rudolfi, appears as a miracle-worker who has, perhaps, had some dealings with Satan in order to keep his magazine afloat. Stanislavsky, in the character of Ivan Vasilievich, is a director of genius who has grown ridiculous through the ministrations of his sycophants. Everything is personal, and nothing in the novel depends on a specific political system to make it work.

In real life, the publication misadventures of *The White Guard* were extremely painful for Bulgakov – it was his first major work and in many ways his most personal (you can sense his attachment to it in his description herein of the novel *Black Snow*), and its fate in the world was worse than farcical. At Lezhnev's urging, Bulgakov had signed a separate contract for the novel's publication with a publisher named Zakhar Kagansky. This was a mistake. Kagansky soon left the country, and in the wake of Bulgakov's success with *Turbins* he used the ill-conceived contract to claim that he was Bulgakov's legal representative in Europe – and for the next fifteen years consistently managed to steal or extort Bulgakov's royalties from theatres and publishers. Fully one-third of Bulgakov's surviving letters are pleas to his brother in Paris to defend his work against Kagansky (Bulgakov himself was never allowed out of the country). Other letters are addressed to the editors of émigré papers, asking them to announce that Kagansky was misleading the public; others still are addressed to the German publisher Fischer-Verlag, asking for protection from Kagansky. The devil in *The Master and Margarita* is usually thought to be Stalin, but the figure of Kagansky should also be considered a possible prototype.

Yet Kagansky's venality is not Bulgakov's concern in the book. Instead he is surprised, in a kind of Gogolian way, at the ability of the world of the Bolsheviks to produce such remarkable types – he is horrified, but also delighted. In the 1929 version of the *Memoir*, the narrator balks at signing a separate contract with the publisher, named Rvatsky (from *rvat'*, meaning literally to tear, or to vomit), explaining that he's seen the publisher and that the publisher wears a fake clip in his tie, so he (the author) would rather sign his contract with the editor. At this, the editor smiles magnanimously and draws a circle on a piece of paper. 'You are a child,' he tells the writer.

'Just like all other writers, you know nothing of life. Do you see this circle? That's you.'

Another circle appeared on the piece of paper.

'And that is me, the editor.'

'All right.'

A third circle represented, it turned out, the publisher Rvatsky.

'Now watch. I, the editor, connect you, the writer, with the publisher. You see? We have before us a geometric figure – an equilateral triangle. One line goes from the publisher to me, and another from me to the writer. You and I are connected only artistically; we read a manuscript, say, or talk about Gogol – we do not have any monetary relations and we cannot. I can talk about Anatole France with you, whereas I cannot do this with Rvatsky, because he does not know what Anatole France is. But with you, on the other hand, I cannot talk about money, for two reasons: first of all, money doesn't interest a writer, and second, you don't understand the first thing about it. In sum, my dove, contracts are signed with publishers, not editors, and what's more Rvatsky is leaving at 2.30 to go to the Commissariat for Enlightenment and it's now quarter to two, so hurry up and don't sit here looking all wan and frightened.'

On the tip of my tongue was the phrase, 'But I signed the first contract with you . . .'

I was already donning my worn-out overcoat in the hall.

You can be sure that this very day, in publishing houses across the world, writers are being ushered out the door by their editors and publishers, assured that they don't know what's best for them, that they had better be going if they wish to catch the train (or do they take the bus?), that if only they knew more about money, and had the cares the publisher had, then they'd know true sorrow and true pain.

And on this day, too, as we speak, young writers are attending literary functions and finding themselves disappointed to the point of aggrievement by the writers they've admired. In one of this book's finest scenes, Bulgakov's surrogate, Sergei Maksudov, attends a dinner in honour of the famous writer Izmail Bondarevsky, based on Alexei Tolstoy. Bulgakov

probably wrote the scene in late 1936. By then, the real-life
Alexei Tolstoy had become Stalin's best-known sycophant.
Another writer, Boris Pilnyak, represented at the dinner in the
form of Egor Agapyonov, 'who had returned from his journey
to China' (p. 27), was just then making his oaths of allegiance
with – in the harsh words of the American then-Trotskyist Max
Eastman – 'a menstrual regularity'. Nowhere does Bulgakov
allude to this; the famous writers at the dinner are condemned
not for lying or cowardice but for their love of pastries, their
loud voices and their narcissism – for going to Paris, a place
Bulgakov could never go, and seeing nothing but Russians. In
the only instances in *A Dead Man's Memoir* where a political
issue, the censorship, is invoked, it is as part of the fabric of
literary life, to be deployed either as a form of jealous criticism
(the auditors of Maksudov's novel-reading criticize the style,
the characterization, and finally declare, precisely as a critical
*coup de grâce*, that the censor will never 'pass it') or as a form
of self-defence (when the satanic editor Rudolfi arrives at his
little room and demands the manuscript, Maksudov responds
that it isn't very good, that under no circumstance will he show
it, that the handwriting is bad, and, of course, that the censor
won't let it through). In the 1929 version of that same scene,
Rudolfi prefaces his lengthy enquiry into the narrator's grooming habits by asking directly if he is not perhaps a monarchist.
(The narrator blanches and declares, 'I beg your pardon!') In
the final version, the reference to monarchism is removed, and
Rudolfi's questions about grooming come to seem to emerge
from some deeper place. You sense, more importantly than that
Rudolfi wonders whether the narrator might be a political
liability, that Maksudov, simply by being a writer, is *strange*.
In Rudolfi's demand to know how Maksudov gets his hair to
look the way it does, we see the unbridgeable gap between even
the most sympathetic editor and his charge.

This is the lesson. Bulgakov's apparent elimination, throughout the book, of the historical springs of much of the action is not
a statement about the irrelevance of history to 'real' human life.
It is, instead, an idea about the nature of history: that at certain
moments, it will allow for the expression, the flowering, of cer-

tain types; that certain other types will adapt, regardless of the compromising situations into which they're placed; and finally, that a third type, the writer committed to his art, will be crushed – this too almost regardless of the time or place he lives in.

For all that, for all the forces ranged against him, the artist continues on. 'It is so fine here in your theatre,' Maksudov says to one of the actors (p. 53) – and he and his creator meant it. In this book, Bulgakov records all the ways in which one's faith can be shaken – even the trip to the bookshop to buy the productions of all one's contemporaries, from the greatest (the world-travelling Bondarevsky) to the least (the unctuous Likospastov), only to find each of them depressingly hollow. 'I had not derived any new insights: from the books of the very finest writers,' laments Maksudov,

> I had not, so to speak, discovered any paths, not glimpsed any lights shining ahead, and I felt sick and tired of everything. And, like a worm, there began gnawing at my heart the appalling thought that I would never actually make any kind of a writer. And immediately I came face to face with an even more terrible thought: what if I turned out like Likospastov? (pp. 39–40)

Bulgakov too was assailed by doubts but also buoyed at times by moments of almost irrational self-belief. 'In this dim room in this dim house,' he wrote in his early diary, seized in 1926 and recovered in 1990 from the KGB archive, 'I sometimes have bursts of confidence and strength. And now I can hear it inside myself, thought taking flight, and I believe that I am stronger as a writer, incomparably stronger, than anyone I know. But in conditions such as these [his poverty, the Soviet regime], I might disappear.' Bulgakov did not disappear and he did not turn out like Likopastov. He turned out like no one else, a genuine original, who kept alive a great tradition in a time that seemed hell-bent on destroying it.

Bulgakov stopped work on the *Memoir* in September 1937 so as to devote himself fully to the completion of his major work, *The Master and Margarita*. (The fair copy would be typed up in a few feverish weeks the next summer by Bulgakov's sister-in-law Olga Bolshanskaya – who appears in the *Memoir* as the genius typist Poliksena Toropetskaya.) Bulgakov was beginning to feel ill (he had less than three years to live), and the essential point of the *Memoir* had been made. There was also a deeper reason to turn to his other novel. The year during which Bulgakov wrote the *Memoir* witnessed the arrest and murder of tens of thousands. Yet the strangest aspect of 1937, for Bulgakov, was that so many of those people were his enemies: Stalin was purging the Party of the true believers, and those were precisely the people who had so railed against Bulgakov's work. Elena Bulgakova's diary for those months is barely more than a series of notations about arrests, rumours of arrests, and public denunciations – many of them of people she genuinely loathed. Meanwhile, there were hints that Bulgakov would soon be back in favour. The whole thing was too grotesque, too confusing, and it needed the mad flights of *The Master and Margarita* to contain it. Bulgakov never returned to the *Memoir* after 1937; technically speaking, the novel is unfinished, though it has a natural ending where Bulgakov left it: in anticipation, finally, of the production of his play.

Keith Gessen

# SOURCES

'To a Secret Friend', in Mikhail Bulgakov, *Sobranie sochinenii v vos'mi tomakh* (St Petersburg, Azbuka-klassika, 2002), volume 1.

Letters and diaries, with commentary by V. I. Losiev, in Mikhail Bulgakov, *Sobranie sochinenii v vos'mi tomakh* (St Petersburg, Azbuka-klassika, 2004), volume 8.

Chudakova, M., *Zhizneopisanie Mikhaila Bulgakova* (Moscow: Kniga, 1988).

Smelianskii, A. M., *Is Comrade Bulgakov Dead? Mikhail Bulgakov at the Moscow Art Theatre*, trans. A. L. Tait (London: Methuen, 1993).

# A Note on the Text

Taking as his starting point a fragment written in 1929 under the title 'To a Secret Friend', Bulgakov began work on this extended satire of Moscow's theatrical life in November 1936, at a time when his relations with the Moscow Art Theatre were in crisis (following the closure of his play *The Cabal of Hypocrites* (*Molière*), he left to work as a librettist at the Bolshoi Theatre). He apparently read the first chapters to friends in early 1937 and in her diary, his wife, Elena Shilovskaya, also notes further readings in September 1938 and May 1939.

The central character and narrator, the 'little man' Sergei Maksudov, is derived from Bulgakov's own experiences during the period when he was largely dependent for earning a living on working for the newspaper *Gudok* (*Siren*) – on 3 September 1923, for instance, he wrote in his diary: 'Every day I go off to work in that *Siren* of mine and waste my day absolutely and irredeemably.' Maksudov's experiences with the 'Independent Theatre' and other writers are clearly drawn from Bulgakov's own dealings with the Moscow Art Theatre and his own contemporaries. The prototypes of the major characters can be identified without too much difficulty as real figures of the time. (Bulgakov's widow drew up a list, which is often cited.)

Bulgakov left his satire unfinished, in the form of a manuscript in three notebooks and a fourth containing amendments and variants. The first page of his manuscript bore two titles: 'A Dead Man's Memoir' and 'A Theatrical Novel'. Both titles are used here.

*

This translation of *A Dead Man's Memoir* was made from the text in Mikhail Bulgakov, *Collected Works in Eight Volumes: Volume 5, The Final Days: A Film Scenario, Plays, a Novel, Librettos* (*Sobranie sochinenii v ros'mi tomakh: Tom pyaty, Poslednie dni: Kinostsenarii, p'esy, roman, libretto*), edited with an introductory article and commentary by V. Petelin (Moscow: Tsentropoligraf, 2004).

The text used in this edition is the same as that in Mikhail Bulgakov, *The Master and Margarita: Novels, Plays*, compiled with an introductory article by V. Petelin (Moscow: Sovremennik, 1991).

The *Collected Works in Eight Volumes* have also provided much of the information used in the notes.

# Further Reading

Barratt, A., *Between Two Worlds: A Critical Introduction to* The Master and Margarita (Oxford: Clarendon Press, 1987).

Bristol, E., 'Turn of a Century: Modernism 1895–1925', in *The Cambridge History of Russian Literature*, ed. Charles A. Moser, rev. edn (Cambridge: Cambridge University Press, 1992), pp. 79–126.

Curtis, J., *Bulgakov's Last Decade: The Writer as Hero*, (Cambridge: Cambridge University Press, 1987).

—, *Manuscripts Don't Burn: Mikhail Bulgakov, a Life in Letters and Diaries* (London: Bloomsbury, 1991).

Gillespie, David C., *The Twentieth-Century Russian Novel: An Introduction* (Oxford: Berg, 1996).

Hunns, Derek J., *Bulgakov's Apocalyptic Critique of Literature* (Lewiston, New York: Edwin Mellen Press, 1996).

Milne, L., The Master and Margarita: *A Comedy of Victory* (Birmingham: University of Birmingham, 1977).

—, *Mikhail Bulgakov: A Critical Biography* (Cambridge: Cambridge University Press, 1990).

Smelianskii, A. M., *Is Comrade Bulgakov Dead? Mikhail Bulgakov at the Moscow Art Theatre*, trans. A. L. Tait (London: Methuen, 1993).

Terry, Garth M., *Mikhail Bulgakov in English: A Bibliography, 1891–1991* (Nottingham, England: Astra Press, 1991).

Weeks, Laura D. (ed.), The Master and Margarita: *A Critical Companion* (Evanston, Ill.: Northwestern University Press, 1996).

## FOREWORD

I should warn the reader that I had absolutely no part at all in writing this memoir and that it came into my possession under extremely strange and sad circumstances.

On the very day of Sergei Leontievich Maksudov's suicide, which took place in Kiev in the spring of last year, I received an extremely thick package and a letter despatched beforehand by the suicide himself.

The package proved to contain this memoir, and the contents of the letter were quite astonishing:

Sergei Leontievich stated that as he left this life he was presenting his memoir to me so that I, his only friend, could correct it, sign it with my name and have it published.

A strange request, but a man's dying wish!

I spent a year making enquiries about Sergei Leontievich's family and friends. In vain! He had not lied in his final letter – he had no one left in the whole world.

And so I accept his gift.

Now for the second thing: I must inform the reader that the suicide had never in his life had any connection whatever with either play-writing or theatres, remaining always what he had been, a lowly employee of the *Shipping Herald* newspaper, who only once assumed the role of a writer of fiction, and then unsuccessfully – for Sergei Leontievich's novel was not published.[1]

Maksudov's memoir therefore represents the fruit of his own fantasy and – alas – a morbid fantasy at that. Sergei Leontievich suffered from an ailment which bears a most disagreeable name: melancholia.

As someone well acquainted with the theatrical life of Moscow, I am prepared to guarantee that nowhere do such theatres and such people as are depicted in the deceased's work exist, nor have they ever existed.

And, to conclude, the third and final thing: my work on the memoir has consisted of providing it with chapter headings and then eliminating the epigraph, which to my eye seemed pretentious, unnecessary and disagreeable.

This epigraph was:

Unto to each according to his deeds . . .[2]

And in addition, I have inserted punctuation marks where they were lacking.

I have not touched Sergei Leontievich's style, although it is clearly rather slipshod. But then, what can one expect from a person who, only two days after he placed the final full stop at the end of his memoir, threw himself headfirst off the Tsepnoi Bridge?[3]

And so . . .

# PART I

## CHAPTER I

### *The Adventures Begin*

A thunderstorm washed Moscow clean on 29 April and the air became sweet and my heart was somehow softened, and I felt I wanted to live.

In my new grey suit and quite passable coat, I walked along one of the central streets of the capital, making my way to a place where I had never been before. The reason for this movement of mine was a letter, received out of the blue, that was lying in my pocket. Here it is:

Highly esteemed Sergei Leontievich!
Would be exceedingly glad to make your acquaintance and likewise also to discuss a certain secret matter which you might very well find of no little interest to yourself.

If you are free, I should be happy to meet with you at the building of the Experimental Stage of the Independent Theatre on Wednesday at four o'clock.

Greetings, X. *Ilchin.*

The letter was written in pencil on a sheet of paper on which the following was printed in the top left corner:

Xavier Borisovich Ilchin
Director, Experimental Stage,
Independent Theatre[4]

It was the first time I had seen Ilchin's name and I did not know that the Experimental Stage existed. I had heard of the Independent Theatre, I knew that it was one of the more distinguished theatres, but I had never been there.

I found the letter extremely interesting, especially since I never used to receive any letters at all. I should tell you that I am a lowly employee of the *Shipping* newspaper. At that time I lived in a poor but separate seventh-floor room in the Krasnye Vorota district beside Khomutovsky Alley.

And so, I was walking along, inhaling the newly freshened air and thinking that the thunderstorm was going to strike again, and also about how Xavier Ilchin could have discovered that I existed, how he had managed to find me and what he could possibly want with me. But no matter how much I thought about it I was unable to fathom the latter question, and I eventually settled on the idea that Ilchin wished to exchange rooms with me.

Of course, I ought to have written to tell Ilchin that he should come to see me, since he was the one who had business with me, but I have to say that I was ashamed of my room, its furniture and the people around it. I am a rather odd person in general and a little afraid of other people. Just imagine it, Ilchin walks in and sees the divan, and its upholstery is ripped open and there is a spring sticking out, the shade on the light bulb above the table is made of newspaper, and the cat is wandering around, and there is the sound of Annushka swearing in the kitchen.

I went in through the fretted cast-iron gates and saw a little shack, where a grey-haired man was selling pin-on badges and spectacle frames.

I jumped over a receding stream of turbid water and found myself facing a yellow building, and I thought how the building had been built a long, long time ago, before either I or Ilchin were even born. The black board with gold letters informed me that this was the Experimental Stage. I went in, and a short little man with a small beard, wearing a jacket with green galloons, immediately blocked my way.

'Who do you want, citizen?' he asked suspiciously and spread his arms wide, as if he were trying to catch a chicken.

'I wish to see the director, Mr Ilchin,' I said, trying to make my voice sound haughty.

The man changed exceedingly in front of my very eyes. He lowered his arms, stood to attention and put on an affected smile.

'Xavier Borisich? Straightaway, sir. Your coat, if you please. Do you have any galoshes?'

The man took my coat with the same care as if it had been some precious sacerdotal vestment.

I walked up the cast-iron stairs, saw the profiles of warriors in helmets and the formidable swords below them in the bas-reliefs, and the antique Dutch stoves with their metal vents polished to a golden gleam.

The building was silent, there was nobody anywhere, there was only the man with the galloons plodding after me, and on turning round I saw that he was making silent gestures of attention, devotion, respect, love and joy to me in connection with the fact that I had come and that although he might be walking behind, he was guiding me, leading me to the place where the solitary, mysterious Xavier Borisovich Ilchin was to be found.

And then it suddenly turned darker, the Dutch stoves shed their rich, whitish lustre and the gloom descended with a crash as the second storm began outside the windows. I knocked at the door, went in and in the half-light I finally saw Xavier Borisovich.

'Maksudov,' I said with dignity.

At that point, far away on the other side of Moscow, lightning cleft the sky, momentarily illuminating Ilchin with a phosphorescent glow.

'So it's you, my dearest Sergei Leontievich!' said Ilchin, smiling cunningly.

And then, putting his arm round my waist, Ilchin drew me over on to a divan exactly like the one in my room – even the spring was sticking out of it in the same place as on mine, in the middle.

And in general to this day I still do not know the function of that room in which the fateful meeting took place. Why the divan? What sheet music was that lying scattered on the floor in the corner? Why was there a set of scales with weighing pans standing on the windowsill? Why was Ilchin waiting for me in this room and not, say, in the hall next door, where in the distance the outlines of a grand piano were dimly visible in the twilight of the storm?

And to the rumbling of the thunder, Xavier Borisovich said ominously:

'I have read your novel.'

I shuddered.

The point is . . .

## CHAPTER 2

### An Attack of Neurasthenia

The point is that, while working in the modest position of a proofreader in the *Shipping*, I hated that job of mine and at night, sometimes working until the light of dawn, I had been writing a novel at home in my garret.

It was conceived one night when I woke after a sad dream. I had been dreaming of my native city, snow, winter, the civil war . . . In the dream a silent blizzard passed before me, and then an old grand piano appeared, with people standing around it who are no longer in this world.[5] In the dream I was astounded by my own loneliness, I began to feel sorry for myself. And I woke in tears. I turned on the light, the dusty bulb suspended above the table. It lit up my poverty – a cheap inkwell, a few books, a bundle of old newspapers. My left side was hurting from the spring, my heart was overwhelmed by fear. I felt I was about to die that very moment at the table; I felt so abased by this pitiful fear of death that I groaned and glanced around, anxiously seeking help and protection against death. And I found that help. The cat that I had once picked up in the gateway gave a quiet miaow. The beast became alarmed. A second later the beast was already sitting on the newspapers, looking at me with its round eyes, asking what had happened.

What the smoky-grey, scrawny beast wanted to know was that nothing had happened. And indeed, who else would feed this old cat?

'It's an attack of neurasthenia,' I explained to the cat. 'It has already taken a hold on me, it will develop and swallow me up. But for the time being I can carry on.'

The house was asleep. I glanced out of the window. Not a single window on five floors was lit up. I realized that it wasn't a house but a multi-decked ship that was flying under a motionless black sky. The idea of movement cheered me up. I calmed down, the cat also calmed down and closed its eyes.

And so I began writing the novel. I described the dream blizzard. I tried to convey the way the side of the piano had gleamed under the lamp with the shade. I didn't manage to do that. But I became stubborn.

The only thing I tried to do during the day was to expend as little energy as possible on my forced labour. I did it mechanically, so that my head was not involved in it. At every convenient opportunity I tried to leave work on the pretext of being ill. Of course, they did not believe me, and my life became unpleasant. But I put up with everything and gradually got used to it. Just as an impatient youth waits for the hour of his assignation, I waited for the hour of night. The accursed flat grew quiet at that time. I sat down at the table ... The concerned cat sat on the newspapers, but she was extremely interested in the novel and she constantly tried to shift across from the newspaper page to the page covered with writing. And I took her by the scruff of the neck and set her back in her place.

One night I lifted up my head and was astonished. My ship was not flying anywhere, the house was standing still and it was absolutely light. The light bulb was not illuminating anything, it was repulsive and irritating. I switched it off, and the disgusting room appeared before me in the light of dawn. Tomcats of various colours strutted stealthily and silently through the asphalt-covered courtyard. Every letter on the sheet of paper could be made out without any lamp.

'My God! It's April!' I exclaimed and, for some reason startled at this thought, I wrote in large letters: 'The End.'

The end of winter, the end of the blizzards, the end of the cold. Over the winter I had gradually lost my few acquaintances, become very shabby and threadbare, fallen ill with rheumatism and become rather unsociable. But I had shaved every day.

Thinking about all this, I let the cat out into the yard, then came back and fell asleep – the first time, I think, in that whole winter that I fell into a sleep without dreams.

It takes a long time to correct a novel. You have to cross out a lot of bits, replace hundreds of words with others. A big job, but necessary.

However, I was overcome by temptation and, having corrected the first six pages, I went back to people. I invited guests. They included two journalists from the *Shipping*, employees like myself, their wives and two writers: one a young man who had astounded me with the quite inimitable dexterity with which he wrote short stories, and the other an elderly man who had seen plenty of the world and proved on closer acquaintance to be an appalling swine.

In one evening I read approximately a quarter of my novel.

The reading made the wives so bleary-eyed that I began to suffer pangs of conscience. But the journalists and the writers proved to be made of stern stuff. Their judgements were fraternally candid, rather severe and, as I now realize, just.

'The language!' exclaimed one writer (the one who proved to be a swine). 'The language, that's the main thing! The language is no good at all.'

He drank a large glass of vodka and swallowed a sardine. I poured him another. He drank it and followed it with a piece of sausage.

'The metaphors!' he cried after his snack.

'Yes,' the young writer politely confirmed, 'the language is pretty poor.'

The journalists said nothing, but they nodded sympathetically and drank up. The ladies did not nod and they did not speak, they flatly refused the port bought especially for them and drank vodka.

'How could it not be poor?' exclaimed the elderly writer. 'Imagery is not a stray dog, please note that! Without it, everything's naked! Naked! Naked! Remember that, old chap.'

The phrase 'old chap' clearly referred to me. I turned cold.

As they left they agreed to come to see me again. And a week later they were back. I read the second portion. The evening was notable for the fact that the elderly writer, entirely unexpectedly and against my will, drank to *Bruderschaft** with me and began calling me 'Leontich'.

'The language is no damn good! But it's amusing. Amusing, damn you to hell (me, that is!),' shouted the elderly writer as he ate the jellied meat cooked by Dusya.

On the third evening a new person showed up, also a writer – with a fierce and Mephistophelean face, a cast in the left eye and unshaven. He said that the novel was bad, but expressed a desire to hear the fourth and final part. There was also someone's divorced wife and a man with a guitar in a case. I picked up a lot of points that were useful to me on that particular evening. My modest comrades from the *Shipping* were now a little more used to the expanded company and also expressed their opinions.

One said that chapter seventeen was too long-winded, the other that the character of Vasienka was not rounded out enough. Both of these things were fair.

The fourth and final reading did not take place at my home but at the home of the young writer who composed short stories so expertly. There were already about twenty people here, and I was introduced to the writer's grandmother, a very pleasant old woman who was spoiled by only one thing – the expression of fright which for some reason never left her face the whole evening. And as well as that I saw the nurse sleeping on a trunk.

The novel was concluded. And then disaster struck. As one man, all the listeners told me that my novel could not be printed for the simple reason that the censor would not pass it.

---

* Brotherhood (German). To drink to *Bruderschaft* is, in effect, to pledge eternal friendship.

It was the first time I had heard this word spoken, and only now did I realize that while I was writing the novel not once had I thought about whether the censor would pass it or not.

One of the ladies began it (later I learned that she was a divorced wife too). What she said was:

'Tell me, Maksudov, will they pass your novel?'

'No-no-no-no!' exclaimed the elderly writer. 'Absolutely not! There's absolutely no question of it being "passed"! Simply no hope at all of that. You've no need to worry, old chap – they won't pass it.'

'They won't pass it!' the lower end of the table echoed in chorus.

'The language . . .' began one, who was the brother of the guitarist, but the elderly writer interrupted him:

'Damn the language!' he exclaimed, heaping salad on to his plate. 'The language is not the point. The old chap's written a bad novel but an amusing one. You have a gift for observation, you scoundrel. Where on earth do these things come from! I'd never have expected it, but! . . . the content!'

'Mm-yes, the content . . .'

'Precisely the content,' shouted the elderly writer, disturbing the nurse. 'Do you know what's required? You don't? Aha! Well now, there you are!'

He winked one eye and drank at the same time. Then he embraced and kissed me, shouting:

'There's something off-putting about you, believe me! I should know these things! But I love you. I do love you, strike me dead where I stand! He's a sly one, the scoundrel! A man with a tricky side to him! Eh? What? Did you notice chapter four? What he said to the heroine? Well now, there you are!'

'In the first place, what kind of way is that to talk?' I began, suffering torment from his familiarity.

'You give me a kiss first,' shouted the elderly writer. 'You don't want to? It's obvious straightaway what kind of comrade you are! No, brother, you're not a straightforward kind of person!'

'Of course he's not straightforward!' the second divorced wife supported him.

'In the first place . . .' I began again in a fury, but absolutely nothing came of it.

'Never mind the first place!' shouted the elderly writer. 'There's a touch of the Dostoevsky about you! Yes, indeed. Well, all right, you don't love me, may God forgive you for it, I'm not offended by you. But we all love you sincerely and wish you well!' At this point he pointed to the brother of the guitarist and another man I didn't know, with a crimson face, who when he arrived had apologized for being late and explained that he had been at the Central Bathhouse. 'And I tell you straight,' the elderly writer went on, 'because I'm used to giving it to everyone straight from the shoulder, Leontich, don't you even bother trying to push this novel through anywhere. You'll just earn yourself a whole lot of trouble and we, your friends, will have to suffer at the thought of your torments. Just you believe me! I'm a man with a lot of bitter experience. I know life! See that,' he shouted resentfully, gesturing to summon everyone to bear witness, 'just look at that: the fierce way he lowers at me. There's his gratitude for the friendly way I treat him! Leontich!' he squealed, so loudly that the nurse behind the curtain got up off the trunk. 'Understand! Understand that the artistic merits of your novel are not so very great (at this point there was the sound of a gentle chord on the guitar from the divan) that you should let yourself be crucified for it. Understand!'

'Understand, understand, understand!' the guitarist sang in a pleasant tenor.

'And now this is the long and the short of it,' shouted the elderly writer, 'if you don't kiss me this moment, I shall get up and go, leave this friendly company, for you have offended me!'

Suffering indescribable torment, I kissed him. As I did so the choir really warmed up, with the tenor floating above the other voices in tones of syrupy tenderness:

'U-understand, understand . . .'

I crept out of the flat like a tomcat, holding the heavy manuscript under my arm. The nurse was leaning over, her red eyes streaming as she drank water from the tap in the kitchen. Without knowing why, I held out a rouble to her.

'Get away with you,' the nurse said angrily, shoving the

rouble aside. 'Three o'clock in the morning! It's too damned awful.'

At this point a familiar voice cut through the choir in the distance:

'But where is he? Has he fled? Catch him! Do you see, comrades...'

But the oilcloth-upholstered door had already released me, and I fled without a backward glance.

## CHAPTER 3

### *My Suicide*

'Yes, this is terrible,' I told myself in my room, 'it is all terrible. That salad, and the nurse, and the elderly writer and that unforgettable "understand", and my whole life in general.'

Outside the windows the autumn wind moaned. A sheet of roofing-metal that had been torn free clattered, streaks of rain trickled down the windowpanes. Since the evening with the nurse and the guitar many events had occurred, but all so repulsive that I do not even want to write about them. First of all, I went dashing to check the novel from the point of view of whether they would pass it or not. And it became clear that they would not. The elderly writer was absolutely right. It seemed to me that every line of the novel cried out that this was so.

Having checked the novel, I spent my last money on having two excerpts typed out and took them to the editorial office of a certain thick journal. Two weeks later I received the excerpts back. Written in the corner of the manuscript was the word 'unsuitable'. After cutting off this resolution with a pair of nail scissors, I took the same excerpts to another thick journal and received them back again two weeks later with exactly the same inscription: 'Unsuitable.'

After that my cat died. She stopped eating, huddled back into the corner and miaowed, driving me into a frenzy. It went on for three days. On the fourth day I found her lying still on her side in the corner.

I took a spade from the yard-keeper and buried her in the empty lot behind our house. I was left absolutely alone in all the world, but I confess that in my heart of hearts I felt glad. The unfortunate beast had been such a burden to me.

And after that the autumn rains began, my shoulder started hurting again, and my left leg at the knee as well.

However, the very worst thing was not this but the fact that the novel was bad. And if it was bad, that meant that the end of my life was approaching.

Spend my whole life working in the *Shipping*! You have to be joking!

Every night I lay there, staring hard into the pitch-black darkness and repeating: 'This is terrible.' If I had been asked: What do you remember about the time you have worked in the *Shipping*? – I would have replied with a clear conscience: Nothing.

Dirty galoshes by the coatstand, someone's wet fur cap with huge long earflaps hanging on the coatstand – and that's all.

'This is terrible,' I repeated, listening to the silence of the night buzzing in my ears.

The insomnia set in about two weeks later.

I took a tram to Samotechnaya-Sadovaya Street, where in one of the houses, the number of which I shall, of course, keep absolutely secret, there lived a certain man who due to the nature of his work had the right to carry arms.

The circumstances under which we made each other's acquaintance are not important.

On entering the flat I found my friend lying on the divan. While he was heating water for tea on the primus stove in the kitchen I opened the left drawer of his desk, stole a Browning out of it, then had a drink of tea and went home.

It was about nine o'clock in the evening. I got home. Everything was the same as always. There was a smell of fried mutton from the kitchen, the corridor was filled with the eternal mist that I knew so well, with a light bulb burning dimly in it on the ceiling. I went into my room. There was a flash of light above me and the room was immediately plunged into darkness. The bulb had burned out.

'It's all the same anyway, and it's all absolutely right,' I said sternly.

I lit the kerosene stove on the floor in the corner. On a sheet of paper I wrote: 'I hereby declare that I stole Browning no. (I've forgotten the number – say, such and such) from Parfyon Ivanovich' (I wrote his surname, the number of the house, the street, everything the way it's supposed to be done). I signed it and lay down on the floor beside the kerosene stove. Mortal terror overcame me. It is terrible to die. Then I pictured our corridor, the mutton and granny Pelagia, the elderly writer and the *Shipping*, cheered myself up by thinking of how they would break in the door of my room with a crash, etc.

I set the barrel to my temple and felt for the trigger with an uncertain finger. Just at that very moment I heard sounds that I knew very well downstairs, a crackly orchestra began playing and the tenor in the gramophone started singing:

But will God return everything to me?

'Good grief! *Faust*!'[6] I thought. 'Now that really is perfect timing. But I'll just wait until Mephistopheles makes his entrance. One last time. I'll never hear it again.'

The orchestra beneath the floorboards kept disappearing and then reappearing, but the tenor kept shouting louder and louder:

My curse on life, faith and all learning!

'One more moment, one more moment,' I thought. 'But how quickly he is singing . . .'

The tenor gave a shriek of despair, and then the orchestra thundered.

My trembling finger was lowered on to the trigger and at that instant a fearsome rumbling deafened me, my heart went hurtling down into some bottomless pit, it seemed to me that the flame from the kerosene stove shot up to the ceiling and I dropped the revolver.

Immediately the rumbling was repeated. From below I heard a terrible bass voice:

'Here I am!'

I turned towards the door.

## CHAPTER 4

### I Have a Sword

Someone had knocked at the door. Imperiously and repeatedly. I put the revolver into the pocket of my trousers and called out feebly:

'Come in!'

The door swung open and I froze on the floor in horror. It was he, beyond a shadow of a doubt. There, suspended in the gloom above me, was a face with a powerful nose and sweeping eyebrows. As the shadows shifted, I seemed to see the point of a black beard protruding from the square chin. The beret was cocked dashingly over one ear. But there was, it is true, no feather.

In short, standing there before me was Mephistopheles. Then I noticed that he was wearing a coat and gleaming high galoshes and he had a briefcase under his arm. 'That's quite natural,' I thought. 'He can't go walking round Moscow looking any other way in the twentieth century.'

'Rudolfi,' the evil spirit said in a tenor voice, not a bass.

In fact he need not have bothered to introduce himself. I had recognized him. There in my room was one of the most prominent individuals in the literary world of that time, the editor and publisher of the country's only private journal, *Motherland* – Ilya Ivanovich Rudolfi.[7]

I got up off the floor.

'Can you not switch on the light?' asked Rudolfi.

'Unfortunately, I can't do that,' I replied, 'since the bulb has burned out, and I don't have another one.'

The evil spirit who had assumed the guise of the editor

performed one of his simple tricks – there and then he took an electric light bulb out of his briefcase.

'Do you always carry light bulbs around with you?' I asked in amazement.

'No,' the spirit explained in a severe tone of voice, 'it is a simple coincidence – I have just been to the shop.'

When the room was illuminated and Rudolfi had taken off his coat I hastily removed from the table the note with the confession to the theft of the revolver, and the spirit pretended that he did not see this.

We sat down. We said nothing for a while.

'You have written a novel?' Rudolfi eventually enquired sternly.

'How do you know that?'

'Likospastov[8] told me.'

'You see,' I began (Likospastov is that self-same elderly writer), 'I really have . . . but . . . in short, it is a bad novel.'

'I see,' said the spirit and looked at me keenly.

It turned out at this point that he did not have a beard at all. It had been a trick of the shadows.

'Show it to me,' Rudolfi said imperiously.

'Not for anything,' I responded.

'Show-it-to-me,' said Rudolfi, emphasizing every word.

'The censor won't pass it . . .'

'Show it to me.'

'Well, you see, it's written by hand, and I have terrible handwriting, the letter "O" comes out like a straight line, and . . .'

And then, before I had realized it, my hands had opened the drawer where the ill-starred novel was lying.

'I can make out any handwriting as if it were print,' Rudolfi explained. 'A professional skill . . .' And there were the notebooks in his hands.

An hour went by. I sat beside the kerosene stove, heating up the water, and Rudolfi read the novel. A multitude of thoughts swirled round inside my head. In the first place, I was thinking about Rudolfi. It should be said that Rudolfi was a remarkable editor and to get into his journal was regarded as not only a pleasure but an honour. I ought to have been glad that the editor had appeared at my home, even in the guise of Mephisto-pheles. But on the other hand, he might not like the novel, and that would be distressing ... Apart from that, I had to offer him tea, and I didn't have any butter. In general, everything in my head was in a jumble, with the revolver that need not have been stolen also tangled up in it.

Meanwhile Rudolfi was swallowing page after page, and I attempted in vain to discover what impression the novel was making on him. Rudolfi's face expressed absolutely nothing.

When he took an interval in order to wipe the lenses of his spectacles, I added one more foolish utterance to those already spoken:

'And what did Likospastov say about my novel?'

'He said that this novel is absolutely no good,' Rudolfi replied coldly and turned the page. (What a swine that Likospastov is! Instead of supporting his friend ... etc.)

At one in the morning we drank tea, and at two Rudolfi finished reading the last page. I started squirming on the divan.

'I see,' said Rudolfi.

We said nothing for a while.

'You imitate Tolstoy,' said Rudolfi.

'Which one of the Tolstoys exactly?' I asked. 'There were a lot of them ... Alexei Konstantinovich, perhaps, the well-known writer, or Pyotr Andreevich, who captured the Tsarevich Alexei abroad, or perhaps the numismatist Ivan Ivanovich, or Lev Nikolaevich?'[9]

'Where did you study?'

At this point I have to reveal a little secret. The fact is that I graduated from two faculties at university, and I had concealed that.

'I graduated from a parish school,' I said, clearing my throat.

'So that's it!' said Rudolfi, and a faint smile flickered across his lips.

Then he asked:

'How many times a week do you shave?'

'Seven times.'

'Pardon my curiosity,' Rudolfi continued, 'but how do you make your parting like that?'

'I rub brilliantine in my hair. But permit me to ask why all this is . . .'

'By all means,' answered Rudolfi. 'No particular reason.' And he added, 'It's interesting. A man has graduated from a parish school, he shaves every day and lies on the floor beside a kerosene lamp. You are a difficult sort of person!' Then he abruptly changed his tone of voice and started speaking sternly: 'Glavlit[10] will not pass your novel, and no one will print it. They won't accept it at either *Daybreak* or *Dawn*.'[11]

'I know that,' I said firmly.

'But nevertheless, I am taking this novel from you,' Rudolfi said strictly (my heart skipped a beat), 'and I shall pay you (and then he named a monstrously tiny sum, I forget how much) per sheet. Tomorrow it will be typed.'

'It is four hundred pages long!' I exclaimed hoarsely.

'I shall divide it into parts,' Rudolfi said in a voice of iron, 'and the twelve typists in the bureau will have typed it by the evening.'

At that point I stopped rebelling and decided to submit to Rudolfi.

'The typing is at your expense,' Rudolfi continued, and I merely nodded, like a puppet. 'And then, we shall have to delete three words: on pages one, seventy-one and three hundred and two.'

I glanced into the notebooks and saw that the first word was 'Apocalypse', the second was 'archangels' and the third was 'devil'. I submissively deleted them; in fact I felt like saying that these were naive deletions, but I glanced at Rudolfi and fell silent.

'And then,' Rudolfi continued, 'you will go with me to Glavlit. And I would ask you please not to say a single word there.'

At this I did take offence.

'If you consider that I might say something . . .' I began mumbling with dignity, 'then I can easily stay at home . . .'

Rudolfi took no notice of this attempt at rebellion and continued:

'No, you can't stay at home, you will go with me.'

'But what am I going to do there?'

'You will sit on a chair,' Rudolfi commanded, 'and you will reply to everything that is said to you with a polite smile . . .'

'But –'

'And I shall do the talking!' Rudolfi concluded.

After that he asked for a clean sheet of paper and wrote something on it in pencil that consisted, as I recall, of several points, signed it himself, made me sign it as well, and then took two crisp banknotes out of his pocket, put my notebooks in his briefcase and disappeared from the room.

I could not sleep all night long, I walked around the room, inspected the banknotes against the light, drank cold tea and imagined the shelves in the bookshops. A lot of people had come into a shop and were asking for the issue of the journal. In the houses people were sitting under their lamps and reading that issue, some of them aloud.

My God! How stupid this is, how stupid this is! But I was relatively young then, it is not right to laugh at me.


## CHAPTER 5

### Extraordinary Events

Stealing something is not difficult. Putting it back – that is the tricky part. With the Browning in its holster in my pocket, I arrived at my friend's place.

My heart began to race when I already heard him shouting through the door:

'Ma! And who else?'

Then came the dull voice of an old woman, his mother:

'The plumber . . .'

'What's happened?' I asked, taking off my coat.

My friend glanced round and hissed:

'Someone pinched my revolver today . . . The bastards . . .'

'Ai-ai-ai!' I said.

His old mum dashed around all over the small flat, crept across the floor in the corridor, glanced into some baskets or other.

'Ma! This is stupid! Stop creeping around on the floor!'

'Today?' I asked happily. (He was mistaken, the revolver had disappeared yesterday, but for some reason he thought that he'd seen it in the desk last night.)

'Well, who's been here?'

'The plumber,' my friend shouted.

'Parfyosha! He didn't go into the study,' his mum said timidly. 'He went straight through to the tap . . .'

'Oh, Ma! Oh, Ma!'

'Has nobody else been here? Who was here yesterday?'

'There was nobody here yesterday either. You were the only one who called in, nobody else.'

And suddenly my friend glared at me.

'I beg your pardon,' I said with dignity.

'Aagh! You intellectuals are all so easily offended!' my friend exclaimed. 'I don't actually think that you pinched it.'

And he went dashing off that instant to see which tap the plumber had walked straight through to. His old mum played the part of the plumber for him and even imitated his accent.

'He came in like this,' the old woman said, 'he said "hello" . . . hung his cap up – and went through . . .'

'Where did he go?'

The old woman set off into the kitchen, imitating the plumber, my friend rushed after her, I made a single deceptive movement, as if I were following them, immediately turned back into the study, put the Browning in the right drawer of the desk instead of the left and set off to the kitchen.

'Where do you keep it?' I asked sympathetically, back in the study.

My friend opened the left drawer and showed me the empty space.

'I don't understand,' I said, with a shrug. 'It really is a mysterious business – yes, it's obvious that it's been stolen.'

My friend became completely upset.

'But I still don't think anyone did steal it,' I said after a little while. 'After all, if there was no one here, who could have stolen it?'

My friend darted away and looked through the pockets of an old greatcoat in the hallway. Nothing turned up there.

'Evidently it must have been stolen,' I said thoughtfully. 'You'll have to report it to the militia.'

My friend whimpered something.

'Couldn't you have put it away somewhere else?'

'I always put it in exactly the same place!' my friend exclaimed, growing nervous, and to prove it he opened the middle drawer of the desk. Then he whispered something with his lips, opened the left drawer and even stuck his hand into it, then the bottom drawer underneath it, and then, with a curse, he opened the right drawer.

'Would you believe it?' he croaked, looking at me. 'Would you believe it? Ma! It's turned up!'

He was exceptionally happy that day and made me stay for dinner.

Having eliminated the matter of the revolver that had been weighing down my conscience, I took a step that could be called risky: I gave up my job at the *Shipping Herald*.

I made the move into a different world; I spent time at Rudolfi's place and began meeting writers, some of whom had major reputations. But now all of that has somehow been erased from my memory, leaving nothing behind but boredom; I've forgotten all of that. And there is only one thing that I can't forget: that is the way that I met Rudolfi's publisher, Makar Rvatsky.[12]

The point is that Rudolfi had everything: intelligence and shrewdness and even a certain erudition, there was only one thing he didn't have – money. But nevertheless, Rudolfi's reckless love for his work drove him on to publish a thick journal no matter what the cost. I believe that he would have died without it.

It was for this reason that I found myself one day in a strange premises on one of the boulevards of Moscow. The publisher Rvatsky was located here, Rudolfi had explained to me. I was struck by the fact that the signboard at the entrance to the premises declared this to be a 'Photographic Accessories Bureau'.

Stranger still was the fact that there were no photographic accessories at all anywhere in the premises, with the exception of several lengths of calico and thick woollen cloth, wrapped up in newspaper.

The whole place was swarming with people. All of them were wearing coats and hats and talking animatedly to each other. I heard two words in passing – 'wire' and 'jars' – and was terribly astonished, but I was also greeted with gazes of astonishment. I said that I was there to see Rvatsky on business. I was immediately and very politely ushered behind a plywood partition, where my astonishment increased to the utmost degree.

Piled up, one on top of the other, on the desk behind which Rvatsky was sitting, were cans of sprats.

But I didn't like the look of Rvatsky himself any more than the sprats in his publishing house. Rvatsky was a short, lean, dried-up man who to my eye, which was used to the smocks in the *Shipping*, seemed to be dressed extremely strangely. He was wearing a morning coat and striped trousers and had a dirty starched collar, with a green tie round the collar, and in this tie there was a ruby pin.

Rvatsky astonished me, but I startled Rvatsky, or rather, upset him, when I explained that I had come to sign a contract with him for the printing of my novel in the journal that he published. But nonetheless, he rapidly recovered his composure, took the two copies of the contract that I had brought, took out a fountain pen, signed them both almost without reading them and thrust both copies towards me, together with the fountain pen. I had already armed myself with the latter when I suddenly glanced at a can with the inscription 'Finest Astrakhan Sprats' and a picture of a net with a fisherman beside it with his trouser legs rolled up, and a certain oppressive thought intruded into my mind.

'Will they pay me the money immediately, as it says in the contract?' I asked.

Rvatsky was transformed into a single smile of sweetness and politeness.

He cleared his throat and said:

'In precisely two weeks' time, there's a little hitch at present . . .'

I put the pen down.

'Or in a week,' Rvatsky said hastily. 'But why don't you sign?'

'Then we'll sign the contract at the same time,' I said, 'when the hitch has been settled.'

Rvatsky gave a bitter smile, shaking his head.

'Don't you trust me?'

'Oh, come now!'

'Very well then, on Wednesday!' said Rvatsky. 'If you are in need of money.'

'I'm sorry, but I can't.'

'It's important to sign the contract,' Rvatsky said in a reasonable tone, 'and I can even get you the money on Tuesday.'

'I'm sorry, but I can't.' And at this point I pushed the contracts away and fastened my coat button.

'Just a moment, ah, you're so tough!' exclaimed Rvatsky. 'And they say that writers are impractical people.'

At that moment an expression of anguish appeared on his pale face and he glanced around anxiously, but a young man came running in and handed Rvatsky a little cardboard ticket wrapped in white paper. 'That's a ticket for a sleeping carriage,' I thought. 'He's going somewhere . . .'

The colour rose in the publisher's cheeks and his eyes sparkled, which I would never have imagined to be possible.

To cut the tale short, Rvatsky gave me the sum that was indicated in the contract and wrote me out promissory notes for the remaining sums. It was the first and the last time in my life that I ever held in my hands promissory notes that had been issued to me. (They ran off to get the promissory-note paper from somewhere, while I waited, sitting on some boxes that gave off a very powerful odour of boot leather.) I felt very flattered that I had promissory notes.

After that about two months have been erased from my memory. All I remember is that at Rudolfi's place I waxed indignant that he had sent me to someone like Rvatsky, that a publisher couldn't possibly have such lacklustre eyes and a ruby tie-pin. I also remember the way my heart sank when Rudolfi said: 'Show me the promissory notes,' and how it returned to its correct place when he said through his teeth: 'It's all in order.' Apart from that, I shall never forget how I arrived to collect on the first of these promissory notes. It all started with the fact that the signboard 'Photographic Accessories Bureau' turned out not to exist any longer; it had been replaced by a signboard saying 'Medicinal Cupping-Glass Bureau'.

I went in and said:

'I need to see Makar Borisovich Rvatsky.'

I remember well the way I went weak at the knees when they replied that M. B. Rvatsky was abroad.

Ah, my heart, my heart! But then, that is not important any more.

Once again, in brief: Rvatsky's brother was there behind the plywood partition (Rvatsky had gone abroad ten minutes after signing the contract with me – remember the sleeping carriage ticket?). In appearance the absolute opposite of his brother, Aloysius Rvatsky, a man of athletic build with grave eyes, paid up against the promissory note.

I received the money for the second note a month later, cursing life, in some official institution to which promissory notes are taken for protestation (a notary's office, perhaps, or a bank, where they have little windows with wire netting).

When the time for the third promissory note came I was wiser, I came to the second Rvatsky two weeks before the due date and said that I was tired.

The gloomy Rvatsky brother turned his eyes on me for the first time and growled:

'I understand. But why should you wait for the dates? You can have it now.'

Instead of eight hundred roubles, I received four hundred and handed over the two oblong pieces of paper to Rvatsky with great relief.

Ah, Rudolfi, Rudolfi! Thank you for Makar and Aloysius. But then, let us not get ahead of ourselves, things will get even worse as they go on.

Ah, but I bought myself a coat.

And at last the day came when I arrived at those same premises in a bitter frost. It was evening. The hundred-candle-power electric bulb glared unbearably into my eyes. Neither of the Rvatskys was there under the lamp behind the plywood partition (need it be said that the second had also gone away?). Sitting under this bulb in his coat was Rudolfi, and lying there in front of him on the desk, and on the floor and under the desk, were the greyish-blue copies of the newly published issue of the journal. Oh, that moment! I find it funny now, but I was younger then.

Rudolfi's eyes were glowing. I have to say that he really loved what he did. He was a genuine editor.

There is a certain kind of young man, you have also met them, of course, in Moscow. These young men are to be found in the editorial offices of journals at the moment when an issue is published, but they are not writers. They can be seen at all the dress rehearsals in all the theatres, although they are not actors; they are present at artists' exhibitions, but they themselves do not paint. They do not address opera prima donnas by their surnames but by their first name and patronymic; they also address individuals who occupy responsible positions by their first names and patronymics, even though they are not personally acquainted with them. At a premiere in the Bolshoi Theatre, as they squeeze their way through between the seventh and eighth rows, they wave an affable hand to someone in the dress circle; in the Metropole Hotel they sit at a table right beside the fountain and the little coloured lamps light up their bell-bottomed trousers.

One of them was sitting in front of Rudolfi.

'Well then, how do you like the latest issue?' Rudolfi asked the young man.

'Ilya Ivanich!' the young man exclaimed with deep feeling, twisting the journal in his hands. 'A quite charming issue, but, Ilya Ivanich, allow me to say to you in all sincerity that we, your readers, do not understand how you, with your taste, could have included this thing of Maksudov's.'

'How do you like that?' I thought, turning cold.

But Rudolfi gave me a conspiratorial wink and asked:

'Why, what's wrong with it?'

'Oh, come now!' the young man exclaimed. 'You know, in the first place ... will you permit me to speak frankly, Ilya Ivanovich?'

'By all means, by all means,' said Rudolfi, glowing.

'In the first place, it is quite simply illiterate . . . I can offer to underline twenty places where there are simply crude errors of syntax.'

'I'll have to reread it straightaway,' I thought with a sinking heart.

'And then, the style!' the young man cried. 'My God, what terrible style! And apart from that, the whole thing is eclectic, imitative, insipid somehow. Cheap philosophy, skimming across the surface . . . It's bad, it's feeble, Ilya Ivanovich! And apart from that, he imitates . . .'

'Who?' asked Rudolfi.

'Averchenko!'[13] the young man exclaimed, twisting and turning the copy of the journal and splitting apart the pages that were stuck together with his finger. 'Perfectly ordinary Averchenko! Here, let me show you.' Then the young man started rifling through the journal while I stretched out my neck like a goose to follow his hands. But unfortunately he failed to find what he was looking for.

'I'll find it at home,' I thought.

'I'll find it at home,' the young man promised. 'The issue is spoilt, really and truly, Ilya Ivanovich. He's simply illiterate. Who is he? Where did he study?'

'He says that he graduated from a parish school,' Rudolfi replied, his eyes flashing, 'but then, why don't you ask him yourself? Allow me to introduce you.'

A green, putrid mould spread across the young man's cheeks and his eyes were filled with indescribable horror.

I bowed to the young man; he bared his teeth and suffering distorted his agreeable features. He gasped and grabbed a handkerchief out of his pocket, and then I noticed that there was blood trickling down his neck. I was dumbfounded.

'What's wrong with you?' exclaimed Rudolfi.

'A nail,' replied the young man.

'Well, I'm off,' I said, stiff-tongued, trying not to look at the young man.

'Take some journals.'

I took a bundle of author's copies, shook Rudolfi's hand

and bowed in farewell to the young man, at which he, while continuing to press the handkerchief against his neck, dropped his copy and his stick on the floor, set off backwards towards the door, struck his elbow against the desk and exited.

Snow was falling in large flakes, New-Year-tree[14] snow.

It is not worth describing how I sat over the thick journal the whole night through, rereading various parts of the novel. It is worth noting that sometimes I liked the novel and then it immediately seemed repulsive. By morning I felt horrified by it.

The events of the following day are engraved in my memory. In the morning the friend I had robbed successfully was at my place and I gave him one copy of the novel, and in the evening I set out to go to a party organized by a group of writers to mark a highly important event – the safe arrival from abroad of the well-known writer Izmail Alexandrovich Bondarevsky. The cause for celebration was augmented by the fact that at the same time it was proposed to honour another well-known writer, Egor Agapyonov,[15] who had returned from his journey to China.

I dressed and walked to the party in a state of great excitement. After all, this was a world that was new to me, the world that I was striving to enter. This world was about to reveal itself to me and from its very best side – the leading representatives of literature, its finest flower, were due to be at the party.

And indeed, when I entered the apartment I felt an upsurge of joy.

The first person to catch my attention was the same young man from the day before, who had torn his ear on a nail. I recognized him despite the fact that he was all bandaged up with fresh gauze.

He was as delighted to see me as if I were a close friend and shook my hands for a long time, adding that he had spent all night reading my novel and that he had started to like it.

'So did I,' I told him. 'I read all night, but I stopped liking it.'

We struck up a warm conversation, and in the course of it the young man informed me that there would be jellied sturgeon and in general he was cheerful and excited.

I looked around – the new world was admitting me into itself, and I liked this world. The apartment was huge, the table was set for about twenty-five places; the crystal glimmered and glittered, there were even sparks glittering in the black caviar; the green, fresh cucumbers provoked nonsensically happy thoughts about picnics, and for some reason about fame and so forth. I was immediately introduced to the extremely well-known author Lesosekov and to Tunsky, the novelist. There were not many ladies, but there were some.

Likospastov was as meek as a lamb, and somehow I immediately sensed that he would probably be a rank below the others, that he couldn't be compared even with a beginner like Lesosekov, with his brown curls, not to mention, of course, Agapyonov or Izmail Alexandrovich.

Likospastov made his way through to me, we said hello.

'Well then,' Likospastov said, sighing for some reason, 'congratulations. Congratulations from the heart. And I'll tell you straight – you're a crafty one, brother. I'd have staked my right hand that your novel couldn't be published, that it was simply impossible. How you managed to get round Rudolfi is beyond me altogether. But I predict that you will go a long way! And to look at you . . . butter wouldn't melt . . . But still waters . . .'

At this point Likospastov's congratulations were interrupted by loud ringing sounds from the front entrance, and the acting host, the critic Konkin (the event was taking place in his apartment), exclaimed: 'It's him!'

And indeed, it proved to be Izmail Alexandrovich. There was the sound of a rich voice in the hallway, then the sounds of kisses, and a short gentleman in a celluloid collar, wearing a short jacket, came into the room. The man was embarrassed, quiet, polite and for some reason he was holding in his hands, having forgotten to leave it in the hallway, a peaked cap with a velvet band and the round dust mark left by a civilian cockade.

'Well, if you please, there's some kind of confusion here . . .' I thought, the appearance of the man who had entered was so out of keeping with the hearty laughter and the word 'pastries' that I had heard from the hallway.

It turned out that there was indeed some confusion. Following the man who had entered, Konkin appeared in the dining room, with an affectionate arm round the waist of the man he was leading in – a tall, solidly built, handsome fellow with a light, wavy, well-tended beard and well-combed curls.

The writer Fialkov, concerning whom Rudolfi whispered to me that his star was rising rapidly, was present and beautifully dressed (in general, everyone there was well dressed), but Fialkov's suit could not even be compared with Izmail Alexandrovich's clothes. A brown suit of the very finest-quality material, sewn by a Parisian tailor, enveloped Izmail Alexandrovich's stately but somewhat full figure. Starched linen, lacquered shoes, amethyst cufflinks. Izmail Alexandrovich was clean, white, fresh, jolly and direct. His teeth sparkled and, casting a glance at the festive board, he shouted:

'Hah! Damnation!'

And then there was a rapid flutter of laughter and applause and the sounds of kisses. Izmail Alexandrovich greeted some by shaking hands, some he kissed on both cheeks, from some he turned away jokingly, covering his face with his white hand, as if he were blinded by the sun, and chortling at the same time.

He kissed me three times, probably having taken me for someone else, and I caught a smell from Izmail Alexandrovich of cognac, eau de Cologne and cigars.

'Baklazhanov!' exclaimed Izmail Alexandrovich, pointing at the man who had come in first. 'Let me introduce him to you. Baklazhanov, my friend.'

Baklazhanov gave a tormented smile, and in his embarrassment at this unfamiliar high society he set his peaked cap on a chocolate-coloured statue of a young maiden who was holding an electric light bulb in her hand.

'I brought him along with me!' Izmail Alexandrovich continued. 'Why should he stay at home? I recommend him – a wonderful chap and most exceptionally erudite. And, mark my words, he'll put the lot of us in our place before a year's gone by! Why did you put your cap on her, you devil? Baklazhanov?'

Baklazhanov burned bright with shame and made a stab at trying to say hello but was prevented by the sudden, swirling vortex of people being shown their places, and then a swollen, glazed *kulebyaka** came gliding through between the people as they took their seats.

The feast started off immediately in a friendly, jolly, cheerful sort of way.

'The pastries have done for us!' I heard Izmail Alexandrovich's voice exclaim. 'Why did we eat those pastries, Baklazhanov?'

The ringing of the crystal was music to my ears; it seemed as if the light in the chandelier had been turned up. After the third glass all eyes turned towards Izmail Alexandrovich. The requests rang out: 'Tell us about Paris! About Paris!'

'Well now, for instance, we were at an automobile exhibition,' Izmail Alexandrovich told us, 'the opening, everything right and proper, the minister, journalists, speeches ... and standing there among the journalists was that petty swindler, Sashka Kondiukov. Well, the Frenchman, of course, was talking away ... some little speech he'd thrown together. Champagne, naturally. Then I look and I see Kondiukov puffing out his cheeks, and before we could even blink he puked! With ladies present, the minister! Ah, the son of a bitch! What on earth got into his head, I still can't understand! A colossal scandal. The minister, of course, pretended not to notice anything, but how could you not notice that ... The tails, the opera hat, the trousers cost a thousand francs. All shot to pieces ... Well, they took him out, gave him some water, drove him away ...'

'More! More!' cried the voices at the table.

By this time a maid in a white apron was already carrying round the sturgeon. The ringing was louder, voices were already starting to be raised. But I desperately wanted to know about Paris, and through the ringing, the clattering and the exclamations I struggled to hear Izmail Alexandrovich's stories.

'Baklazhanov! Why aren't you eating?'

'More! Please!' shouted the young man, applauding ...

'What happened afterwards?'

'Well, afterwards those two swindlers ran into each other on the Champs-Elysées, nose to nose ... What a tableau! And

---

* A large Russian pie of fish, meat, cabbage, etc.

before he had time to look round that fraud Katkin went and spat right in his face!'

'Ai-ai-ai!'

'Yes, indeed ... Baklazhanov! Don't sleep, damn you! Well now, and he was so agitated – he's a te-rr-rr-ible neurasthenic – that he missed and hit a lady, a lady he didn't know at all, right on her hat ...'

'On the Champs-Elysées?'

'Just imagine! Well, they don't take any nonsense there ... And her hat alone's worth three thousand francs! Well, of course, some gentleman struck him across the face with his stick ... An absolutely terrible scandal!'

At this point there was a pop in the corner and the yellow Abrau began sparkling in a narrow glass before my eyes ... I recall that we drank to Izmail Alexandrovich's health.

And I listened to more about Paris.

'He said to him, without the slightest embarrassment: "How much?" And he said ... the s-s-swindler! (Izmail Alexandrovich even screwed up his eyes.) "Eight thousand," he said. And then the first one answers: "Here you are!" and he takes out his hand and cocks a snook at him.'

'At the Grand Opéra?'

'Just imagine! He couldn't give a damn for the Grand Opéra! There were two ministers there in the second row.'

'Well, and the other one? What did the other one say?' someone asked, laughing.

'Something unmentionable, of course!'

'Good Lord!'

'Well, they took them both out, they don't take any nonsense there.'

The festivity became more expansive. Smoke was already drifting above the table, separating into layers. I felt something soft and slippery under my foot and on bending down saw that it was a piece of salmon, and I couldn't understand how it had got under my foot. Laughter drowned what Izmail Alexandrovich was saying and the subsequent astonishing tales of Paris remain unknown to me.

Before I had time to reflect adequately on the oddities of life

abroad the doorbell announced the arrival of Egor Agapyonov.
Things were already getting a bit confused. I could hear a piano
in the next room, somebody quietly playing a foxtrot, and I
saw my young man shuffling about, holding a lady and pressing
her against himself.

Egor Agapyonov entered briskly; he came sweeping in and
he was followed by a Chinese, small, skinny and yellowish,
wearing spectacles with black frames. Behind the Chinese came
a lady in a yellow dress and a sturdy man with a beard by the
name of Vasily Petrovich.

'Is Izmash here?' exclaimed Egor, and he dashed towards
Izmail Alexandrovich, who started shaking in joyful mirth and
exclaimed: 'Hah! Egor!' and plunged his beard on to Agapyonov's shoulder. The Chinese smiled sweetly at everyone but
didn't make a single sound, nor did he subsequently make any.

'Let me introduce you to my Chinese friend!' Egor shouted
after he and Izmail Alexandrovich had finished kissing each
other.

But after that things got noisy and muddled. I remember that
we danced on the carpet in the room, which made it uncom-
fortable. There was coffee standing in a cup on the writing desk.
Vasily Petrovich drank cognac. I saw Baklazhanov sleeping in
an armchair. The air reeked of smoke. And somehow I got the
feeling that it was really time to be going home.

And then quite unexpectedly I had a conversation with
Agapyonov. I noticed that as soon as it began to get close to
three in the morning he started showing signs of some kind of
anxiety. He started talking with a few people about something
and, as far as I could understand through the mist and the
smoke, he received firm refusals from them. Having submerged
myself in an armchair by the writing desk, I was drinking coffee,
without understanding why my heart was aching and why Paris
suddenly seemed somehow boring, so that I had even abruptly
stopped wanting to visit the place.

And then a broad face with perfectly round spectacles leaned
down over me. It was Agapyonov.

'Maksudov?' he asked.

'Yes.'

'I've heard of you, I have,' said Agapyonov. 'Rudolfi told me. They say you've published a novel?'

'Yes.'

'A fine hefty novel, they say. Ugh, Maksudov!' Agapyonov said with a wink, suddenly starting to whisper. 'Take a look at that individual . . . You see?'

'The one with the beard.'

'That's him, my brother-in-law.'

'A writer?' I asked, studying Vasily Petrovich, who was drinking his cognac with a smile of endearing anxiety.

'No! A cooperative businessman from Tetiushi . . . Maksudov, waste no time,' Agapyonov whispered, 'or you'll be sorry. Such an astonishing character! You need him for your writing work. In a single night you could trim a dozen stories out of him and sell every one of them for good money. An ichthyosaurus, the Bronze Age! He tells his stories fantastically well! Just imagine all the things he's seen in that Tetiushi of his! Catch him, or else the others will beat you to it and ruin everything.'

Sensing that he was being talked about, Vasily Petrovich smiled even more anxiously and took a drink.

'And the very best thing . . . Yes, that's an idea!' wheezed Agapyonov. 'I'll introduce you right away . . . Are you a bachelor?' he asked anxiously.

'I am,' I said, gaping wide-eyed at Agapyonov.

An expression of joy appeared on his face.

'Marvellous! You get to know him, and you take him home for the night! What an idea! Do you have some kind of divan? He'll fall asleep on the divan, nothing will happen to him! And in two days' time he'll leave.'

Due to being absolutely stupefied I was unable to think of anything to say apart from:

'I only have one divan . . .'

'A wide one?' Agapyonov asked anxiously.

But at this point I recovered my senses a little. And just in time, because Vasily Petrovich had already begun fidgeting in obvious readiness to make my acquaintance, and Agapyonov had begun pulling on my arm.

'I'm sorry,' I said, 'unfortunately there's absolutely no way I can take him. I live in a connecting room in someone else's apartment, and the landlady's children sleep behind a screen (I was about to add that they had scarlet fever, then decided that would be an excessive aggregation of falsehood, and then added it anyway) . . . and they have scarlet fever.'

'Vasily,' Agapyonov exclaimed, 'have you had scarlet fever?'

The number of times in my life I have heard the word 'cultured' used to describe me . . . I won't argue, possibly I have deserved this sad title. But this time I gathered up all my strength and before Vasily Petrovich had time to smile imploringly and say: 'I ha–' I told Agapyonov firmly:

'I categorically refuse to take him. I can't.'

'But just perhaps,' Agapyonov whispered quietly. 'Eh?'

'I can't.'

Agapyonov hung his head and chewed on his lips.

'But, I beg your pardon, surely he came to see you? Where is he staying?'

'He's staying with me, damn him,' Agapyonov said miserably.

'Well, and . . .'

'Well, my mother-in-law and her sister arrived today, you understand, my dear man, and then there's the Chinese . . . What the hell do they come for,' Agapyonov added abruptly, 'these brothers-in-law? Why couldn't he stay in Tetiushi . . .'

And at that point Agapyonov walked away from me.

For some reason I was overcome by a vague sense of alarm and without saying goodbye to anyone except Konkin, I left the apartment.


## CHAPTER 6

### The Catastrophe

Yes, this chapter will probably be the shortest. At dawn I felt a chill shudder run across my back. Then it was repeated. I huddled up tight and pulled the blanket right over my head and that felt better, but only for a moment. I suddenly felt hot. Then cold again, so cold that my teeth started chattering. I had a thermometer. It showed 38.8. I must have fallen ill.

When it was very nearly morning I tried to go to sleep, and I remember that morning to this day. The moment I closed my eyes a face in spectacles leaned down towards me and murmured: 'Take him,' and I kept repeating the same thing: 'No, I won't.' Either I was dreaming about Vasily Petrovich or he really had moved into my room, and the really horrifying thing was that he kept pouring cognac for himself but I was the one who drank it. Paris had become absolutely intolerable. The Grand Opéra, and someone in it cocking a snook at someone else. Shaping their hand, showing it and hiding it away again. Shaping it, showing it.

'I want to tell the truth,' I muttered, when the day had already spilled itself across the tattered, unwashed curtain, 'the whole truth. I saw a new world yesterday, and I found that world repulsive. I will not enter it. It is an alien world. A repulsive world! This has to be kept a total secret, sh-sh-sh!'

My lips somehow dried out exceptionally quickly. I don't know why, but I put a copy of the journal down beside me, intending to read it I can only suppose. But I didn't read anything. I wanted to put the thermometer in position again, but I didn't. The thermometer was lying on a chair beside me, but for some reason I had to go somewhere else to get it. Then I began losing contact with reality completely. I can remember the face of my colleague from the *Shipping* but the doctor's face has blurred. In short, it was the flu. I stopped seeing the Champs-Elysées, and there was nobody spitting on a hat, and Paris no longer extended for a hundred miles in front of me.

I started to feel hungry, and my kind neighbour, a foreman's wife, boiled me some broth. I drank it from a cup with its handle broken off, and kept trying to read my own composition, but only read about ten lines before giving up.

On about the twelfth day I was well. I was astonished by the fact that Rudolfi had not visited me, although I had written him a note asking him to come.

On the twelfth day I went out of the house, walked to the

'Medicinal Cupping-Glasses Bureau' and saw a new lock on it. Then I got into a tram and rode for a long time, holding on to the rails because I was so weak and breathing on the frozen window. I reached the place where Rudolfi lived. I rang the bell. Nobody answered. I rang again. A little old man opened the door and looked at me in disgust.

'Is Rudolfi home?'

The little old man looked at the toes of his bedroom slippers and replied:

'He's not here.'

In reply to my questions – where had he gone, when would he be back, and even the absurd question of why there was a new lock on the 'Bureau' – the little old man hummed and hawed and asked who I was. I explained everything, even told him about the novel. Then the little old man said:

'He went away to America a week ago.'

I'll be damned if I know where Rudolfi went and why.

Where the journal got to, what happened to the 'Bureau', why America, how he went away – I don't know and I never will know. And who that little old man was, the devil only knows!

Under the influence of my weakness after the flu, the thought even flashed through my exhausted brain that I might have dreamed the whole thing – that is, Rudolfi himself, and the novel in print, and the Champs-Elysées, and Vasily Petrovich, and the ear torn by the nail. But when I arrived home I found nine light-blue copies of the journal in my room. The novel had been printed. It had. There it was.

Unfortunately, I didn't know any of the people who were printed in the journal. And so I could not enquire from anybody about Rudolfi.

On making another trip to the 'Bureau', I became convinced that there was no bureau there any longer, but there was a café with tables covered with oilcloth.

But you tell me, if you can: where did several hundred copies of the journal go to? Where are they?

There has never been anything so mysterious in my life as the case of this novel and Rudolfi.

## CHAPTER 7[16]

The most reasonable thing to do in such strange circumstances seemed to be simply to forget all this and stop thinking about Rudolfi and about the issue of the journal that had disappeared with him. And that was what I did.

However, this did not relieve me of the cruel necessity to carry on living. I examined my past.

'And so,' I said to myself as I sat by the kerosene stove during the March blizzard, 'I have visited the following worlds.

'World one: the university laboratory, in which I remember the fume cupboard and flasks on tripods. I left that world during the civil war. Let us not argue over whether I acted frivolously or not. After incredible adventures (although why really incredible? – who did not go through incredible adventures during the civil war?), in short, after that I found myself in the *Shipping Herald*. Due to what reason? Let us hold nothing back. I cherished hopes of being a writer. Well, so what? I quit the world of the *Shipping Herald* too. And, in fact, there then opened up before me the world that I had been striving to enter, and then the odd thing was that I immediately found it unbearable. The moment I think of Paris a kind of cramp runs right through me and I can't go in through that door. And always that damned Vasily Petrovich! Why couldn't he have stayed in Tetiushi? And Izmail Alexandrovich may be very talented, but Paris is really disgusting. So I would appear to have been left in some kind of void? Precisely so.

'Well then, stay here and compose another novel, since that's what you have set your hand to; and you do not have to go to the parties. It is not a matter of parties, the real nub of the matter is that I have absolutely no idea what subject this second novel should be written about. What story should I tell to mankind? That is the disaster of the whole thing.'

By the way, about the novel. Let us look the truth in the face. Nobody read it. They couldn't read it, since Rudolfi had no time to distribute the journal before he disappeared. And my friend, the one I gave a copy to, he didn't read it either. I assure you of that.

Yes, and by the way: I am sure that after reading these lines many people will call me a cultured intellectual and a neurasthenic. As far as the first thing goes, I won't argue, but as for the second, I warn you very seriously that it is a delusion. I don't have even a shred of neurasthenia in me. And in general, before you start throwing that word about you should find out more precisely what neurasthenia is and listen to Izmail Alexandrovich's stories. But that is by the way. First and foremost I had to live, and for that I had to earn money.

And so, having put an end to my pointless March jabbering, I went looking for ways to earn a living. At this point life took me by the scruff of the neck and brought me back to the *Shipping Herald* again, like the prodigal son. I told the secretary that I had written a novel. That failed to move him. In a word, I agreed that I would write four features a month, receiving for them remuneration in accordance with the provisions of the law. A certain financial basis was thus beginning to take shape. The plan was to churn out these features as quickly as possible and write at night once again.

I carried out the first part, but the second part went right off the rails. The first thing I did was go off to the bookshops and buy the works of my contemporaries. I wanted to find out what they wrote about, how they wrote, what was the magic secret of this craft.

In buying I did not spare my resources, purchasing all the very best that happened to be on the market. In the first place, I acquired Izmail Alexandrovich's works, Agapyonov's book, two novels by Lesosekov, two collections of stories by Flavian Fialkov and a lot more besides. First of all, of course, I threw myself on Izmail Alexandrovich. But when I glanced at the cover I was stung by a disagreeable presentiment. The book was called *Parisian Trifles*. They all turned out to be familiar to me, from the first trifle to the last. I recognized the accursed Kondiukov, who was sick at the automobile exhibition, and those two who had a fight on the Champs-Elysées (it turned out that one was Pomadkin and the other Sherstyanikov), and the troublemaker who cocked a snook at someone at the Grand Opéra. Izmail Alexandrovich wrote with exceptional brilliance, I must give him that, and he inspired me with a distinct feeling of horror for Paris.

It turned out that Agapyonov had managed to publish a book of stories during the time that had elapsed since the party: *Tetiushi Fidget*. It was not difficult to guess that he had failed to find Vasily Petrovich a lodging for the night anywhere, that he had stayed the night at Agapyonov's place and that Agapyonov had been obliged to make use of the homeless brother-in-law's stories. Everything was clear, apart from the absolutely incomprehensible word 'fidget'.

Twice I attempted to read Lesosekov's novel *The Swans*; twice I read as far as page forty-five and started reading again from the beginning because I had forgotten what happened at the beginning. This gave me a serious fright. Something was going wrong with my head – I had stopped being able, or was not yet able, to understand serious things. And so, setting aside Lesosekov, I took up Flavian and even Likospastov, and in the latter I came across a surprise. To be precise, as I read a story which described a certain journalist – the story was called 'The Authorized Tenant' – I recognized a tattered divan with a spring that had forced its way out, a blotter on the table . . . In other words, the person described in the story was . . . me!

The trousers were the same, the head pulled down into the neck and that lowering look . . . In short, it was me! But I swear by all that I have ever held dear that I was described unfairly. I am not in the least bit cunning, nor greedy, nor sly, nor mendacious, nor a careerist, and I have never uttered the kind of nonsense that there is in this story! My sadness at reading Likospastov's story was inexpressible, and I decided after that to take a stricter look at myself from the outside, for which decision I am greatly obliged to Likospastov.

However, my sadness and my reflections concerning my own imperfection effectively meant nothing by comparison with the terrible awareness that I had not derived any new insights: from the books of the very finest writers I had not, so to speak, discovered any paths, not glimpsed any lights shining ahead, and I felt sick and tired of everything. And, like a worm, there began gnawing at my heart the appalling thought that I would never actually make any kind of a writer. And immediately I came face to face with an even more terrible thought: what if I turned out like Likospastov? Speaking even more boldly, let me say even: what if I even turned out like Agapyonov? Fidget? What is fidget? And why Kaffirs? This is all nonsense, I assure you!

Away from my feature-writing I spent a lot of time on the divan, reading various books, which, as I acquired them, I stacked up on the crooked bookcase and on the table and simply in the corner. With my own work I proceeded as follows: I put the remaining nine copies and the manuscript away in the drawer of the table, locked them in and decided never, ever in my life to go back to them.

A blizzard woke me up one day. March was still full of blizzards and wild winds, even though it was already approaching its end. And again, like that other time, I woke in tears! What weakness, ah, what weakness! And again the same people, and again the distant city and the side of the grand piano, and the shots and somebody sprawled out on the snow.

These people were born in dreams, they emerged from the dreams and settled in the most solid manner possible in my monk's cell. It was clear that I could not part with them so easily. But what was I to do with them?

At first I simply talked to them, and I had to extract the journal with the novel from the drawer after all. And then in the evenings I began getting the impression that there was something coloured projecting up out of the white page. On looking more closely and screwing up my eyes, I became convinced that it was a picture. And even more, that it was not a flat picture but a three-dimensional one, like a little box, and in it, through the lines of words, I could see a light burning and the same little figures that were described in the novel moving about. Ah, what an amusing game it was, and more than once I regretted that the cat was no longer alive and there was no one to whom I could show the people moving on the page in the little room. I am sure that the beast would have reached out its paw and started scraping the page. I can imagine how the cat's eyes would have blazed with curiosity, how its paw would have scratched at the letters!

As time went by the chamber in the book acquired sounds. I quite clearly heard the sounds of a piano. Of course, if I had told anyone about this, I must assume that they would have advised me to see a doctor. They would have said someone was playing under the floor downstairs and even, perhaps, have said precisely what they were playing. But I would not have paid any attention to these words. No, no! The piano is being played here on my table, this is where the keys are producing that quiet tinkling. But that is still not everything. When the house falls quiet and there is nobody downstairs playing anything at all, I hear an accordion forcing its way through the blizzard in miserable fury, and the accordion is joined by angry and sad voices that whine on and on. Oh no, this is not down there under the floor! Why does the little room fade away, why does a winter's night on the Dnepr appear on the pages, why do horses' faces emerge, and above them the faces of men in tall astrakhan hats? And I see sharp sabres and I hear a whistling sound that rends my very soul.

There is a man running, gasping for breath. Through the tobacco smoke I follow him, I strain my eyes and I see: a sudden flash behind the man – a shot – with a gasp he falls flat on his back, as if he has been stabbed to the heart with a sharp knife from the front. He lies without moving and a small, dark puddle spreads out from his head. And high above there is the moon and in the distance a string of sad little reddish lights in the village.

I could go on playing this game all my life, looking at the page ... But how could I record these little figures so that they would never go away anywhere again?

Then one night I decided to describe this magical chamber. But how was I to describe it?

Why, it's very simple. Just write down what you see, and if you don't see something, there's no need to write it. Look: the little picture lights up; the little picture acquires different colours. Do I like what I see? Very much. And so that is what I write: scene one. I see an evening, the lamp is burning. The fringe of the lampshade. Music lying open on the piano. They are playing *Faust*. Suddenly *Faust* falls silent, but a guitar starts to play. Who is playing? There he is, entering through the door, holding the guitar. I listen – he sings. I write: '*He sings*.'

Yes, this proves to be a charming game! There is no need to go to parties, and no need to go to the theatre either.

I spent three nights like that, tinkering with the first scene, and by the end of the third night I realized that I was writing a play.[17]

In April, when the snow disappeared from the courtyard, the first scene was already worked out. My heroes moved and walked about and spoke.

It was at the end of April that the letter from Ilchin arrived.

And now, when the reader is already familiar with the story of the novel, I can continue my narrative from the moment when I met Ilchin.

## CHAPTER 8

### The Golden Horse

'Yes,' Ilchin repeated, squinting cunningly and mysteriously, 'I have read your novel.'

I gaped wide-eyed at my interlocutor as he was alternately illuminated by the flickering light and faded away. The water lashed against the windows. For the first time in my life I saw before me a reader.

'But how did you get hold of it? You see . . . The issue . . .' I said, hinting at the journal.

'Do you know Grisha Aivazovsky?'

'No.'

Ilchin raised his eyebrows, he was astounded.

'Grisha is the literary director at the Unanimous Cohort.'

'And what sort of Cohort is that?'

Ilchin was so astounded that he waited for the lightning in order to study me.

The flash came and faded, and Ilchin continued:

'The Cohort is a theatre. Have you never been there?'

'I have never been in any theatres. You see, I have not been in Moscow long.'

The force of the storm abated and the day began to return. I saw that I provoked a jolly astonishment in Ilchin.

'Grisha was quite delighted,' Ilchin said in an oddly mysterious manner, 'and he gave me the journal. An excellent novel.'

Not knowing how to behave in such circumstances, I bowed to Ilchin.

'And you know, I had an idea,' Ilchin whispered, screwing up his left eye in mysterious fashion. 'You ought to make a play out of this novel!'

'The finger of fate,' I thought, and I said:

'You know, I have already begun to write it.'

Ilchin was so astounded that he began scratching his left ear with his right hand and screwed up his eyes even more. I think that at first he could not even believe in such a coincidence, but he managed to control himself.

'Wonderful, wonderful! You must carry on, do not stop even for a second. Do you know Misha Panin?'

'No.'

'Our literary director.'

'Aha.'

Ilchin went on to say that in view of the fact that only a third of the novel had been printed in the journal, and he desperately needed to know how it continued, I should read the continuation from the manuscript to him and Misha, and also to Evlampia Petrovna, and, having already learned from experience, he did not bother to ask if I knew her but explained himself that she was a stage director.

All of Ilchin's projects aroused in me the very greatest excitement.

Then he whispered:

'You will write the play, and we shall stage it. Won't that be wonderful? Ah?'

My chest was heaving, I was drunk on the afternoon storm and vague premonitions. And Ilchin said:

'And you never know, stranger things have happened, what if we even manage to prevail upon the old man? . . . Ah?'

On learning that I did not know the old man either, he actually shook his head, and I clearly read in his eyes the words: 'What a child of nature!'

'Ivan Vasilievich!'[18] he whispered. 'Ivan Vasilievich! What? You don't know him? You haven't heard that he is the head of the Independent?' And he added: 'Well, I never!'

Everything was spinning round in my head, primarily because there was something about the world around me that I found intriguing. As if I had already seen it in some long-ago dreams, and now here I was in it.

Ilchin and I went out of the room, walked through the hall with the fireplace, and the affection I felt for that hall was like a drunken joy. The sky cleared and a ray of light suddenly lay across the parquet flooring. And then we walked past the strange doors and, seeing that my interest was aroused, Ilchin seductively beckoned me inside with his finger. Our footfalls disappeared, there was silence and total subterranean darkness. My companion's rescuing hand pulled me out of it and artificial brightness dawned in an elongated aperture – my companion had parted the other curtains – and we found ourselves in a small auditorium with about three hundred seats. On the ceiling two light bulbs were glowing feebly in a chandelier; the curtain was open and the stage gaped wide. It was solemn, mysterious and empty. Its corners were flooded with darkness, but towering up in the middle, gleaming ever so faintly, there was a prancing golden horse.

'Today is our day off,' Ilchin whispered solemnly, as if he were in a church, then suddenly he was at my other ear and continued: 'Your little play will work a treat with our young people, you couldn't ask for anything better. Don't let it bother you that the hall looks small; in actual fact it's big, and by the way, the houses here are always full. And if we can get round the old man, who knows, it might even move on to the big stage! Ah?'

'He is trying to seduce me,' I thought, and my heart skipped a beat and trembled in anticipation, 'but why is he talking about all the wrong things? These full houses are really not important, the only important thing is that golden horse, and this highly mysterious old man is also extremely interesting, the one who has to be prevailed upon and got round so that the play can be put on . . .'

'This is my world,' I whispered, not noticing that I was beginning to speak out loud.

'Ah?'

'Nothing, it is not important.'

When Ilchin and I parted I even took away a little note from him:

Highly respected Pyotr Petrovich! Please be so kind as to arrange a seat at *The Favourite* for the author of *Black Snow*.

Yours cordially, *Ilchin*

'That is called a free pass,' Ilchin explained to me, and I left the building in an excited state, bearing away the first free pass of my life.

From that day on my life changed abruptly. By day I worked feverishly on the play, though in the daylight the pictures no longer appeared from the pages and the box had expanded to the dimensions of the Experimental Stage.

In the evening I waited impatiently for my appointment with the golden horse.

I cannot say whether the play *The Favourite* was good or bad. I was not interested in that anyway. But there was a certain inexplicable charm about this production. The moment the lights went out in the tiny little auditorium music started up somewhere behind the stage and people dressed in eighteenth-century costumes entered the box. The golden horse stood at one side of the stage, the characters sometimes entered and sat at the hooves of the horse or conducted passionate convers-ations beside its muzzle, and I revelled in it.

Bitter feelings overwhelmed me when the performance came to an end and I had to go out into the street. I wanted so badly to put on a caftan exactly like those the actors wore and take part in the action. For instance, it seemed to me that it would be very good if I appeared suddenly from the side with a colossal snub nose glued on my face, in a snuff-coloured caftan, holding a cane and a snuffbox in my hand, and said something very funny, and I tried to invent this very funny thing, sitting there in the tightly packed row of spectators. But it was other people who said funny things composed by someone else, and at times the audience laughed. Never in my life, before or after, has there ever been anything that has given me more delight than this.

To the astonishment of the sullen and unsociable Pyotr Petrovich, who sat at the little window with the inscription 'Business Manager, Experimental Stage', I saw *The Favourite* three times, the first time in the second row, the second time in the sixth and the third time in the eleventh. And Ilchin carried on punctiliously providing me with little notes, and I watched another play too, in which the characters entered in Spanish costumes and one actor played a servant so funnily and magnificently that the enjoyment of it brought out little beads of sweat on my forehead.

Then May began, and at last one evening Evlampia Petrovna and Misha and Ilchin and I gathered together. We went to a narrow little room in that same Experimental Stage building. The window was already open wide and the honking of the city could be heard.

Evlampia Petrovna proved to be a regal lady with a regal face and diamond earrings in her ears, and Misha astonished me with his laugh. He would start laughing all of a sudden – 'ah-ha-ha' – and then everybody stopped talking and waited. When he finished laughing he suddenly looked older and lapsed into silence.

'What mournful eyes he has,' I thought, fantasizing according to my morbid habit. 'He once killed his friend in a duel in Pyatigorsk,' I thought, 'and now this friend comes to him in the night, nodding his head in the moonlight at the window.' I took a great liking to Misha.

Both Misha and Ilchin, and Evlampia Petrovna, demonstrated their exceptional patience, and in a single sitting I read them the third of the novel that followed the published part. Then I suddenly stopped, stricken by pangs of conscience, saying that after that everything was clear anyway. It was late.

There was a conversation between my listeners, and even though they were talking Russian I did not understand a thing, it was so puzzling.

Misha was in the habit, when he was discussing something, of running around the room, occasionally stopping suddenly.

'Osip Ivanich?' Ilchin asked in a quiet voice, screwing up his eyes.

'No-no-no,' Misha replied and suddenly started shaking with laughter again. When he finished laughing he remembered the man he had shot and became old.

'In general, the elders . . .' Ilchin began.

'I don't think so,' muttered Misha.

After that I heard: 'But with just the Galins and the subsidiary, you won't really get . . .' (That was Evlampia Petrovna.)

'I'm sorry,' Misha started speaking suddenly and sawing the air with his hand, 'I've been saying for a long time that it's time to raise this matter in the theatre!'

'But what about Sivtsev Vrazhek Lane?' (Evlampia Petrovna.)

'Yes, and India, we still don't know what he'll make of this little matter,' added Ilchin.

'If we could put it all on the turntable at once,' Ilchin whispered quietly, 'they could turn to the music.'

'Sivtsev!' Evlampia Petrovna said significantly.

At this point my face must clearly have expressed total despair, because the listeners abandoned their incomprehensible conversation and turned to me.

'We all request you most urgently, Sergei Leontievich,' said Misha, 'to have the play ready no later than August. We really, really need to be able to read it for the beginning of the season.'

I do not remember how May ended. June has also been erased from my memory, but I remember July. Exceptionally hot weather set in. I sat there naked, wrapped in a sheet, composing the play. The further I went, the harder it became. My little box had long ago ceased making any sounds, the novel had gone dark and lay dead, as if it were unloved. The little coloured figures did not move on the table, no one came to my assistance. Now it was the box of the Experimental Stage that stood before my eyes. The characters sprang up and entered it very adroitly and briskly, but evidently they liked being there beside the golden horse so much that they had no intention of ever leaving, and the events developed, and there was no end to them in sight. Then the heat abated, the glass jug from which I had been drinking boiled water was almost empty and there was a dead fly floating in the bottom of it. It started to rain and August arrived. That was when I received a letter from Misha Panin. He asked about the play.

I plucked up my courage and that night I halted the flow of events. The play had thirteen scenes.

## CHAPTER 9

### It Has Begun

Raising my head, I saw above me a frosted globe filled with light, to one side a silver wreath of colossal proportions in a glass cupboard with ribbons bearing the inscription: 'To our beloved Independent Theatre from the Moscow Barristers' . . .' (one word was bent under); ahead of me I saw the smiling faces of the actors, mostly with shifting expressions.

In the distance I could hear silence, and occasionally a kind of mournful singing in chorus, then some kind of hubbub like in a bathhouse. There was a performance going on over there while I read my play.

I kept wiping my forehead with a handkerchief all the time and in front of me I could see a stocky, thickset man, smoothly shaven, with a thick head of hair. He was standing in the doorway with his eyes fixed on me, as if he were pondering something.

He is the only thing I remember, everything else was twitching, gleaming and shifting – except only that the wreath remained unchanged. I remember it most sharply of all. Such was the reading; no longer, however, at the Experimental Stage but at the Main Stage.

As I left that night I turned round and looked at where I had been. In the centre of the city, where there was a delicatessen next to the theatre, and opposite it a 'Trusses and Corsets' shop, there stood a quite unremarkable building looking like a tortoise, with dull, cube-shaped bay windows.

The following day the interior of this building presented itself to my gaze in the autumn twilight. I recall that I walked across the soft carpeting of soldier's greatcoat fabric around something which, it seemed to me, was the internal wall of the auditorium, and a great many people went bustling past me. The season was beginning.

I walked across the soundless fabric and came to an office furnished in an extremely agreeable fashion, where I found an elderly, equally agreeable man with a shaved face and jolly eyes. This was the repertoire manager, Anton Antonovich Knyazhevich.

There was a bright, happy picture hanging above Knyazhevich's desk . . . I recall that the stage curtain in it had crimson tassels and behind the curtain there was a jolly, pale-green garden . . .

'Ah, comrade Maksudov,' Knyazhevich exclaimed affably, inclining his head to one side, 'we have been waiting for you to get here, waiting for you! Please, please, have a seat, have a seat!'

And I sat down in an extremely agreeable leather armchair.

'I heard your p-lay, I did, I heard it,' said Knyazhevich, smiling, and for some reason spreading his hands wide. 'A wonderful play! Of course, we have never staged any plays like that before, but why don't we just take this one and stage it anyway, stage it . . .'

The longer Knyazhevich talked, the merrier his eyes became.

'. . . and you'll become terribly rich,' continued Knyazhevich. 'You'll be riding around in carriages! Yes indeed, in carriages!'

'Well, well,' I was thinking, 'he's a tricky man, this Knyazhevich . . . very tricky . . .'

And to my astonishment, the jollier that Knyazhevich became, the more uneasy I felt.

After talking to me a bit more Knyazhevich rang a bell.

'We'll send you to Gavriil Stepanovich now, hand you over, so to speak, directly to him, into his hands! A quite wonderful man, our Gavriil Stepanovich is ... He wouldn't hurt a fly! Not a fly!'

But the man with green galloons who came in at the sound of the bell delivered the following announcement:

'Gavriil Stepanovich has not arrived in the theatre yet.'

'If he hasn't yet, he soon will,' Knyazhevich responded as joyfully as ever. 'No more than half an hour will elapse before he arrives! And you, in the meanwhile, take a walk round the theatre, feast your eyes on everything, have a good time, take tea in the buffet and sandwiches, do not be mean with the sandwiches, do not wound the feelings of our buffet manager Ermolai Ivanovich!'

And I set out to walk round the theatre. It gave me physical pleasure to stroll across the fabric, and I was also gladdened by the mysterious semi-darkness everywhere and the silence.

In the semi-darkness I made another acquaintance. A man of about the same age as myself, thin and tall, approached me and introduced himself:

'Pyotr Bombardov.'

Bombardov was an actor at the Independent Theatre; he said that he had heard my play and that in his opinion it was a good play.

Somehow from the very first moment Bombardov and I became friends. He impressed me as being a very intelligent, observant man.

'Would you like to take a look at our gallery of portraits in the foyer?' Bombardov asked politely.

I thanked him for the offer and we went into the immense foyer, also carpeted with grey fabric. The piers between the windows were hung with several rows of portraits and enlarged photographs in gilded oval frames.

From the first frame there gazed out at us a woman of about

thirty painted in oils, with ecstatic eyes and a tall back-combed fringe, wearing décolleté.

'Sarah Bernhardt,'[19] Bombardov explained.

Located in the frame beside the famous actress was a photographic representation of a man with a moustache.

'Andrei Pakhomovich Sevastianov, manager of the theatre's lighting apparatus,' Bombardov said politely.

I recognized Sevastianov's neighbour myself, it was Molière.[20]

In the position following Molière there was a lady wearing a tiny saucer hat on one side of her head, with a small shawl pinned with an arrow at her breast and holding a little lace handkerchief, which the lady grasped in a hand with the little finger extended.

'Ludmila Silvestrovna Pryakhina, an actress in our theatre,' said Bombardov, and a certain twinkle appeared briefly in his eyes. But squinting sideways at me, Bombardov added nothing more.

'I beg your pardon, but who is that?' I asked in astonishment, gazing at the cruel face of a man wearing laurel leaves in his curly hair. The man was dressed in a toga and he was holding a five-stringed lyre in his hand.

'The Emperor Nero,'[21] said Bombardov, and once again his eye glinted brightly, then dimmed.

'But why?'

'On the orders of Ivan Vasilievich,' said Bombardov, maintaining the immobility of his face. 'Nero was a singer and an actor.'

'I see, I see.'

Located beyond Nero was Griboedov,[22] beyond Griboedov came Shakespeare in a starched turn-down collar, beyond him an unidentified man I did not know, who turned out to be Plisov, who had been in charge of the turntable in the theatre for forty years.

After that came Givochini, Goldoni, Beaumarchais, Stasov and Shchepkin.[23] And then gazing out at me from the frame was a dashingly cocked uhlan shako, and beneath it a haughty

face, a waxed moustache, a cavalry general's epaulettes, a red
lapel and a cartridge belt.

'The late Major-General Klavdii Alexandrovich Komarovsky-
Echapart de Billancourt, commander of the life guards of
His Majesty's uhlan regiment.' And thereupon, observing my
interest, Bombardov told me:

'His story is perfectly extraordinary. He once came from
Peter to Moscow for two days, had dinner at Testov's[24] and in
the evening ended up in our theatre. Well, naturally, he sat
in the first row, and he watched ... I don't remember what
play they were performing, but the eyewitnesses say that during a scene in which a forest was shown something happened
to the general. A forest in the sunset, the birds starting to
sing before going to sleep, behind the scenes the church bells
summoning people to vespers in a distant village ... they looked
and saw the general wiping away the tears with his cambric
handkerchief.

'After the performance he went to Aristarkh Platonovich's
office. The usher said afterwards that as he walked into the
office the general spoke in a subdued and frightened voice:
"Teach me what to do!"

'Well, then he and Aristarkh Platonovich locked themselves
in ...'

'I beg your pardon, but who is this Aristarkh Platonovich?'
I asked.

Bombardov glanced at me in amazement but immediately
wiped the amazement from his face and explained:

'Our theatre is headed by two directors – Ivan Vasilievich
and Aristarkh Platonovich.[25] Pardon me, but are you not a
Muscovite?'

'No, I am not ... Please go on.'

'... they locked themselves in, what they talked about, no
one knows, but we do know that that night the general sent a
telegram stating the following to St Petersburg: "St Petersburg.
His Majesty. Having realized my vocation to be an actor at
Your Majesty's Independent Theatre, I most humbly request
permission to retire. Komarovsky-Billancourt."'

I gasped and asked:

'And what happened?'

'The mess that was stirred up was simply charming,' replied Bombardov. 'Alexander the Third was given the telegram at two o'clock in the morning. They woke him up especially. There he is in just his nightwear, beard and little cross ... he said: "Give me that! What's happened to my Echapart?" He read it and for two minutes he couldn't say a thing, he just turned crimson and started breathing heavily, then he said: "Give me a pencil!" – and there and then he wrote a resolution on the telegram: "Let him never set foot in St Petersburg. Alexander." And he went to bed.

'And next day the general came straight to a rehearsal, wearing a morning coat and trousers.

'They varnished the resolution and after the Revolution the telegram was sent to the theatre. You can see it in our museum of curiosities.'

'And what parts did he play?' I asked.

'Kings, generals and valets in rich houses,' replied Bombardov. 'You know, here Ostrovsky's[26] more in our line, merchants and such ... And then we gave *The Power of Darkness*[27] for a long time ... Well naturally, our manners here, you understand yourself ... And he knew all that inside out, whether to give a lady a handkerchief, whether to pour the wine, he spoke French ideally, better than the French do ... And he had a special passion: he was terribly fond of playing birds offstage. When we had plays on with the action in the countryside in spring he always used to sit on a stepladder in the wings and whistle away merrily. It's such a strange story!'

'No! I don't agree!' I exclaimed passionately. 'It is so fine here in your theatre that if I were in the general's place I would have acted in exactly the same way ...'

'Karatygin, Taglioni,' Bombardov listed off as he led me from portrait to portrait. 'Catherine the Great, Caruso, Feofan Prokopovich, Igor Severyanin, Battistini, Euripides,[28] Bobylyova – the head of the women's sewing shop.'

But then one of those men in green galloons came trotting into the foyer and announced in a whisper that Gavriil Stepanovich had arrived in the theatre. Bombardov broke off in mid-word, shook my hand firmly and uttered the following mysterious words in a low voice:

'Be firm . . .' And he faded away into the semi-darkness.

I set off after the man in galloons, who trotted along in front of me, occasionally beckoning me on with his finger and smiling a weak, forced smile.

At every ten steps we encountered flaming electrical inscriptions on the walls of the wide corridor along which we were moving: 'Quiet! Rehearsal in progress!'

A man who was wearing gold pince-nez and also had green galloons, sitting in an armchair at the end of this corridor that ran in a circle, leapt up when he saw me being led along and barked in a whisper: 'Good health to you!' and then pulled back a heavy door curtain with the theatre's monogram, 'IT', embroidered on it in gold.

I now found myself in a tent. Green silk covered the ceiling, radiating out from its centre, at which a crystal lamp was lighted. There was soft silk furniture standing there. Another door curtain, and behind it a door glazed with matt glass. My new guide in the pince-nez did not approach it, but he gestured to indicate: 'Please do knock!' and instantly disappeared.

I knocked once quietly and took hold of the handle, made in the shape of a silver eagle's head, the pneumatic spring hissed and the door admitted me. My face came up against a door curtain, I got tangled up in it, cast it aside . . .

I shall cease to exist, I shall cease to exist very soon now. I have made up my mind, but even so it is rather frightening . . . But as I die I shall remember the office in which I was received by the theatre's assets manager Gavriil Stepanovich.

No sooner had I entered than the immense clock in the left corner chimed delicately and began playing a minuet.

My eyes were dazzled by all sorts of different lights. Green from the writing desk, or rather, that is, not a desk, but a bureau, that is, not a bureau, but some kind of very complicated construction with dozens of drawers, with vertical compartments for letters, with another lamp on a flexible silvery leg and an electric lighter for cigars. An infernal red light from under the desk of rosewood, with three telephones on it. A tiny white light from a little table with a compact foreign typewriter, with a fourth telephone and a pile of gold-edged paper with the crest 'IT'. Reflected light, from the ceiling.

The floor of the office was covered with cloth, not greatcoat fabric but billiard-table cloth, and lying on top of it was a cherry-red rug almost two inches thick. Beside it a colossal divan with cushions and a Turkish hookah. Outside it was day-time in the centre of Moscow, but not a single ray of light, not a single sound penetrated into the office through the window, which was hermetically sealed off with three layers of curtains. Here it was eternal, wise night, here it smelt of leather, cigars, perfume. The heated air caressed my face and hands.

Hanging on a wall that was covered with morocco leather embossed in gold there was a large photographic portrait of a man with a fine artistic mane of hair, squinting eyes and curled moustaches, holding a lorgnette in his hands. I guessed that this was Ivan Vasilievich or Aristarkh Platonovich, but exactly which of the two I did not know.

Swinging round abruptly on the pivot of his stool, a short man with a little black French goatee and a moustache with arrow-points directed towards his eyes turned his face towards me.

'Maksudov,' I said.

'Excuse me,' my new acquaintance replied in a thin, high tenor and gestured as if to say: 'I'll just finish reading this paper and . . .'

. . . he finished reading the paper, took off his pince-nez on a black cord, rubbed his weary eyes and, turning his back com-pletely towards the bureau, fixed his gaze on me without saying anything. He looked me directly and frankly in the eye, studying me closely, the way people study some new machine that they have just bought. He did not conceal the fact that he was studying me, he even screwed his eyes up. I averted my eyes – it did not help; I began squirming on the divan . . . Eventually I thought: 'A-ha-ha . . .' and, admittedly by dint of very great effort, I forced myself to begin staring back into the man's eyes. As I did so for some reason I felt a vague annoyance with Knyazhevich.

'What a strange way to behave,' I thought. 'Either he is blind, this Knyazhevich, or . . . not a fly . . . not a fly . . . I don't know . . . Steely, deep-set little eyes . . . there is a will of iron in them, a diabolical boldness, an inflexible determination . . . a little French goatee . . . why wouldn't he hurt a fly? He's terribly like the captain of the musketeers in Dumas . . . What was his name . . . I've forgotten, damn it!'

The silence that followed became unbearable, and it was broken by Gavriil Stepanovich. He smiled playfully for some reason and suddenly squeezed my knee.

'Well then, contractual party, perhaps it's time to sign?' he said.

A turn on the stool, a turn back again and there was the contract in Gavriil Stepanovich's hands.

'Only I don't know, can we really sign it without agreeing it with Ivan Vasilievich?' And at this point Gavriil Stepanovich cast a brief, involuntary glance at the portrait.

'Aha! Well, thank God . . . now I know,' I thought. 'It's Ivan Vasilievich.'

'We wouldn't want any trouble,' Gavriil Stepanovich continued. 'Well then, perhaps just for you!' He gave a friendly smile.

And then the door opened without a knock, the curtain was thrown back and a lady with a masterful face of a southern cast entered the room and glanced at me. I bowed to her and said: 'Maksudov . . .'

The lady shook my hand firmly, like a man, and answered: 'Avgusta Menazhraki.'

She sat down on a stool, took a gold cigarette holder out of the little pocket of her green jumper, lit a cigarette and started tapping quietly on the typewriter.

I read the contract and can say quite honestly that I didn't understand a thing and did not even try to understand anything.

I felt like saying: 'Put my play on; I don't want anything except to be granted the right to come here every day, lie on this divan for two hours, breathe the honeyed scent of tobacco, listen to the chiming of the clock and dream!'

Fortunately, I did not say this aloud.

I recall that the phrases 'should there be' and 'insofar as' occurred quite frequently in the contract and that every point began with the words: 'The author does not have the right . . .'

The author did not have the right to transfer his play to another theatre in Moscow.

The author did not have the right to transfer his play to any theatre in the city of Leningrad.

The author did not have the right to transfer his play to any city in the RSFSR.

The author did not have the right to transfer his play to any city in the Ukrainian SSR.[29]

The author did not have the right to print his play.

The author did not have the right to demand something from the theatre, but exactly what I have forgotten (point 21).

The author did not have the right to appeal against something, but exactly what I don't remember either.

One point, however, did disrupt the uniformity of this document – it was point 57. It began with the words: 'The author undertakes . . .' According to this point, the author undertook 'unconditionally and immediately to introduce into this play such amendments, changes, additions or abridgements, should these be required by the board of directors or any commissions, or institutions, or organizations, or corporations, or individuals invested with the relevant authority, without requiring for this any remuneration in addition to that indicated in point 15'.

Upon turning my attention to this point I saw that the word 'remuneration' in it was followed by a blank space.

I underlined this space with an interrogative fingernail.

'And what remuneration would you regard as acceptable to you?' asked Gavriil Stepanovich, gazing at me fixedly.

'Anton Antonovich Knyazhevich,' I said, 'told me that I would be given two thousand roubles . . .'

My interlocutor inclined his head respectfully.

'I see,' he said, then paused for a moment and continued: 'Ah, money, money! How much evil it causes in the world! We all think of nothing but money, but how many of us have ever given a thought to our soul?'

In the course of my hard life I had grown so unaccustomed

to such high-flown sentiments that I must confess I was flustered
. . . I thought: 'Who knows, perhaps Knyazhevich is right . . . I
have simply become callous and suspicious . . .' In order to
maintain decent appearances, I heaved a sigh, and my interlocutor replied to me, in turn, with a sigh, then suddenly winked at
me playfully, which did not tally with the sigh at all, and
whispered in an intimate tone:

'Four hundred roubles? Eh? Just for you? Eh?'

I must confess that I felt upset. The fact is that I did not have
a single kopeck to my name and had very much been counting
on those two thousand.

'Perhaps you can manage one thousand eight hundred?'
I asked. 'Knyazhevich told me . . .'

'He tries to make himself popular,' Gavriil Stepanovich
responded bitterly.

At this point there was a knock at the door and a man in
green galloons brought in a tray covered with a white napkin.
Standing on the tray were a silver coffee pot, a milk jug, two
china cups – orange on the outside and gilded inside – two
sandwiches with caviar, two with transparent orange sturgeon,
two with cheese and two with cold roast beef.

'Did you take the package to Ivan Vasilievich?' Avgusta
Menazhraki asked the man who had come in.

The man's expression changed and he tilted the tray.

'Avgusta Avdeevna, I dashed off to the buffet, and Ignutov
ran to take the package,' he said.

'I told you to do it, not Ignutov,' said Menazhraki. 'It's not
Ignutov's job to take packages to Ivan Vasilievich. Ignutov is
stupid, he'll get something confused, say the wrong thing . . .
Do you really want Ivan Vasilievich's temperature to go up?'

'He'll be the death of us,' Gavriil Stepanovich said coldly.

The man with the tray gave a quiet groan and dropped a
teaspoon.

'Where was Pakin while you were wasting your time in the
buffet?' asked Avgusta Avdeevna.

'Pakin ran to get the car,' explained the man under inter-
rogation, 'I ran to the buffet, I told Ignutov: "Run to Ivan
Vasilievich."'

'And Bobkov?'

'Bobkov ran off to get the tickets!'

'Put it down here!' said Avgusta Avdeevna. She pressed a button and a table top popped out of the wall.

Delighted, the man in galloons abandoned the tray, parted the curtain with his backside, opened the door with his foot and squeezed out through it.

'Your soul, think of your soul, Kliukvin!' Gavriil Stepanovich called after him, and turning to me he said in an intimate tone:

'Four hundred and twenty-five. Eh?'

Avgusta Avdeevna took a nibble at a sandwich and began tapping quietly with one finger.

'Perhaps one thousand three hundred? I really do feel very awkward, but at the moment I have no money and I have to pay my tailor . . .'

'Did he sew that suit?' asked Gavriil Stepanovich, pointing at my trousers.

'Yes.'

'Well, he sewed it badly, the scoundrel,' observed Gavriil Stepanovich. 'Give him the boot!'

'But you see . . .'

'We don't have,' Gavriil Stepanovich said with some uncertainty, 'any precedent here for paying authors money when the contract is signed, but for you . . . four hundred and twenty-five!'

'One thousand two hundred,' I responded more briskly. 'Without that much I cannot extricate myself from . . . my difficult circumstances . . .'

'Have you not tried betting on the races?' Gavriil Stepanovich enquired sympathetically.

'No,' I replied regretfully.

'One of our actors also got into difficulties; he went to the races, and just imagine, he won one and a half thousand. And there's no point in your taking money from us. Let me tell you as a friend, take too much and you're finished! Ah, money! What is it good for? I haven't got any, and my heart is so light, so peaceful . . .' And Gavriil Stepanovich turned out a pocket in which there was indeed no money but there was a bunch of keys on a little chain.

'A thousand,' I said.

'Ah, to hell with everything!' Gavriil Stepanovich exclaimed wildly. 'Let them tear me asunder afterwards, but I'll give you five hundred roubles. Sign!'

I signed the contract, and meanwhile Gavriil Stepanovich explained to me that the money which would be given to me was an advance, which I undertook to redeem from the first performances. We agreed that today I would receive seventy-five roubles, in two days' time a hundred roubles, then on Saturday another hundred and the remainder on the fourteenth.

My God! How prosaic, how dismal the street appeared to me after that office. It was drizzling, a cart loaded with firewood was stuck in the gates and the carter was yelling at the horse in a terrible voice; the citizens were walking along with disgruntled expressions because of the weather. I went rushing home, trying not to see the scenes of sad prose. The cherished contract was in safekeeping next to my heart.

I found my friend in my room (see the story with the revolver).

I tugged the contract out of my coat with wet hands and exclaimed:

'Read it!'

My friend read the contract and, to my great surprise, he became angry with me.

'What sort of useless drivel is this? What sort of things do you sign, dimwit?'

'You don't understand anything about theatrical matters, so don't talk about them!' I said, also angry now.

'What is this – "undertakes, undertakes" – and do they undertake to do anything at all?' my friend muttered.

I began heatedly explaining to him what the picture gallery was like, what an open-hearted man Gavriil Stepanovich was; I mentioned Sarah Bernhardt and General Komarovsky. I tried to convey the chiming of the minuet in the clock, the way the coffee steamed, the quiet, magical sound of steps on the fabric, but although the clock was chiming inside my head, and I could see the gold cigarette holder and the infernal fire in the electric stove and even the Emperor Nero, I was not able to convey any of this.

'Does Nero draw up the contracts for them?' my friend quipped in a wild voice.

'That's enough from you!' I exclaimed and tore the contract out of his hands.

We decided to have breakfast and sent Dusya's brother to the shop.

A fine autumn rain was falling. What ham that was, what butter! Moments of happiness.

The climate of Moscow is well known for its caprices. Two days later it was a fine, almost summery, warm day. And I was hurrying to the Independent. As I approached the theatre with a sweet feeling, anticipating the receipt of a hundred roubles, I saw a modest poster on the central doors.

I read it:

## REPERTOIRE

## PLANNED FOR THE CURRENT SEASON

Aeschylus – *Agamemnon*

Sophocles – *Philoctetus*

Lope de Vega – *Fenisa's Nets*

Shakespeare – *King Lear*

Schiller – *The Maid of Orleans*[30]

Ostrovsky – *Not of This World*

Maksudov – *Black Snow*

I stood there open-mouthed on the pavement – I am amazed that nobody took my wallet while I did it. People shoved me and said unpleasant things to me, but I went on standing there, contemplating the poster. Then I moved off a little to one side, intending to see what impression the poster made on the citizens walking past.

It turned out that it made no impression whatever. If you did not count the three or four people who gave it a brief glance, you could say that no one even read it.

But less than five minutes had passed before I was rewarded a hundred times over for my wait. In the stream of people walking towards the theatre I clearly spied the head of Egor

Agapyonov. He was walking towards the theatre with an entire
entourage, in which I caught a glimpse of Likospastov with a
pipe in his teeth and a man I did not know with a fat, pleasant-
looking face. Straggling along behind everyone else was a Kaffir
in an exceptionally yellow summer coat, for some reason without any hat. I withdrew deeper into a niche occupied by a blind
statue and watched.

The company drew abreast with the poster and halted. I do
not know how to describe what happened to Likospastov. He
was the first to linger and read it. The smile was still playing on
his face, his lips were still uttering the final words of some joke.
Then he reached *Fenisa's Nets*. Suddenly Likospastov turned
pale and seemed somehow to age instantly. His face expressed
unfeigned horror.

Agapyonov read it and said: 'Hmm . . .'

The fat man I did not know blinked . . . 'He is trying to
remember where he has heard my name . . .'

The Kaffir began asking in English what his companions had
seen . . .

Agapyonov said: 'A poster, a poster,' and started tracing out
a rectangle in the air. The Kaffir shook his head, not understanding a thing.

The public piled past, alternately concealing and revealing
the heads of the company, their words alternately reaching my
ears and being drowned in the noise of the street.

Likospastov turned to Agapyonov and said:

'But did you see, Egor Nilich? What on earth is going on?'
He glanced around miserably. 'They've gone totally insane!'

The wind blew away the end of the phrase.

I caught scraps of Agapyonov's bass and then Likospastov's
tenor.

'. . . But where did he come from? I was the one who discovered him . . . That same . . . Ugh . . . ugh . . . ugh . . . Dreadful
fellow . . .'

I emerged from my niche and walked straight towards the
poster-readers. Likospastov was the first to catch sight of me,
and I was astounded by the change that had taken place in his
eyes. They were Likospastov's eyes but something new had

appeared in them, some sort of estrangement, an abyss had opened up between us . . .

'Well, brother,' exclaimed Likospastov, 'well, brother! Thank you, I never expected it! Aeschylus, Sophocles and you! I don't know how you pulled it off, but it's brilliant! And now, of course, you won't want to know your friends! What kind of friends would we make for the Shakespeares of this world?'

'Why don't you just stop playing the fool!' I said timidly.

'There you see, can't even say a word! Just look at you, I swear to God! Well, I bear you no grudge. Give me a hug and a kiss, old man!' And I felt the touch of Likospastov's cheek, strewn with short, stiff wires.

'Let me introduce you!' And I was introduced to the fat man, who was staring fixedly at me. He said: 'Krupp.'

I was also introduced to the Kaffir, who pronounced a very long phrase in broken English. Since I did not understand this phrase, I did not say anything to the Kaffir.

'They'll be performing it on the Experimental Stage, of course?' Likospastov enquired.

'I don't know,' I replied. 'They said on the Main Stage.'

Likospastov turned pale again and cast a miserable glance up at the radiant sky.

'Well then,' he said hoarsely, 'God grant. God grant. Perhaps it is here that success will finally overtake you. It didn't work out with the novel, who knows, perhaps with the play it will. Only do not become proud. Remember, there's nothing worse than forgetting your friends.'

Krupp kept looking at me, for some reason becoming more and more thoughtful, and I noticed that he was studying my hair and my nose most attentively of all.

We had to part. It was distressing. Squeezing my hand, Egor enquired whether I had read his book. I turned cold with fear and said that I had not. At this Egor turned pale.

'How could he have read it?' said Likospastov. 'He has no time to read modern literature . . . I'm joking, only joking . . .'

'You read the book,' Egor said with authority. 'It turned out well.'

I walked into the entrance of the dress circle. The window

looking out on to the street was open. A man with green galloons was wiping it with a piece of cloth. The heads of the writers drifted by outside the cloudy glass and I heard Likospastov's voice:

'You struggle . . . struggle so hard to get by . . . It's offensive!'

The poster had turned everything in my head upside down, and the only thing I could feel was that my play was, strictly speaking and just between us, extremely bad, and that something ought to be done about it but it was not clear what.

. . . And then, right by the stairs leading to the dress circle, there appeared before me a stocky, blond-haired man with a resolute face and anxious eyes. The blond man was holding a plump briefcase.

'Comrade Maksudov?' the blond man asked.

'Yes, I . . .'

'I've been looking for you all over the theatre,' my new acquaintance began. 'Allow me to introduce myself – stage director Foma Strizh. Well, everything's in good order. Don't worry and don't be concerned, your play's in good hands. Have you signed the contract?'

'Yes.'

'Now you're ours,' Strizh continued decisively. His eyes glittered. 'You know what you ought to do, conclude a contract with us for all your future work! For all the rest of your life! So that it will all come to us. If you wish, we'll do it this very moment. Quick as a spit!' And Strizh spat smartly into a spittoon. 'Well now, I'll be putting on the play. We'll break the back of it in two months. On the fifteenth of December we'll have the dress rehearsal. Schiller won't hold us up. Schiller's a smooth job . . .'

'I beg your pardon,' I said timidly, 'but I was told that Evlampia Petrovna would be directing . . .'

Strizh's expression changed.

'What has Evlampia Petrovna to do with it?' he asked me severely. 'No Evlampias here.' His voice had turned to metal. 'Evlampia has nothing to do with this, she and Ilchin are going to put on *In the Outhouse in the Yard*. I have a firm understanding with Ivan Vasilievich! And if anyone tries to undermine it,

I shall write to India! By registered post, if it comes to that,' Foma Strizh cried menacingly, for some reason becoming quite agitated. 'Give me the copy,' he commanded me, holding out his hand.

I explained that the manuscript had not yet been typed up.

'What can they have been thinking of?' Strizh exclaimed, looking around indignantly. 'Have you been to see Poliksena Toropetskaya[31] in the antechamber?'

I did not understand a thing and merely gazed wildly at Strizh.

'You haven't? She's not in today. Tomorrow take the manuscript, go to her and act in my name! Boldly!'

At this point a very well-mannered, elegant man who burred his 'r's appeared beside us and said politely but insistently:

'Please come to the rehearsal hall, Foma Sergeevich! We are starting.'

And Foma adjusted the briefcase under his arm and disappeared, calling out to me in farewell:

'Tomorrow to the antechamber! In my name!'

I was left standing there and I stood there without moving for a long time.

## CHAPTER 10

### Scenes in the Antechamber

It hit me! It hit me! My play had thirteen scenes. Sitting in my little room, I held my old silver watch in front of me and read the play aloud to myself, evidently to the great astonishment of my neighbour on the other side of the thin wall. As I finished reading each scene I made a note on the paper. When I finished it emerged that the reading had taken three hours. At this point I realized that in a performance there are intervals, in the course of which the public goes out to the buffet. Having added on time for the intervals, I realized that my play could not be performed in a single evening. The nocturnal torments resulting from this problem led to my crossing out one scene. That shortened the play by twenty minutes, but it did not save the situation. I recalled that in addition to intervals there were also pauses. For instance, an actress stands there crying and adjusts a bouquet of flowers in a vase. She does not actually say anything, but time goes by. Clearly, mumbling the text at home was one thing but declaiming it from the stage was quite a different matter.

Something else had to be thrown out of the play but it was not clear what. Everything seemed important to me and, apart from that, the moment I marked something down for expulsion the entire structure, erected with such great effort, began to crumble, and I dreamed of falling cornices and collapsing balconies, and these dreams were prophetic.

Then I expelled one character, and as a result one of the scenes became somehow lopsided, then dropped out altogether, and there were eleven scenes.

After that, no matter how I racked my brains or how much I smoked, I was unable to cut anything. Every day my left temple ached. Realizing that nothing else would work, I decided to allow the problem to work itself out.

And then I set out to see Poliksena Toropetskaya.

'No, without Bombardov I won't be able to manage . . .' I thought.

And Bombardov did help me immensely. He explained that this India that I had encountered for the second time, and the antechamber, were not gibberish and I had not imagined hearing them. It now became clear at long last that the Independent Theatre was headed by two directors: Ivan Vasilievich, as I already knew, and Aristarkh Platonovich . . .

'Tell me, by the way, why was there only one portrait – of Ivan Vasilievich – in the office where I signed the contract?'

At this Bombardov, usually very perky, faltered.

'Why? Downstairs? Hmm . . . hmm . . . no . . . Aristarkh Platonovich . . . he is . . . his portrait is upstairs . . .'

I realized that Bombardov was not yet used to me, he was still shy of me. It was clear from this incomprehensible reply. And I did not press him for an answer out of a sense of delicacy

... 'This world enchants, but it is full of mysteries...'
I thought.

India? That is very simple. At that time Aristarkh Platonovich
was in India and that was why Foma was intending to write to
him by registered post. As for the antechamber, that is an
actors' joke. That was the nickname given (and which had
stuck) to the room in front of the upper director's office, in
which Poliksena Vasilievna Toropetskaya worked. She was
Aristarkh Platonovich's secretary...

'And Avgusta Avdeevna?'

'Why, naturally, Ivan Vasilievich's.'

'Aha, aha...'

'Aha's all very well and good,' said Bombardov, glancing at
me thoughtfully, 'but I advise you very seriously, try to make a
good impression on Toropetskaya!'

'But I don't know how!'

'Well, just you try!'

Holding the manuscript rolled up into a tube, I walked upstairs to the upper section of the theatre and reached the place
where, according to my instructions, the antechamber was
located.

In front of the antechamber there was a kind of porch with
a divan; here I stopped for a moment, feeling anxious, and
adjusted my tie, thinking about how I could make a good
impression on Poliksena Toropetskaya. And immediately it
seemed to me that I could hear sobbing coming from the antechamber. 'I just imagined it...' I thought and walked in, when
it immediately became obvious that I had not imagined it at all.
I guessed that the lady with the magnificent complexion in the
scarlet jumper behind the yellow writing desk must be Poliksena
Toropetskaya, and she it was who was sobbing.

Astounded and unnoticed, I halted in the doorway.

The tears were running down Toropetskaya's cheeks, she
was crumpling a handkerchief in one hand and hammering on
the writing desk with the other. A pockmarked, compactly built
man with green galloons was standing in front of the little
writing desk with his eyes rolling in horror and grief, jabbing
his hands up into the air.

'Poliksena Vasilievna!' the man exclaimed in a voice wild with despair. 'Poliksena Vasilievna! They haven't signed it yet! They'll sign it tomorrow!'

'This is villainous!' exclaimed Poliksena Toropetskaya. 'You have acted villainously, Demyan Kuzmich! Villainously!'

'Poliksena Vasilievna!'

'Those people downstairs have intrigued against Aristarkh Platonovich, taking advantage of the fact that he is in India, and you have helped them!'

'Poliksena Vasilievna! My lady!' the man cried in a terrible voice. 'What are you saying? How could I possibly undermine my benefactor . . .'

'I won't hear a word of it,' cried Toropetskaya. 'It's all lies, despicable lies! You have been bought!'

When he heard that Demyan Kuzmich cried out:

'Poli . . . Poliksena,' and he suddenly began sobbing himself, in a terrible, dull, barking bass.

But Poliksena, swinging her hand up to smash it against the writing desk, stuck the end of a pen protruding from a little vase into her palm. At this she whined quietly, leapt up from behind the little desk, collapsed into an armchair and tucked up her feet, clad in foreign shoes with glass diamonds on the buckles.

Demyan Kuzmich did not even cry out but howled in a strange, hollow tone of voice: 'Good grief! A doctor!' He went dashing out, and I followed him out into the porch.

A minute later a man in a grey lounge suit, clutching some muslin and a bottle, ran past me and disappeared into the antechamber.

I heard him shout:

'My dear! Calm yourself!'

'What has happened?' I whispered to Demyan Kuzmich in the porch.

'Be so good as to observe,' boomed Demyan Kuzmich, turn-ing his despairing, tear-filled eyes towards me, 'that I was sent to the commission for the travel warrants to Sochi for our people for October . . . Well then, sir, they gave me four war-rants, but somehow they'd forgotten to sign the warrant for

Aristarkh Platonovich's nephew in the commission ... Come tomorrow, they said, at twelve ... And now be so good as to observe – I have hatched a plot!' And from the suffering in Demyan Kuzmich's eyes it was clear that he was innocent, that he had not hatched any plot and did not deal in plots at all.

There came a weak cry of 'ai' from the antechamber, and Demyan Kuzmich scooted out of the porch and disappeared without trace. About ten minutes later the doctor also left. I sat for a while on the divan in the porch, until I could hear the sound of a typewriter from inside the antechamber, at which I felt emboldened and entered.

Poliksena Toropetskaya, powdered and calm now, was sitting behind the little writing desk and typing. I bowed, trying to make my bow pleasing and at the same time full of dignity, and began speaking in a voice at once dignified and pleasant, which to my surprise made it sound muffled.

Having explained that I was so-and-so and had been sent here by Foma in order to dictate the play, I received from Poliksena an invitation to sit down and wait, which I did.

The walls of the antechamber were thickly hung with photographs, daguerrotypes and pictures, dominant among which was a large portrait painted in oils of an imposing man in a frock coat with side whiskers in the fashion of the 1870s. I guessed that this was Aristarkh Platonovich, but I could not understand who was the ethereal, white maiden or lady peeping out from behind Aristarkh Platonovich's head and holding a transparent veil in her hand. This riddle tormented me so greatly that, having chosen an appropriate moment, I cleared my throat and asked about it.

There was a pause, during which Poliksena rested her gaze on me as if she were studying me, finally replying in an oddly strained manner:

'That is the muse.'

'Ah-ah,' I said.

The typewriter began rattling again, and I started looking round the walls, becoming convinced that in every one of the photos or drawings Aristarkh Platonovich was depicted in the company of other persons.

Thus a yellowed old photograph depicted Aristarkh Platonovich on the edge of a forest. Aristarkh Platonovich was dressed
in autumn-season city clothes, in high galoshes, a coat and top
hat. But his companion was wearing a sort of padded coat,
with a game bag and a double-barrelled shotgun. The companion's face, his pince-nez and grey beard seemed familiar
to me.

At this point Poliksena Toropetskaya demonstrated a remarkable quality: the ability at one and the same time to type
and also in some magical manner to see what was going on in
the room. I actually shuddered when, without waiting for the
question, she said:

'Yes, yes, Aristarkh Platonovich out hunting with Turgenev.'[32]

In the same way I discovered that the pair in fur coats at the
entrance to the 'Slavyansky Bazaar',[33] beside the two-horse cab,
were Aristarkh Platonovich and Ostrovsky.

The foursome at the dinner table, with the rubber plant behind them, were Aristarkh Platonovich, Pisemsky, Grigorovich
and Leskov.[34]

There was no need even to ask about the next photo: the old
man standing barefoot in a long peasant shirt, with his hands
stuck into his rope belt, with eyebrows like bushes, a neglected
beard and a bald head, could not be anyone else but Leo
Tolstoy. Aristarkh Platonovich was standing facing him in a
flat straw hat and a raw-silk summer jacket.

But the next watercolour astounded me beyond all measure.
'It is not possible!' I thought. There, sitting in an armchair in a
poor room, was a man with an extremely long, bird-like nose,
eyes with a sick and anxious expression and hair that fell in
straight strands on to emaciated cheeks, wearing tight, light-
coloured trousers with footstraps, shoes with square toes and
a little light-blue tail coat. A manuscript on his knees, a candle
in a candlestick on the table.

A young man of about sixteen, as yet without any side whiskers but with that same haughty nose, in short, undoubtedly
Aristarkh Platonovich, wearing a short jacket, was standing
leaning with his hands on the table.

I gaped at Poliksena, and she replied drily:

'Yes, yes. Gogol reading Aristarkh Platonovich the second part of *Dead Souls*.'[35]

The hair stood up on the top of my head, as though someone had blown on me from behind, and the question somehow slipped out involuntarily:

'But how old is Aristarkh Platonovich?'

To this improper question I received an appropriate answer, and moreover I detected a certain vibration in Poliksena's voice:

'For people like Aristarkh Platonovich age does not exist. You are apparently greatly surprised that in the course of Aristarkh Platonovich's activities many people have had the opportunity of enjoying his company?'

'Why no!' I exclaimed, frightened. 'Quite the opposite! I . . .' But I said nothing sensible after that, because I thought: 'But what is the opposite? What nonsense am I jabbering?'

Poliksena fell silent, and I thought: 'No, I have not succeeded in making a good impression on her. Alas! That much is clear!'

At that point the door opened and a lady entered the antechamber with a lively stride, and I only had to glance in order to recognize her as Ludmila Silvestrovna Pryakhina from the portrait gallery. Everything the lady was wearing was the same as in the portrait; the plait, too, and the same handkerchief in her hand, and she was holding it the same way, with her little finger jutting out.

I thought that it would not be a bad thing to try to make a good impression on her as well, all at the same time, and gave a polite bow, but somehow it went unnoticed.

After running in, the lady burst into shimmering laughter and exclaimed:

'No, no! Surely you must see it! Surely you must see it!'

'Why, what is it?' asked Toropetskaya.

'Why, it's the sunshine, the sunshine!' exclaimed Ludmila Silvestrovna, toying with her handkerchief and even dancing on the spot a little. 'The Indian summer! The Indian summer!'

Poliksena glanced at Ludmila Silvestrovna with mysterious eyes and said:

'There's a form here that you will have to fill in.'

Ludmila Silvestrovna's merriment ceased immediately, and her face changed so greatly that now I would never have been able to recognize her in the portrait.

'What form is that? Ah, my God! My God!' And I did not recognize her voice any longer either. 'Just a moment ago I was delighting in the sunshine, I had focused inwardly, I had just developed something and cultivated the grain, the strings had just begun to sing, I was walking as if on my way to a shrine ... and now this ... Well, give it to me, give it here!'

'There's no need to shout, Ludmila Silvestrovna,' Toropetskaya remarked in a quiet voice.

'I'm not shouting! Not shouting! And I can't see a thing. The printing's abominable.' Pryakhina ran her eyes over the grey sheet of the form and suddenly pushed it away: 'Ah, write it yourself, you write it, I understand nothing about these matters!'

Toropetskaya shrugged and picked up a pen.

'All right, Pryakhina, Pryakhina,' Ludmila Silvestrovna exclaimed nervously, 'all right, Ludmila Silvestrovna! Everybody knows that, I'm not hiding anything!'

Toropetskaya entered three words into the form and asked:

'When were you born?'

This question produced an astonishing effect on Pryakhina – red spots appeared on her cheeks and she suddenly began speaking in a whisper:

'Holy Mother of God! What is this? I don't understand who needs to know that, what for? Why? Oh, very well, very well. I was born in May, in May! What else do you need from me? What?'

'I need the year,' Toropetskaya said quietly.

Pryakhina's eyes squinted inwards towards her nose and her shoulders began to shake.

'Oh, how I wish,' she whispered, 'that Ivan Vasilievich could see how they torment an artiste before rehearsal!'

'No, Ludmila Silvestrovna, this is impossible,' responded Toropetskaya. 'You take the form home and fill it in yourself as you like.'

Pryakhina grabbed the sheet of paper and began stuffing it into her handbag in disgust, with her mouth twitching.

At this point the telephone pealed loudly and Toropetskaya shouted into it sharply.

'Yes! No, comrade! What tickets? I haven't got any tickets! What? Citizen? You are wasting my time! I don't have any . . . What? Ah?' Toropetskaya turned red in the face. 'Ah! I beg your pardon! I didn't recognize your voice! Yes, of course! Of course! They'll be left right there at the door. And I'll instruct them to leave a programme! But will Feofil Vladimirovich himself not be here? We shall regret that greatly! Greatly! All the very, very best to you!'

Embarrassed, Toropetskaya hung up the phone and said:

'Thanks to you I was rude to a person one should not be rude to.'

'Ah, don't you tell me, don't you tell me all that!' Pryakhina exclaimed nervously. 'The grain is destroyed, the day is ruined!'

'Ah, yes,' said Toropetskaya, 'the company manager asked you to call in to see him.'

A faint pink glow coloured Pryakhina's cheeks, she raised her eyebrows haughtily.

'What could he possibly want with me? This is extremely interesting!'

'The costume-maker Korolkova has complained about you.'

'What Korolkova do you mean?' exclaimed Pryakhina. 'Who is she? Ah, yes, I remember! How could I possibly forget?' And then Ludmila Silvestrovna laughed in a way that sent a cold shiver running down my spine, with an 'oo' sound and without parting her lips. 'How could I possibly forget this Korolkova, who ruined my hem? What tales has she been telling about me?'

'She complains that you were so furious you pinched her in the changing room in front of the hairdressers,' Toropetskaya said sweetly, and just for a moment a glitter appeared in her crystal-clear eyes.

The effect produced by Toropetskaya's words astounded me. Pryakhina suddenly opened her mouth wide and crooked, as if she were at the dentist's, and two torrents of tears gushed out of her eyes. I squirmed in my chair and lifted my feet up for some reason. Toropetskaya pressed the button of the bell and Demyan Kuzmich's head was immediately thrust in at the door and then instantly disappeared.

But Pryakhina pressed her fist against her forehead and cried in a sharp, high voice:

'They're hounding me to death! Oh, Lord God! Oh, Lord God! Lord God! You at least, Holy Mother, just look at what they do to me in the theatre! Pelikan is a scoundrel! And Gerasim Nikolaevich is a traitor! I can imagine what nonsense they talked about me on Sivtsev Vrazhek Lane! But I shall cast myself at the feet of Ivan Vasilievich! I shall implore him to hear me!' Her voice sank and cracked.

At this point the door opened and in ran the same doctor. In his hands he was holding a bottle and a glass. Without asking anyone about anything, he splashed the liquid from the bottle into the glass with an accustomed gesture, but Pryakhina exclaimed hoarsely:

'Leave me alone! Leave me alone! You base people!' And she ran out.

The doctor dashed after her, exclaiming 'My dear!', and Demyan Kuzmich went flying after the doctor, stomping his gouty feet in opposite directions.

Through the open doors there came a tinkling of piano keys and in the distance a powerful voice sang passionately:

'. . . and you shall be the queen of all the wor – or – or . . .' It started expanding, soaring swiftly upwards, then the doors slammed shut and the voice disappeared.

'Very well, I am free now, let us get started,' said Toropetskaya, smiling gently.

## CHAPTER II

### *I Become Acquainted with the Theatre*

Toropetskaya had a perfect mastery of the art of typing. I have never seen anything like it. There was no need to dictate the punctuation marks to her or to repeat the instructions about who was speaking. I even reached the point of striding to and fro round the antechamber and dictating, halting, pondering, then saying: 'No, wait . . .' then changing what I had written, and I completely stopped reminding her who was speaking, I muttered or spoke loudly, but no matter what I did, Toropetskaya's hands produced a perfectly regular page of the play, almost without corrections, without a single grammatical error – good enough to hand straight in to the printer's.

In general Toropetskaya knew her job and coped with it very well. We typed to the accompaniment of telephone calls. Initially they bothered me, but afterwards I got so used to them that I even enjoyed them. Poliksena dealt with the callers with her own exceptional dexterity. She immediately shouted:

'Yes? Speak more quickly, comrade, I'm busy! Yes?'

This approach made the comrade at the other end of the wire flustered and he would begin babbling all sorts of nonsense and was immediately brought to order.

The scope of Toropetskaya's activities was extremely wide. I was convinced of this by the telephone calls.

'Yes,' said Toropetskaya, 'no, you're calling the wrong place. I don't have any tickets . . . I'll shoot you!' (That was to me, repeating a phrase already typed.)

Another ring.

'All the tickets are sold already,' said Toropetskaya. 'I don't have any free passes . . . That doesn't prove a thing.' (To me.)

'Now I'm beginning to understand,' I thought, 'just how many people there are who want to go to the theatre for free in Moscow. But isn't it strange: none of them tries to ride the tram for free. And none of them would walk into a shop and ask to be given a tin of sprats for free. Why do they think they don't have to pay at the theatre?'

'Yes! Yes!' Toropetskaya shouted into the telephone. 'Calcutta, the Punjab, Madras, Allahabad ... No, we don't give out the address! Yes?' she said to me.

'I won't have him singing Spanish serenades under my fiancée's window!' I said passionately, running around the antechamber.

'Fiancée's window! ...' repeated Toropetskaya. The typewriter tinkled constantly. The telephone pealed out again.

'Yes! The Independent Theatre! No, I haven't got any tickets! Fiancée's window! ...'

'Window!' I said. '*Yermakov throws the guitar on the floor and runs out on to the balcony*.'

'Yes? Independent! I haven't got any tickets! *Balcony*.'

'*Anna dashes* ... no, simply *walks out after him*.'

'*Walks out* ... yes? Ah, yes. Comrade Butovich, tickets will be left for you with Filya in the office. All the best.'

'*Anna*: He'll shoot himself!

'*Bakhtin*: He won't shoot himself!'

'Yes! Hello. Yes, with her. After that the Andaman Islands. I'm afraid I can't give the address, Albert Albertovich ... He won't shoot himself!'

It must be said in all fairness that Poliksena Toropetskaya really knew her job. She typed with ten fingers – with both hands; as soon as the phone rang she typed with one hand, picked up the receiver with the other and shouted: 'He didn't like Calcutta! He's feeling well ...' Demyan Kuzmich came in often, ran up to the little writing desk and handed her some papers. Toropetskaya read them with her right eye, applied the seals and with her left hand she typed: '*The accordion plays merrily, but that only ...*'

'No, wait, wait!' I exclaimed. 'No, not *merrily*, but *in a bravura sort of style* ... No, no ... wait.' I stared wildly at the wall, not knowing how an accordion plays. Meanwhile Toropetskaya powdered her face and spoke on the phone, telling some Missy that Albert Albertovich would get the plaques for the corsets in Vienna. Various different people appeared in the antechamber and at first I felt shy of dictating in front of them, it felt as if I were naked among people wearing clothes, but I quickly got used to it.

Misha Panin kept appearing and every time as he went past, in order to encourage me, he would squeeze my shoulder and walk on through the door behind which, as I had already discovered, lay his analytical office.

A smooth-shaven man would appear, with a decadent Roman profile and a capriciously jutting lower lip – the chairman of the production corporation, Ivan Alexandrovich Poltoratsky.

'A thousand pardons. Are you already typing the second act? Magnificent!' he exclaimed and walked through to another door, lifting his feet comically in order to demonstrate that he was trying not to make a noise. If the door opened slightly, he could be heard talking on the telephone.

'It's all the same to me . . . I'm a man without prejudices . . . It's quite original, actually, them arriving at the races in their underpants. But India won't accept it . . . He sewed the same for everyone – for the prince, and the husband and the baron . . . perfect underpants, both the colour and the cut! But you tell him that we need trousers. It's not my business! Let them do them over again. Then send him to hell! He's just lying! Petya Dietrich couldn't draw costumes like that! He drew trousers. I have the sketches on my desk! Petya . . . He may or may not be very refined, but he walks around in trousers himself! He's a man of experience!'

At the very height of the day, as I was pulling on my hair and trying to imagine how to express more precisely that there is the man . . . falling . . . dropping the revolver . . . is the blood flowing or not?, a young, modestly dressed actress came into the antechamber and exclaimed:

'Hello, my darling Poliksena Vasilievna! I've brought you some flowers!'

She kissed Poliksena and put four yellowish asters on the little counter.

'Is there anything about me from India?'

Poliksena answered that there was, and she took a

plump-looking envelope out of the writing desk. The actress became excited.

'"Tell Veshnyakova,"' Toropetskaya read out, '"that I have solved the riddle of Ksenya's role" . . .'

'Ah, well, well!' exclaimed Veshnyakova.

'"I was on the bank of the Ganges with Praskovya Fyodorovna and it struck me. The point is that Veshnyakova must not enter through the central doors but from the side, where the piano is. She should not forget that she has only recently lost her husband and could never bring herself to enter through the central doors for anything. She walks with the stride of a nun, with her eyes lowered, holding a bunch of wild daisies in her hand, which is typical for any widow" . . .'

'My God! How true! How profound!' exclaimed Veshnyakova. 'So true. That's why I felt awkward in the central doors.'

'Wait,' Toropetskaya continued, 'there's something else here,' and she read: '"But in general, let Veshnyakova make her entrance from wherever she wishes! When I get there everything will become clear. I did not like the Ganges, in my opinion there is something lacking in this river . . ." Well, that does not concern you,' Poliksena remarked.

'Poliksena Vasilievna,' Veshnyakova began, 'write and tell Aristarkh Platonovich that I am quite insanely, insanely grateful to him!'

'Very well.'

'But can I not write to him myself?'

'No,' replied Poliksena, 'he has expressed the wish that no one should write but me. It would tire him while he is musing on his thoughts.'

'I understand, I understand!' exclaimed Veshnyakova, then she kissed Toropetskaya and left.

A plump, middle-aged, energetic man came in, beaming and exclaiming while still in the doorway:

'Have you heard the new joke? Ah, are you typing?'

'Never mind, we're having an interval,' said Toropetskaya, and the plump man, evidently bursting at the seams with the joke, leaned down, positively glowing with joy, to Toropetskaya. At the same time he beckoned people to gather round with his hands. Misha Panin and Poltoratsky and someone else as well came to hear the joke. Their heads leaned down over the writing desk. I heard: 'And just then the husband comes back into the drawing room . . .' Behind the writing desk they started laughing. The plump man whispered a little bit more, after which Misha Panin was seized by a paroxysm of laughter – 'hah, hah, hah' – Poltoratsky exclaimed: 'Magnificent!' and the plump man started laughing merrily and immediately went dashing out, shouting:

'Vasya! Vasya! Stop! Have you heard it? I'll sell you the new joke!'

But he wasn't able to sell the new joke to Vasya, because Toropetskaya called him back.

It turned out that Aristarkh Platonovich had written about the plump man too.

' "Tell Elagin," ' Toropetskaya read, ' "that the thing he should be most afraid of is playing the result, which is what he is always tempted to do." '

Elagin's expression changed and he glanced into the letter.

' "Tell him," ' Toropetskaya continued, ' "that in the scene at the general's soirée he must not immediately greet the colonel's wife but first of all walk round the table, smiling in confusion. He owns a distillery, and there is no way that he would say hello immediately, but" . . .'

'I don't understand!' began Elagin. 'I beg your pardon, but I don't understand.' Elagin made a circle round the room, as if he were walking round something. 'No – I don't feel it. It seems awkward! The colonel's wife is there in front of him, and he walks off . . . I don't feel it!'

'Do you mean to say that you understand this scene better than Aristarkh Platonovich?' Toropetskaya asked in an icy voice.

Elagin was disconcerted by this question.

'No, I'm not saying that . . .' He blushed. 'But, you judge . . .' and he made the circle round the room again.

'I think that you ought to bow down at Aristarkh Platonovich's feet because he has written from India . . .'

'Why do we keep hearing about his feet all the time?' Elagin muttered suddenly.

'Ah, well said, that man,' I thought.

'You'd better listen to what Aristarkh Platonovich writes after that,' and she read: ' "But in general, let him do as he wishes. When I get there the play will become clear to everyone." '

Elagin brightened up and played the following trick. He waved his hand past one cheek, then past the other, and I had the impression that he had sprouted side whiskers before my very eyes. Then he became less tall and flared his nostrils haughtily and then, speaking through his teeth while at the same time plucking hairs from the imaginary side whiskers, recited everything that was written about him in the letter.

'What an actor!' I thought. I realized that he was representing Aristarkh Platonovich.

The blood rushed to Toropetskaya's face and she began breathing heavily.

'Please, if you don't mind!'

' "But in general," ' Elagin said through his teeth, then shrugged his shoulders and said in his usual voice: 'I don't understand!' and went out. I saw him make another circle in the porch of the antechamber, shrug his shoulders in bewilderment and disappear.

'Oh, these in-betweeners!' said Poliksena. 'Nothing is sacred. Did you hear the way they were talking?'

'Ghm,' I replied, not knowing what to say and, most importantly, not knowing what the term 'in-betweeners' meant.

By the end of the first day it became clear that it was not possible to type the play in the antechamber. Poliksena was released from her own direct responsibilities for two days, and she and I were moved into one of the female changing rooms. Demyan Kuzmich carried the typewriter there, puffing and panting.

The Indian summer surrendered and gave way to a wet autumn. A grey light poured in at the window. I sat on a couchette, reflected in a wardrobe with a mirror, and Poliksena sat on a little stool. I felt as if I had two storeys. Taking place in the upper storey was all the bustle and disorder that had to be transformed into order. The demanding characters of the play filled my heart with quite exceptional anxiety. Each of them requiring the correct words, each of them trying to occupy the first place, shoving the others aside. Correcting the proofs of a play is an extremely fatiguing business. The upper storey in my head was full of noise and movement that prevented me from enjoying the lower storey, where a secure and stable peace reigned. From the walls of the small changing room, which was like a bonbon box, women with exaggeratedly full lips and shadows under their eyes looked out, smiling artificial smiles. These women were wearing crinolines or farthingales. Set between them, their teeth glinting from the photographs, were men holding top hats in their hands. One of them was wearing thick epaulettes. His fat, drunkard's nose hung down to his lips, his cheeks and his neck were segmented into folds. I did not recognize him as Elagin until Poliksena told me who it was.

I looked at the photographs and, getting up from the couchette, touched the unlit lampions and the empty powder case, breathed in the barely perceptible smell of some kind of paint and the aromatic scent of Poliksena's *papyrosas*. It was quiet here, and the only sounds cutting through this quietness were the typewriter's clacking and its soft jingling, and sometimes the parquet floor would creak as well. Through the open door I could see some rather withered-looking elderly ladies occasionally walking past on tiptoe, carrying heaps of starched petticoats.

Occasionally the great silence of this corridor was broken by dull explosions of music from somewhere and distant menacing cries. I knew now that on the stage, somewhere deep behind the cobweb of old corridors, ramps and stairways, they were rehearsing the play *Stepan Razin*.[36]

We would begin typing at twelve o'clock and at two there was a break. Poliksena went to her antechamber in order to keep an eye on her own affairs, and I went to the tearoom.

In order to get to it, I had to leave the corridor and go out on to the stairs. Here the charm of the silence was disrupted. There were actresses and actors walking up the stairs, a telephone

ringing behind a white door, another telephone responding
from somewhere downstairs. One of the couriers schooled by
Avgusta Menazhraki was on duty at the bottom of the stairs.
Then the iron medieval door, the mysterious steps behind it
and what seemed to me a boundlessly high brick ravine, solemn
and dark. In this ravine the stage flats stood, towering up
against its walls in several layers. On their white wooden frames
I glimpsed mysterious abbreviations in black: 'I left back.',
'Count's rear.', 'Bedroom Act III'. There were wide, tall gates,
black with age, with a wicket gate cut into them on the right,
with a massive lock, and I learned that they led on to the stage.
There were similar gates on the left, and they led out into
the courtyard, and through these gates workmen handed in
from the sheds the stage flats that did not fit into the ravine. I
always lingered in the ravine in order to indulge my dreams in
solitude, and this was easy to do, for I encountered only a rare
traveller coming towards me along that narrow track between
the stage sets, where we had to turn sideways in order to pass
each other.

The spring-cylinder on the iron door sucked the air with a
quiet serpent's hiss as it let me out. The sounds made by my
feet disappeared as I found myself on the carpet and from
the bronze lion's head I recognized the doorway to Gavriil
Stepanovich's office. I walked over that familiar greatcoat fabric
towards the place where I could already glimpse people and
hear them – the tearoom.

The multi-gallon, gleaming samovar behind the counter was
the first thing to catch my eye, followed by a short, elderly man
with a drooping moustache, bald-headed and with such sad
eyes that everyone who was not yet used to him was overcome
by pity and alarm. Sighing miserably, the sad man stood behind the counter and gazed at a heap of red caviar and sheep's
cheese sandwiches. The actors approached the buffet and took
these provisions, and then the counterman's eyes filled with
tears. He took no joy in either the money that they paid for
the sandwiches or the awareness that he was standing in
the very best spot in the capital, in the Independent Theatre.
Nothing brought him any joy; his heart evidently ached at the

thought that now they would eat up everything that lay on the dish, eat it up and leave nothing behind, and drink his gigantic samovar dry.

The light of the tearful autumn day came in through the two windows, behind the buffet the lamp that was lit in a glass tulip on the wall never went out, the corners were drowned in eternal twilight.

I felt shy of the unfamiliar people sitting at the tables, afraid to approach them, although I wanted to. I could hear muffled laughter at the tables, everywhere they were telling each other about something.

After drinking a glass of tea and eating a sheep's cheese sandwich, I walked to other places in the theatre. Best of all I came to love the place that bore the name of 'the office'.

This place differed quite dramatically from all the other places in the theatre, for it was the only noisy place where life poured in, so to speak, from the outside.

The office consisted of two parts. The first was a narrow little room on the way into which there were so many intricate steps that everyone entering the theatre for the first time always fell over. Sitting in the first little room were two couriers, Katkov and Bakvalin. Standing in front of them on the table were two telephones. And these telephones rang constantly, almost never falling silent.

I very quickly realized that the calls on both the telephones were for the same man, and this man was located in the adjoining room, on the door of which there hung the following notice:

Head of Internal Order
*Filipp Filippovich Tulumbasov*

No one in Moscow was more popular than Tulumbasov, and probably no one ever will be. It seemed to me that the entire city was desperately trying to reach Tulumbasov on those telephones, and Katkov and Bakvalin by turns connected Filipp Filippovich with those who were longing to talk to him.

Either somebody told me or else I dreamed that Julius Caesar had the ability to do several different things at the same time, for instance read something and listen to what someone was saying.

I can testify here that Julius Caesar would have been reduced to a most pitiful state if he had been put in Filipp Filippovich's place.

In addition to those two telephones that jangled under the hands of Bakvalin and Katkov there were another two of them standing in front of Filipp Filippovich himself and one of the old type hanging on the wall.

Filipp Filippovich, a plump, blond-haired man with a pleasant, round face and exceptionally lively eyes, in the depths of which there lurked a concealed sadness that no one could see, evidently eternal and incurable, sat behind a barrier in a corner that was extremely cosy. Whether it was day or night outside, for Filipp Filippovich it was always evening, with his lamp lit under its green shade. Located in front of Filipp Filippovich on the writing desk were four calendars, completely covered with mysterious inscriptions such as: 'Pryan. 2, st.4', '13 matin. 2', 'Mon 77727' and the like.

The five notepads open on the desk were also covered with the same kind of signs. Towering up above Filipp Filippovich there was a stuffed brown bear with little electric bulbs set in its eyes. Filipp Filippovich was separated off from the outside world by the barrier, and at any hour of the day there were people dressed in the most various kinds of costumes lying with their bellies pressed up against this barrier. The entire country passed in front of Filipp Filippovich here, I can say that with confidence; here before him were representatives of every class, group, stratum, persuasion, sex and age. Poorly dressed female citizens in battered hats were followed by military men with collar tabs of various colours. The military men gave way to well-dressed men in beaver coat-collars and starched shirt-collars. Among the starched collars I occasionally glimpsed a collarless cotton shirt. A cap set on wild curls. A sumptuous lady with ermine on her shoulders. A cap with earflaps, a black eye. A juvenile individual of the female sex with a powdered little nose. A man wearing high waders, in a cloth caftan, girded round with a belt. Another military man, one pip. Some man with his head shaved and bandaged. An old woman with a trembling jaw and lifeless eyes who for some reason spoke to her female companion in French, and her female companion was wearing men's galoshes. A sheepskin coat.

Those who could not lie with their bellies on the barrier jostled behind, occasionally lifting up crumpled notes, occasionally exclaiming timidly: 'Filipp Filippovich!' Sometimes women or men without any outside clothing, dressed simply in blouses or jackets, would worm their way into the crowd besieging the barrier, and I realized that they were actresses and actors from the Independent Theatre.

But whoever might come to the barrier, they all, with only the very rarest of exceptions, wore a flattering expression and smiled ingratiatingly. Everyone who had come was asking Filipp Filippovich for something, they were all hanging on his reply.

The three telephones rang without ever falling silent, and sometimes all three at once filled the little office with a deafening jangling. This did not fluster Filipp Filippovich in the slightest. With his right hand he picked up the receiver of the right telephone, put it on his shoulder and held it in place with his cheek, then took the left telephone in his left hand and pressed it against his left ear and with his free right hand he took one of the notes held out to him, starting to speak to three people at once – into the left telephone and the right, then to the visitor. Into the right telephone, to the visitor, into the left, the left, the right, the right.

He dropped both telephones on to their cradles at the same time and, since he had freed both hands, took two notes. Declining one of them, he picked up the receiver of the yellow telephone, listened for a moment and said: 'Phone tomorrow at three,' then hung up the receiver and told the visitor: 'There's nothing I can do.'

As time passed I began to understand what it was they were asking Filipp Filippovich for. They were asking him for tickets.

They requested tickets from him in every possible manner of way. There were those who said that they had come from Irkutsk and were leaving that night and could not go away

without having seen *The Dowryless Bride*.[37] Someone said that
he was a tour guide from Yalta. A member of some delegation.
Someone else was neither a Siberian nor leaving to go anywhere
but simply said: 'Petukhov, remember me?' The actresses and
actors said: 'Filya, ah Filya, fix it . . .' Someone said: 'For any
price, I don't care about the price . . .'

'Knowing Ivan Vasilievich for twenty-eight years as I do,'
some old woman with a hole eaten in her beret by a moth
suddenly mumbled, 'I am sure that he will not refuse me . . .'

'I'll give you a standing place,' Filipp Filippovich said unexpectedly and, without waiting for the astounded old woman
to say anything else, held out a piece of paper to her.

'There are eight of us . . .' some brawny fellow began, and
again the rest of his words never passed his lips, for Filya was
already saying:

'For places left free!' and holding out a piece of paper.

'I've come from Arnold Arnoldovich,' began some young
man dressed with pretensions to luxury.

'I'll give you a standing place,' I prompted in my head, but
I guessed wrong.

'I can't help you, sir,' Filya unexpectedly replied after running
his glance once across the young man's face.

'But Arnold . . .'

'Can't help you, sir!'

And the young man disappeared, seeming to vanish into
thin air.

'My wife and I . . .' began a plump citizen.

'For tomorrow?' Filya asked, abruptly and swiftly.

'Next please.'

'Go to the ticket office!' exclaimed Filya, and the plump man
squeezed his way out, with a scrap of paper in his hand, as
meanwhile Filya was already shouting into the telephone: 'No!
Tomorrow!' and at the same time reading a piece of paper
handed to him with his left eye.

As time went by I realized that he was not guided at all by
people's appearance and, of course, not by grubby pieces of
paper. There were modestly, even poorly dressed people who,
unexpectedly for me, would receive two free seats in the fourth

row, and there were certain well-dressed people who went away with nothing. People would bring huge, beautiful warrants from Astrakhan, Eupatoria, Vologda, Leningrad, and they had no effect, or they could only have an effect five days later in the morning, and sometimes quiet, unassuming people who said nothing at all would come and simply stretch their hands out across the barrier and immediately be given a seat.

Enlightened, I realized that here I beheld a person who possessed a perfect knowledge of people. Having realized this, I felt a stirring of excitement and a chill sensation in the region of my heart. Yes, the person here before me was a great reader of hearts. He knew people in their most intimate depths. He could guess their secret desires, their passions and shortcomings were revealed to him, he knew everything that was concealed within them, but he also knew the good things. And, most importantly, he knew their rights. He knew who should come to the theatre and when, who had the right to sit in the fourth row and who had to languish in the upper circle, squatting on a narrow projection in the insane hope that in some magical way a seat would be left empty for him.

I realized that Filipp Filippovich's training had been truly magnificent.

And how could he not have known people, when in the fifteen years that he had been doing this job tens of thousands of people had passed in front of him? Among them there had been engineers, surgeons, actors, women's organization leaders, embezzlers, housewives, typists, teachers, mezzo-sopranos, building contractors, guitarists, pickpockets, dentists, firemen, young women of no specific profession, photographers, economic planners, pilots, Pushkin scholars, collective-farm chairmen, underground demi-mondaines, race jockeys, electricians, sales assistants from department stores, students, hairdressers, design engineers, lyric poets, criminals, professors, former property owners, female pensioners, village-schoolteachers, wine-makers, cellists, circus magicians, divorced wives, managers of cafés, poker-players, homeopaths, piano accompanists, graphomaniacs, women from the Conservatory ticket office, chemists, orchestral conductors, athletes, chess-players,

laboratory assistants, petty crooks, accountants, schizo-
phrenics, wine-tasters, manicurists, bookkeepers, former ser-
vants of the church, speculators and photographic technicians.

What did Filipp Filippovich need little pieces of paper for?

A single glance and the first words spoken by someone who
appeared before him were enough for him to know what that
person was entitled to, and Filipp Filippovich gave his replies,
and those replies were always unerringly correct.

'Yesterday,' said a lady in some agitation, 'I bought two
tickets for *Don Carlos*,[38] put them in my handbag, and when
I got home . . .'

But Filipp Filippovich was already pressing the bell button
and, no longer looking at the woman, saying:

'Bakvalin! Two lost tickets . . . which row?'

'Elev–'

'Row eleven. Let them in, seat check . . . Check!'

'Yes sir,' barked Bakvalin, and the lady was already gone,
and someone was already tumbling on to the barrier, saying
that he was going away tomorrow.

'You can't do that!' a lady declared angrily, and her eyes
glittered. 'He's already sixteen! Never mind that he's wearing
short trousers . . .'

'Madam, we don't mind who wears what kind of trousers,'
Filya replied in a steely voice. 'By law children under fifteen are
not allowed in. Sit here a moment, please,' he said at the same
time in an intimate tone to a clean-shaven actor.

'Begging your pardon,' shouted the quarrelsome lady, 'but
right here beside me they let through three little children in long
flared trousers. I'm going to complain!'

'Those little children, madam,' Filya replied, 'were midgets
from Kostroma.'

A total silence ensued. The light in the lady's eyes faded
and then Filya bared his teeth in a smile that made the lady
shudder. The people kneading each other at the barrier giggled
spitefully.

An actor with a pale face and dull, tormented eyes suddenly
fell against the barrier from the side and whispered:

'A terrible migraine . . .'

Filya, quite unsurprised, reached his hand out backwards without turning round, opened a little cupboard on the wall, found a little box by touch, took a paper packet out of it and held it out to the suffering man, saying:

'Take it with water . . . Yes, citizen, what can I do for you?'

Tears sprang to the lady citizen's eyes, her hat slid over on to one ear. The lady's grief was very great. She blew her nose into a dirty handkerchief. Apparently when she got home yesterday from that performance of *Don Carlos*, her handbag was missing. And in the handbag there had been a hundred and seventy-five roubles, a powder-case and a handkerchief.

'That's very bad, citizen,' Filya said sternly. 'You should keep money in the savings bank, not in your handbag.'

The lady goggled at Filya wide-eyed. She had not expected anyone to take such a callous attitude to her misfortune.

But Filya immediately opened the drawer of the desk with a clatter, and a moment later the crumpled handbag with its metal naiad yellowed by age was in the lady's hands. She babbled words of gratitude.

'The dead man's arrived, Filipp Filippovich,' Bakvalin reported.

That very moment the lamp went out and the drawers were shut with a clatter. Hastily pulling on his coat, Filya squeezed his way through the crowd and went out. I followed like someone spellbound. After hitting my head against the wall at the turn in the staircase, I came out into the yard. There was a truck draped with red ribbons standing at the door of the office, and lying on the truck, staring up into the autumn sky with closed eyes, was a fireman. His helmet gleamed at his feet and there were fir-tree branches lying at his head. Filya was standing beside the truck, without a cap and with a solemn face, giving some sort of silent instructions to Kuskov, Bakvalin and Kliukvin.

The truck sounded its horn and drove out into the street. Immediately there was the harsh sound of trombones from the theatre entrance. The public halted in languid astonishment and the truck halted too. In the theatre entrance I could see a man with a light-brown imperial below his lip, dressed in a coat and waving a conductor's baton about. In obedience to it, several gleaming brass instruments were filling the street with deafeningly loud sounds. Then the sounds broke off just as suddenly as they had begun, and the golden bellmouths and the little brown beard disappeared into the entrance.

Kuskov leapt into the truck, three firemen positioned themselves at the corners of the coffin and, despatched by Filipp Filippovich's parting gesture, the truck drove off to the crematorium, and Filya went back to the office.

The vast city pulsates, and everywhere in it there are waves – the tide coming in or going out. Sometimes, for no apparent reason, the tide of Filya's visitors would slacken and Filya would allow himself the liberty of leaning back in his chair, sharing a joke with someone and unbending.

'They sent me to see you,' said an actor from some other theatre.

'Couldn't they find anyone better – you troublemaker?' Filya replied, smiling with just his cheeks (Filya's eyes never smiled).

A very pretty lady in a magnificently tailored coat with a silver fox on her shoulders came in through Filya's door. Filya smiled amiably and shouted:

'*Bonjour*, Missy!'

The lady laughed merrily in reply. The lady was followed into the room at a slack waddle by a lad of about seven in a sailor's hat, his quite exceptionally haughty features smeared with soya chocolate and with three fingernail marks under his eye. The lad was hiccuping quietly at regular intervals. He was followed in by a plump and agitated lady.

'Fie, Alyosha!' she exclaimed with a German accent.

'Amalia Ivanna!' the lad said with quiet menace, surreptitiously showing Amalia Ivanovna his fist.

'Fie, Alyosh!' Amalia Ivanovna said in a quiet voice.

'Ah, greetings all!' exclaimed Filya, holding out his hand to the lad.

The lad hiccuped, bowed and shuffled his foot.

'Fie, Alyosh,' whispered Amalia Ivanovna.

'What's that under your eye?' asked Filya.

'I had,' the lad whispered, hiccuping and hanging his head, 'a fight with George . . .'

'Fie, Alyosha,' Amalia Ivanovna whispered with just her lips, entirely automatically.

'*C'est dommage!*'* Filya barked and took a chocolate sweet out of the drawer.

The lad's eyes, dulled by chocolate, blazed brightly for a moment and he took the sweet.

'Alyosha, you've eaten fourteen today,' Amalia Ivanovna whispered timidly.

'Don't lie, Amalia Ivanovna,' the lad hooted, thinking that he was talking quietly.

'Fie, Alyosha!'

'Filya, you have completely forgotten about me, you horrible man!' the lady exclaimed in a quiet voice.

'*Non, madame, impossible!*' barked Filya. '*Mais les affaires toujours!*'†

The lady gave a gurgling laugh and struck Filya on the hand with her glove.

'You know what?' the lady said, inspired. 'My Darya baked pies today, come for supper. Eh?'

'*Avec plaisir!*'‡ Filya exclaimed and lit up the bear's eyes in the lady's honour.

'What a fright you gave me, you nasty Filka!' the lady exclaimed.

'Alyosha! Just look at the big bear,' Amalia Ivanovna said in feigned ecstasy. 'He looks alive!'

'Let me go,' the lad yelled and dashed to the barrier.

'Fie, Alyosha . . .'

'Bring Argunin along,' the lady exclaimed, as if inspired afresh.

'*Il joue!*'§

'He can come after the show,' said the lady, turning her back to Amalia Ivanovna.

'*Je transporte lui.*'¶

'Yes, my dear, that's good. Yes, and I have a favour to ask

* It's a pity (French)
† No, madam, impossible . . . But there is always work to do (French)
‡ With pleasure (French)          § He's performing (French)
¶ I'll bring him (French)

you. Can you fit in one old lady somewhere for *Don Carlos*? Eh? In the upper circle at least? Eh, my precious?'

'A dressmaker?' asked Filya, fixing the lady with an all-comprehending eye.

'How horrible you are!' the lady exclaimed. 'Why does she have to be a dressmaker? She is the widow of a professor and now . . .'

'She sews underwear,' Filya said as if he were sleeping, writing in his notebook: 'Seamstr. Mi. side upcirc. 13th.'

'How clever of you to guess!' exclaimed the lady, looking even prettier.

'Filipp Filippovich, you're wanted on the phone in the director's office,' Bakvalin growled.

'Coming!'

'And meanwhile I'll phone my husband,' said the lady.

Filya bounded out of the room and the lady picked up a handset and dialled a number.

'Manager's office. Well, how's everything there? I've invited Filya round for pies today. Well, never mind. You sleep for an hour. Yes, and Argunin asked to come as well . . . But that would be impolite. Goodbye then, my darling. Why does your voice sound upset like that? Kiss-kiss.'

Pressing myself hard into the oilcloth back of the divan and closing my eyes, I dreamed. 'Oh, what a world . . . a world of pleasure, of calm . . .' I pictured this unknown lady's apartment. For some reason it seemed to me that it was a huge apartment, that there was a picture hanging in a golden frame in the boundless white entrance hall, that the parquet floors gleamed everywhere in the rooms. That there was a grand piano in the middle room, that the immense carp . . .'

My dreaming was suddenly interrupted by a quiet groan and an intestinal rumbling. The lad was sitting on the divan, pale with the pallor of death, his eyes rolled up under his forehead, with his legs sprawling out across the floor. The lady and Amalia Ivanovna came dashing across to him. The lady herself turned pale.

'Alyosha,' exclaimed the lady, 'what's wrong with you?'

'Fie, Alyosha, what's wrong with you?' Amalia Ivanovna also exclaimed.

'My head hurts,' the lad replied in a trembling, weak baritone, and his cap slid down over one eye. He suddenly puffed
out his cheeks and turned even paler.

'Oh, God!' exclaimed the lady.

A few minutes later an open-topped motor-taxi came flying
into the yard with Bakvalin also flying along, standing in it.

Wiping the lad's mouth with a handkerchief, they led him
out of the office by the hand.

Oh, wonderful world of the office! Filya! Farewell! Soon
I shall be gone. You, also, remember me!

## CHAPTER 12

### Sivtsev Vrazhek Lane

I had no time even to notice that Toropetskaya and I had
finished typing out the play. And I had no time even to think
about what would come next, before fate prompted me.

Kliukvin brought me a letter.

Highly esteemed Leontii Sergeevich! . . .

Why in damnation did they want me to be Leontii Sergeevich?
No doubt because it was easier to pronounce than Sergei
Leontievich? . . . But then, that's not important!

. . . You are to read your play to Ivan Vasilievich. For this you
are due to arrive at Sivtsev Vrazhek Lane on Monday the 13th
at 12 noon.

Your profoundly devoted servant,
*Foma Strizh*

I became extremely agitated, realizing that this letter was of
exceedingly great importance.

I decided on a starched collar, a blue tie and a grey suit. The

last item was not difficult to decide, for the grey suit was my
only decent one.

I would behave politely but with dignity and without any
hint, God forbid, of obsequiousness.

The thirteenth, as I remember very well, was the next day,
and in the morning I met Bombardov in the theatre.

His instructions seemed to me strange in the extreme.

'As soon as you pass the big grey building,' Bombardov said,
'turn to the left, into the little cul-de-sac. After that you'll find
it easily. Fancy wrought-iron gates, a house with columns.
There's no entry from the street, so walk round the corner of
the building in the yard. You'll see a man in a sheepskin coat
there; he'll ask you: "What do you want here?" and you say
just one word to him: "Appointment".'

'Is that the password?' I asked. 'And if the man's not there?'

'He will be,' Bombardov said coldly and continued: 'Exactly
opposite the man in the sheepskin coat round the corner you'll
see an automobile without any wheels on a jack, and beside it
a bucket and a man washing the automobile.'

'Have you been there today?' I asked excitedly.

'I was there a month ago.'

'Then how do you know that the man will be washing the
automobile?'

'Because he washes it every day, after he takes the wheels
off.'

'But when does Ivan Vasilievich ride in it?'

'He never rides in it.'

'Why?'

'Where would he want to ride to?'

'Well, let's say, the theatre?'

'Ivan Vasilievich comes to the theatre twice a year for the
dress rehearsals, and then they hire the cabby Drykin for him.'

'Well, I'm blowed! Why the cabby, if he has an automobile?'

'What if the driver has a heart attack and dies at the wheel,
and the automobile goes driving into a window, then what
would you have us do?'

'I beg your pardon, but what if the horse bolts?'

'Drykin's horse won't bolt. It only moves at a walking pace.

Directly opposite the man with the bucket there's a door. Go in and walk up the wooden stairs. Then another door. Go in. You'll see a black bust of Ostrovsky there. And opposite it little white columns and a pitch-black stove, with a man in felt boots squatting beside it and stoking it.'

I laughed.

'Are you sure that he's going to be there and he'll definitely be squatting?'

'Definitely,' Bombardov replied drily, not laughing at all.

'It will be interesting to check!'

'Then check. He will ask in alarm: "Where are you going?" And you answer him . . .'

'Appointment?'

'Ughu. Then he'll say to you: "Take your coat off here," and you'll go into the entrance hall, and then a nurse will come out to you and say: "What are you here for?" And you'll answer . . .'

I nodded.

'The first thing that Ivan Vasilievich will ask you is who your father was. Who was he?'

'A deputy provincial governor.'

Bombardov frowned.

'Er . . . no, I don't think that will do. No, no. You tell him he worked in a bank.'

'Now that's something I really don't like. Why do I have to lie from the very first moment?'

'Because that might frighten him, and . . .'

I could only blink.

'. . . and it's all the same to you, a bank or whatever else. Then he'll ask what you think about homeopathy. And you tell him that last year you took drops for your stomach and they helped you a lot.'

At this point a bell pealed several times and Bombardov started hurrying, he had to go to rehearsal, and he gave his remaining instructions in abbreviated form.

'You don't know Misha Panin, you were born in Moscow,' Bombardov informed me, rattling off the words. 'As for Foma, say you didn't like him. When you talk about the play don't object to anything. There's a shot in the third act, but don't read it . . .'

'How can I do that, when he's shot himself?'

The bell pealed again. Bombardov set off at a run into the semi-darkness and his low shout reached me from the distance:

'Don't read the shot! And you haven't got a cold in the nose!'

Still completely astounded by Bombardov's riddles, I was in the cul-de-sac on Sivtsev Vrazhek Lane on the dot of midday.

There was no man in a sheepskin coat in the yard, but there was a woman with a shawl on her head at the very spot that Bombardov had mentioned. She asked me: 'What do you want?' and gave me a suspicious look. The word 'appointment' reassured her completely and I turned the corner. Standing there exactly at the very spot that had been indicated was a coffee-coloured car, but on its wheels, and there was a man polishing the body with a cloth. Standing beside the car were a bucket and some kind of big bottle.

Following Bombardov's instructions, I proceeded unerringly and found myself at the bust of Ostrovsky. 'Eh . . .' I thought, remembering Bombardov's instructions: the birchwood logs were blazing merrily in the stove but there was no one squatting beside it. Only before I even had time to laugh an old, dark-lacquered oak door opened and out came a little old man in patched felt boots, with a poker in his hands. When he saw me he was frightened and began blinking. 'What do you want, citizen?' he asked. 'Appointment,' I replied, revelling in the power of the magic word. The little old man brightened up and waved his poker in the direction of another door. There was an old-fashioned lamp burning up on the ceiling above it. I took off my coat, put the play under my arm and knocked at the door. Immediately there was the sound of a chain being removed on the other side, and then a key turned in the lock and out glanced a woman in a white headscarf and white coat. 'What do you want?' she asked. 'Appointment,' I said. The woman moved aside, let me through and took a good look at me.

'Is it cold outside?' she asked.

'No, it's fine, an Indian summer,' I replied.

'Have you got a cold in the nose?'

I shivered, remembering Bombardov, and said:

'No, I haven't.'

'Knock here and go in,' the woman said sternly and disappeared.

Before knocking on the dark door bound with strips of metal I glanced round.

A white stove, huge cupboards of some kind. There was a smell of mint and of some other pleasant herb as well. There was absolute quiet, and suddenly it was shattered by a hoarse chiming. It struck twelve, and then a cuckoo clock behind a cupboard cuckooed alarmingly.

I knocked on the door, then pressed my hand down on the huge, heavy ring and the door admitted me into a large, bright room.

I was anxious, I could hardly make anything out, apart from the divan on which Ivan Vasilievich was sitting. He was exactly the same as in his portrait, only a little fresher and younger. The ends of his black moustache, with just a hint of grey, were curled up magnificently. He had a lorgnette hanging on a gold chain at his chest.

Ivan Vasilievich astounded me with the charming quality of his smile.

'Pleased to meet you,' he said, lisping slightly. 'Please sit down.'

I sat down in an armchair.

'Your first name and patronymic?' Ivan Vasilievich asked, looking at me endearingly.

'Sergei Leontievich.'

'Very pleased to meet you! Well now, tell me, how are you getting on, Sergei Pafnutievich?' And looking at me affectionately, Ivan Vasilievich drummed his fingers on the table, on which there was the stump of a pencil and a glass of water, for some reason covered with a sheet of paper.

'I am most obliged, well, thank you.'

'You don't feel you have a cold?'

'No.'

Ivan Vasilievich gave an odd croak and asked:

'And how is your good father's health?'

'My father is dead.'

'Terrible,' replied Ivan Vasilievich. 'And who did you consult? Who treated him?'

'I can't say exactly, but I think it was Professor . . . Professor Yankovsky.'

'That was a mistake,' responded Ivan Vasilievich. 'You ought to have consulted Professor Pletushkov, then everything would have been all right.'

I assumed an expression of regret that we had not consulted Pletushkov.

'Or even better . . . hmm . . . hmm . . . the homeopaths,' Ivan Vasilievich continued. 'It's quite terrifying how much better they make everyone feel.' So saying, he cast a fleeting glance at the glass. 'Do you believe in homeopathy?'

'Bombardov is an astonishing man,' I thought, and I began saying something vague and indefinite:

'On the one hand, of course . . . I personally . . . Although many people don't . . .'

'They should,' said Ivan Vasilievich. 'Fifteen drops and you won't feel another thing.' He croaked again and went on: 'And who was your father, Sergei Panfilich?'

'Sergei Leontievich,' I said gently.

'A thousand pardons!' exclaimed Ivan Vasilievich. 'And so, who was he?'

'I'm not going to lie!' I thought and said:

'He was a deputy provincial governor.'

This news drove the smile off Ivan Vasilievich's face.

'Well, well, well,' he said anxiously, was silent for a moment, drummed a little and said: 'Well then, sir, let us get started.'

I opened the manuscript, cleared my throat, froze in fear, cleared my throat again and began to read.

I read the title, then the long list of characters and began reading the first act:

'*Lights in the distance, a courtyard sprinkled with snow, the door of an outhouse. The muffled sound of* Faust *being played on a piano can be heard coming from the outhouse . . .*'

Have you ever had occasion to read a play to another person tête-à-tête? It is a very difficult thing, I assure you. I occasionally raised my eyes to look at Ivan Vasilievich and wiped my brow with my handkerchief.

Ivan Vasilievich sat entirely motionless and watched me through his lorgnette, without looking away. I was extremely flustered by the fact that he never smiled even once, although there were funny places already in the first scene. The actors had laughed a lot when they heard them at the reading, and one had laughed until he cried.

But not only did Ivan Vasilievich not laugh, he even stopped croaking. And every time I raised my eyes to look at him I saw the same thing: the gold lorgnette with its unblinking eye fixed on me. The result was that I began to feel that these funny places were not funny at all.

And so I reached the end of the first scene and began on the second. In the total silence the only thing I could hear was my own monotonous voice, it was like a sexton reading prayers for a dead person.

I felt myself beginning to be overcome by a strange apathy and a desire to close the thick notebook. I had the feeling that Ivan Vasilievich would say menacingly: 'Is this ever going to end?' My voice became hoarse, I hemmed occasionally to clear my throat, read sometimes in a tenor voice, sometimes in a deep bass; a couple of times my voice cracked and broke, but it did not make anyone laugh – neither Ivan Vasilievich nor myself.

A certain relief was provided by the appearance of the woman in white. She entered without a sound; Ivan Vasilievich glanced quickly at the clock. The woman handed Ivan Vasilievich a small glass, Ivan Vasilievich drank the medicine, followed it with water from the other glass, replaced its cover and glanced at the clock again. The woman bowed to Ivan Vasilievich in the old Russian style and left haughtily.

'Right, sir, carry on,' said Ivan Vasilievich, and I started reading again.

The cuckoo called in the distance. Then a telephone rang somewhere behind the screens.

'Excuse me,' said Ivan Vasilievich. 'That's a call for me from a certain institution.'

'Yes,' I heard his voice say behind the screens, 'yes . . . Hmm . . . hmm . . . It's all that gang's work. I order you to keep all this absolutely secret. I'll have a certain reliable man here this evening, and we'll work out a plan . . .'

Ivan Vasilievich came back, and we reached the end of the fifth scene. And then, at the beginning of the sixth, something quite astounding happened. My ear detected the sound of a door slamming, there was also loud and – so it seemed to me – false weeping, a door opened, not the one that I had entered but evidently the one leading into the inner chambers, and flying into the room, absolutely crazed, one must assume from fear, came a fat, striped tomcat. He streaked past me to the muslin curtain, stuck his claws into it and started climbing upwards. The muslin could not support his weight and holes appeared in it immediately. Continuing to tear the curtain apart, the cat climbed all the way to the top, from where he glanced round with a furious expression. Ivan Vasilievich dropped his lorgnette and Ludmila Silvestrovna Pryakhina came running into the room. The moment the cat saw her he made an attempt to climb even higher, but the only thing above him was the ceiling. The animal fell off the round cornice and hung there, frozen, on the curtain.

Pryakhina ran in with her eyes closed, pressing a fist clutching a crumpled, wet handkerchief against her forehead and holding the lace handkerchief, dry and clean, in her other hand. Having run as far as the centre of the room, she went down on one knee, bowed her head and extended one arm in front of her, as if she were a captive surrendering his sword to his conqueror.

'I shall not move from this spot,' Pryakhina proclaimed shrilly, 'until I am granted protection, my teacher! Pelikan is a traitor! God sees everything, everything!'

At this point the muslin made a cracking sound and a hole about a foot wide appeared in it below the cat.

'Shoo!' Ivan Vasilievich suddenly shouted despairingly and clapped his hands.

The cat slid down off the curtain, ripping it right to the bottom, and darted out of the room, while Pryakhina began sobbing in stentorian tones, putting her hands over her eyes and exclaiming as she choked on her tears:

'What do I hear? What do I hear? How could my teacher and benefactor drive me away? My God! My God! Do you see?'

'Look behind you, Ludmila Silvestrovna,' Ivan Vasilievich shouted out in despair, and then an old woman appeared in the doorway and called:

'Milochka! Come back! There's a stranger here!'

At that Ludmila Silvestrovna opened her eyes and saw my grey suit in the grey armchair. She gaped at me wide-eyed and the tears seemed to me to dry on her face in the twinkling of an eye. She leapt up from her knees, whispered: 'Oh, Lord . . .' and rushed out. The old woman also instantly disappeared and the door closed.

Ivan Vasilievich and I said nothing. After a long pause he drummed his fingers on the table.

'Well then, sir, how did you like that?' he asked and added miserably: 'The damn curtain's ruined.'

We said nothing again for a while.

'I suppose you must be amazed by this scene?' Ivan Vasilievich enquired and croaked.

I croaked too and began fidgeting in the chair, having no idea at all how to reply – the scene had not astounded me in the least. I had understood perfectly well that it was the continuation of the scene that had taken place in the antechamber and that Pryakhina had carried out her promise to throw herself at Ivan Vasilievich's feet.

'We were rehearsing,' Ivan Vasilievich suddenly declared, 'but you probably thought that it was simply a scandal! Did you not? Eh?'

'Astonishing!' I said, averting my eyes.

'Occasionally we like to refresh our memory of some scene or other all of a sudden like that . . . hm . . . hm . . . exercises are very important. And don't you believe that about Pelikan. Pelikan is a most valorous and helpful individual!'

Ivan Vasilievich glanced miserably at the curtain and said:

'Well then, sir, let us continue!'

We were not able to continue, since the same old woman who had been in the doorway came in.

'My aunty, Nastasya Ivanovna,' said Ivan Vasilievich.

I bowed. The pleasant-looking old woman looked at me amiably, sat down and asked:

'How is your health?'

'Thank you most kindly,' I replied, bowing, 'I am perfectly well.'

We said nothing for a while, although the aunty and Ivan Vasilievich looked at the curtain and exchanged a bitter glance.

'What is the occasion for your visit to Ivan Vasilievich?'

'Leontii Sergeevich,' responded Ivan Vasilievich, 'has brought me a play.'

'Whose play?' the old woman asked, looking at me with sad eyes.

'Leontii Sergeevich has written the play himself!'

'But what for?' Nastasya Ivanovna asked in alarm.

'How do you mean, what for? . . . Hmm . . . hmm . . .'

'Are there no plays left, then?' Nastasya Ivanovna asked in endearing reproach. 'There are such good plays already. And so many of them! If you start performing them, you won't get through them all in twenty years. Why bother yourself with writing more?'

She was so convincing that I could not think of anything to say. But Ivan Vasilievich drummed his fingers and said:

'Leontii Leontievich has written a contemporary play!'

At this the old woman became alarmed.

'We do not rebel against the authorities,' she said.

'Indeed, why rebel?' I agreed with her.

'But don't you like *The Fruits of Enlightenment*?'[39] Nastasya Ivanovna asked with timid anxiety. 'It's such a good play, after all. And there's a part for Milochka . . .' She sighed and stood up. 'Please give my best regards to your father.'

'Sergei Sergeevich's father is dead,' Ivan Vasilievich informed her.

'God rest his soul,' the old woman said politely. 'I suppose he doesn't know that you write plays? And what did he die of?'

'They consulted the wrong doctor,' Ivan Vasilievich informed her. 'Leontii Pafnutievich told me the woeful story.'

'I somehow can't seem to catch what your name is,' said Nastasya Ivanovna. 'Sometimes Leontii, sometimes Sergei. Do they let people change their first names as well now? We had one person who changed his surname. Now how can you tell who he is?!'

'I am Sergei Leontievich,' I said in a husky voice.

'A thousand pardons!' exclaimed Ivan Vasilievich. 'It was my mistake.'

'Well, I won't stop you working,' responded the old woman.

'That cat should be flogged,' said Ivan Vasilievich. 'It's a bandit, not a cat. We've been quite overrun by bandits,' he remarked confidentially, 'we really don't know what to do!'

As the twilight advanced, disaster struck.

I read out:

'*Bakhtin (to Petrov)*: Well, goodbye! Very soon you will follow me ...

'*Petrov*: What are you doing?

'*Bakhtin*: (*shoots himself in the temple, falls; in the distance there is the sound of an accordi–*'

'That's no good!' exclaimed Ivan Vasilievich. 'What's that for? You have to cut that out, this very second. For goodness' sake. Why have shooting?'

'But he has to commit suicide,' I replied with a cough.

'That's excellent. Let him commit suicide by stabbing himself with a dagger!'

'But don't you see, the action takes place during the civil war ... Daggers weren't used any more ...'

'Yes, they were,' objected Ivan Vasilievich. 'That what's-his-name, I forget, he told me that they were used ... You cut out that shot!'

I said nothing, which was a grievous error, and carried on reading:

'*–dion and a few isolated shots. A man with a rifle in his hand has appeared on the bridge. The moon –*'

'My God!' exclaimed Ivan Vasilievich. 'Shots! More shots! What sort of calamity is this? I tell you what, Leo . . . I tell you what, you cut out this scene, it's superfluous.'

'I thought this scene,' I said, trying to speak as gently as possible, 'was the most important . . . You see, here . . .'

'You are absolutely mistaken,' Ivan Vasilievich snapped. 'Not only is this scene not the most important, it is simply not necessary at all. What is it for? This what's-his-name of yours . . .'

'Bakhtin.'

'Well then . . . yes, he has stabbed himself over there in the distance,' – Ivan Vasilievich waved his hand towards something very far away – 'and somebody else comes to his house and says to his mother: "Bekhteev has stabbed himself!"'

'But he has no mother,' I said, gazing in stupefaction at the glass with the lid.

'He has to have one! You write her part. It's not hard. It seems hard at first – he had no mother, and all of a sudden he has – but that's a misconception, it's very easy. And there's the old woman sobbing at home, and the man who brought the news . . . Call him Ivanov . . .'

'But Bakhtin is the hero. He has monologues on the bridge . . . I expected . . .'

'But Ivanov will speak all his monologues! Your monologues are good, they should be retained. Ivanov will speak them – say that Petya has stabbed himself and before he died he said such-and-such and such-and-such . . . It will be a really strong scene.'

'But how can I do it, Ivan Vasilievich; after all, I have a crowd scene on the bridge . . . masses of people have clashed there . . .'

'Well, let them clash behind the scenes. We must not see it under any circumstances. It's terrible when they clash on the stage! It is your good fortune, Sergei Leontievich,' said Ivan Vasilievich, getting my name right for the only time, 'that you do not happen to be acquainted with a certain Misha Panin! . . .' (I turned cold.) 'Let me tell you, he is an amazing individual! We keep him for a rainy day, when something suddenly goes wrong we set him going . . . He has also supplied us with a little play, a friendly gesture, you might say – *Stenka Razin*. I came to the theatre, and as I approached I could hear it from a distance, the windows were open: rumbling, whistling, shouting, swearing, and they were firing guns! The horse almost bolted, I thought there was a rebellion in the theatre! It was awful! It turned out that Strizh was rehearsing! I said to Avgusta Avdeevna, what were you thinking of, I said? Do you, I asked her, want me to get shot myself? And what if Strizh burns down the theatre, they won't give me a pat on the back for that, will they now? Avgusta Avdeevna, such a noble woman, replied: "Blame me, Ivan Vasilievich, I can't do a thing with Strizh!" That Strizh is a pestilence in our theatre. If you ever see him coming, run a mile.' (I turned cold.) 'Well, of course, this is all with the blessing of a certain Aristarkh Platonich, but then you don't know him, thank God! And you have shots! Do you know what those shots could lead to? Well now, sir, let us continue.'

And we did continue, and when it had already begun to get dark I said in a hoarse voice: 'The end.'

And I was immediately overcome by horror and despair; it seemed to me that I had built a house and had only just moved into it when the roof had collapsed.

'Very good,' said Ivan Vasilievich at the conclusion of my reading. 'Now you need to work on this material.'

I almost shrieked: 'What?'

But I didn't.

And Ivan Vasilievich, relishing the details as he went along, began telling me how to work on this material. The sister who was in the play ought to be transformed into the mother. But since the sister had a fiancé, and the 55-year-old mother (Ivan Vasilievich immediately christened her Antonina) could not, of course, have a fiancé, an entire role would be thrown out of my play and, moreover, it was one that I was very fond of.

The twilight came creeping into the room. The medical attendant was there for a while and Ivan Vasilievich again took some drops. Then some wrinkled old woman brought a table lamp, and it was evening.

There was some sort of confusion in my head. There were hammers pounding at my temple. I was so hungry I had a falling sensation and the room occasionally twisted out of shape in front of my eyes. But most important of all was that the scene on the bridge was vanishing, and my hero was vanishing with it.

No, I suppose the most important thing of all was that there was obviously some sort of misunderstanding taking place. The poster with the play already on it would suddenly appear before my eyes, and I seemed to hear the final, unspent ten-rouble note from the ones that I had received for the play rustling in my pocket. Foma Strizh seemed to be standing behind my back and assuring me that he would put the play on in two months, but here it was absolutely clear that there was no play at all and that it needed to be written all over again from the beginning to the end. Misha Panin, Evlampia, Strizh and the scenes from the antechamber swirled round and round me in a furious dance, but there was no play.

But then something happened that was quite unforeseen, even – so it seemed to me – unimaginable.

Having demonstrated (and demonstrated very well) how Bakhtin, now firmly renamed Bekhteev, stabs himself, Ivan Vasilievich gave a sudden croak and delivered the following speech:

'I'll tell you what kind of play you ought to write . . . You can earn colossal money in an instant. A profound psychological drama . . . The fate of an actress. Let us say that in a certain kingdom there lives an actress, and a band of enemies persecutes her, torments her and makes her life a misery . . . And she only offers up prayers for her enemies . . .'

'And makes scandalous scenes,' I thought in a sudden surge of spite.

'Does she offer up her prayers to God, Ivan Vasilievich?'

This question perplexed Ivan Vasilievich. He croaked and replied:

'To God? Hmm . . . Hmm . . . No, not under any circumstances. Don't write to God . . . Not to God but . . . to the art to which she is utterly devoted. But she is persecuted by a gang of scoundrels, and this gang is urged on by a wizard called Chernomor.[40] You write that he has gone away to Africa and delegated his power to a certain lady X. A terrible woman. She sits at a little desk and is capable of anything. If you sit down to drink tea with her, watch out, you never know what kind of sugar she'll put in your glass . . .'

'Good grief, why he's talking about Toropetskaya!' I thought.

'. . . one sip and you'll turn up your toes. Her and that terrible villain Strizh . . . that is, I mean . . . a certain director . . .'

I sat there gazing stupidly at Ivan Vasilievich. The smile gradually slid from his face and I suddenly saw that the expression in his eyes was not at all benign.

'It is clear that you are a stubborn man,' he said in a rather bleak voice and chewed on his lips.

'No, Ivan Vasilievich, it is simply that I have little experience of the world of the stage.'

'Then study it! It is very simple. We have characters in our theatre that are a real feast for the eyes . . . One and a half acts of a play, ready-made for you! Some of the people walking about there have you just waiting for them to steal your boots from the changing room or plunge a bowie knife into your back.'

'That's terrible,' I said in a sickly voice and put a hand to my temple.

'I see you do not find that fascinating . . . You are an inflexible man! But then, your play is good too,' said Ivan Vasilievich, peering at me keenly. 'Now all you have to do is write it and everything will be ready . . .'

I left the room on unsteady legs and glanced at the black Ostrovsky with my head pounding. I muttered something as I went down the creaky wooden stairs, with the play that I now hated weighing down my arms.

The wind tore the hat from my head as I came out into the yard and I caught it in a puddle. There was not a trace left of the Indian summer. The rain was slanting down, my steps made a squelching sound, the wet leaves were falling from the trees in the garden. Water trickled down behind my collar.

Whispering some meaningless curses on life and myself, I walked along, looking at the street lamps burning wanly behind the streaks of rain.

On the corner of some side street there was light flickering feebly in a kiosk. The newspapers, weighted down with bricks, were getting soaked on the counter, and without knowing why I bought the magazine *Melpomene's Face*[41] with a drawing of a man in a skintight leotard, with a little feather in his little cap and affected, made-up eyes.

My room seemed incredibly loathsome to me. I flung the rain-swollen play on the floor, sat down at the table and pressed my hand against my temple to calm it. With my other hand I pinched off little pieces of black bread and chewed them.

Removing my hand from my temple, I began leafing through the thoroughly damp *Melpomene's Face*. I saw some girl or other in a farthingale, caught a glimpse of a heading, 'Pay attention', and another, 'The unbridled tenor di grazia', and suddenly glimpsed my own name. I was so surprised that my headache even disappeared. I glimpsed my name again and again, and then I glimpsed Lope de Vega's as well. There was no doubt about it, what I was looking at was a satirical article, entitled 'In someone else's sleigh', of which I myself was the hero. I have forgotten what the main point of the article was. I can vaguely recall its beginning:

Things were dull on Mount Parnassus.

'There doesn't seem to be anything new,' said Jean-Baptiste Molière with a yawn.

'Yes, things are a bit dull,' replied Shakespeare . . .

I recall that after that the door opened and I entered – a dark-haired young man with an immensely thick drama under my arm.

They were laughing at me, there could be no doubt about that. All of them were laughing spitefully. Shakespeare, and Lope de Vega and the malicious Molière, asking me if I had written anything like *Tartuffe*, and Chekhov, whom from his books I had taken to be a most sensitive individual, but the one who mocked me most facetiously of all was the author of the satire, who had the name 'Wolfhound'.

It is funny to recall it now, but my bitter resentment knew no bounds. I strode around the room, feeling that I had been insulted unjustly, wrongly, for absolutely no reason at all.

Wild dreams of shooting 'Wolfhound' alternated with puzzled reflections on what I could possibly have done wrong.

'It's the poster!' I whispered. 'But I didn't write it, did I? Take that!' I whispered, and I had visions of 'Wolfhound' lying on the floor in front of me, oozing blood.

There was a sudden stale-tobacco smell from a pipe, the door creaked and Likospastov was standing there in the room in a wet raincoat.

'Have you read it?' he asked gleefully. 'Yes, brother, congratulations, they really tore into you. Well, what is there to be done? You must lie in the bed you've made for yourself. As soon as I saw it I set out to see you, I had to visit my friend' – and he hung his stiff raincoat on a nail.

'Who is this "Wolfhound"?' I asked in a faint voice.

'Why do you need to know?'

'Ah, so you do know! . . .'

'Yes, but you're acquainted with him yourself.'

'I don't know any "Wolfhound"!'

'But of course you know him! I was the one who introduced you. Remember, in the street . . . And there was that funny poster . . . Sophocles . . .'

At this point I remembered the fat, thoughtful man looking at my hair . . . 'Black hair! . . .'

'But what did I do to that son of a bitch?' I asked vehemently.

Likospastov shook his head.

'Oh, brother, that's bad, that's ve-ry bad. I can see that your pride has completely consumed you. What's this now, can't anyone dare say a single word about you? You won't get through life without criticism.'

'What kind of criticism is this? He taunts me . . . Who is he?'

'He's a playwright,' Likospastov replied. 'He's written five plays. And he's a fine chap, you're wrong to be angry. Why, of course, he's a little offended. Everyone's offended . . .'

'But I didn't write the poster, did I? Is it supposed to be my fault that their repertoire includes Sophocles and Lope de Vega ... and ...'

'But, after all, you're not Sophocles,' said Likospastov with a malicious chuckle. 'I've been writing for twenty-five years, brother, but I still haven't become a Sophocles.' He sighed.

I realized there was nothing I could say in reply to Likospastov. Nothing! How could I say: 'You haven't become a Sophocles because you wrote badly, but I wrote well!' Can you say that to anyone, I ask you? Can you?

I said nothing, and Likospastov continued:

'Of course, that poster upset the general public. Lots of people have already asked me about it. That poster upsets them! But anyway, I didn't come to argue, when I learned about your second misfortune I came to console you, to have a chat with a friend ...'

'What misfortune is that?'

'Why, that Ivan Vasilievich didn't like the play,' said Likospastov, and his eyes glittered. 'You read it to him today, they say?'

'How do you know that?'

'The earth is full of rumours,' Likospastov said with a sigh – he was fond of speaking in proverbs and sayings. 'Do you know Nastasya Ivanna Koldybaeva?' He continued without waiting for my answer: 'A most respectable lady, Ivan Vasilievich's aunty. The whole of Moscow knows her, why they used to absolutely adore her at one time. She was a famous actress! And there's a dressmaker, Anna Stupina, who lives in our building. She was at Nastasya Ivanovna's just now, she only just got back. Nastasya Ivanna told her. She said some new man had been to see Ivan Vasilievich today and read him a play, as black as a beetle he was (I guessed it was you straightaway). Ivan Vasilievich didn't like it, she said. So that's it. But didn't I tell you then, remember, when you read it? I said the third act is lightweight and superficial; I'm sorry, but I'm only trying to help. But you didn't listen, did you? Well brother, Ivan Vasilievich, he knows his business, you can't hide anything from him, he saw how things were straightaway. And if he didn't like it, then the play won't be produced. That means you'll be stuck with that poster of yours. Then people will laugh, just look at this Euripides! And Nastasya Ivanovna says that you were actually insolent to Ivan Vasilievich? You upset him? He started offering you advice, and Nastasya Ivanovna says you just snorted back at him, snorted! Forgive me now, but that's going too far! That's getting above your station. Your play's obviously not valuable enough (to Ivan Vasilievich, that is) for you to go snorting . . .'

'Let's go to a restaurant,' I said in a low voice. 'I don't feel like staying at home, I don't feel like it.'

'I understand! Ah, how well I understand!' exclaimed Likospastov. 'Gladly. Only you see . . .' He rummaged uneasily in his wallet.

'I've got some.'

About half an hour later we were sitting at a stained tablecloth by the window of the 'Napoli' restaurant. An agreeable man with blond hair was busily setting our table with various kinds of hors d'oeuvres, speaking in affectionate tones about the 'wee cucumbers' and the 'lovely caviar', and he made everything feel so warm and cosy that I forgot that outside the gloom was impenetrable and Likospastov even stopped seeming like a serpent.

## CHAPTER 13

### I Learn the Truth

There is nothing worse, comrades, than cowardice and lack of faith in oneself. They were what led me to start wondering whether perhaps I really ought to transform the engaged sister into the mother.

'It couldn't possibly be, surely,' I thought to myself, 'that he could say that and be wrong? After all, he knows about these things!'

And taking up a pen, I began writing something on the page. I confess quite frankly that what I produced was some kind of gibberish. The worst thing was that I hated the unwelcome mother, Antonina, so badly that I began gritting my teeth the moment she appeared on the paper. So of course, nothing could possibly come of it. One has to love one's characters: if you don't have that, I advise anyone not to take up the pen – you will only suffer great distress, and it will serve you right.

'And serve you right!' I wheezed, tearing the page to shreds and swearing to myself that I would not go to the theatre. It was agonizingly difficult to keep my oath. I still wanted to know how this would all end. 'No, let them send for me,' I thought.

However, one day passed, and then a second, three days, a week, and they didn't send for me. 'Evidently that scoundrel Likospastov was right,' I thought. 'They won't stage the play. So much for that poster and *Fenisa's Nets*. Ah, how unlucky I am!'

But the world is not empty of good people, let me say, in imitation of Likospastov. One day there was a knock at my door and in came Bombardov. I felt so glad to see him that my eyes started to itch.

'All this was only to be expected,' said Bombardov, sitting on the windowsill and tapping his foot against the steam-heating pipe, 'and it has happened. After all, I warned you, didn't I?'

'But think, think, Pyotr Petrovich!' I exclaimed. 'How can one not read out a shot? How can one not read it?'

'Well, you did read it! And there you are,' Bombardov said harshly.

'I will not give up my hero,' I said angrily.

'You wouldn't have had to give him up . . .'

'How can you say that!'

Choking on my words, I told Bombardov about everything: about the mother, and about Ivanov, who was supposed to acquire the hero's precious monologues, and about the dagger that had driven me particularly wild.

'How do you like these plans?' I asked vehemently.

'Madness,' replied Bombardov, glancing over his shoulder for some reason.

'Well, you see!'

'What you ought to have done was not argue,' Bombardov said quietly, 'and reply like this: "I am very grateful to you for your guidance, Ivan Vasilievich, I will definitely put it into effect." You must not object, do you understand that or not? At Sivtsev Vrazhek Lane nobody objects.'

'How is that possible? Nobody ever objects?'

'Nobody, not ever,' Bombardov replied, rapping out every word. 'Nobody ever has, nobody does and nobody ever will.'

'Whatever he says?'

'Whatever he says.'

'And what if he says that my hero must go away to Penza? Or that this mother, Antonina, must hang herself? Or that she sings and she's a contralto? Or that this stove is black? What am I supposed to say to that?'

'That this stove is black.'

'And how will it turn out on stage?'

'White, with a black spot.'

'But that's quite monstrous, outrageous! . . .'

'Never mind, we get by,' replied Bombardov.

'Oh, come on now! Can Aristarkh Platonovich not say anything to him?'

'Aristarkh Platonovich cannot say anything to him since Aristarkh Platonovich has not spoken to Ivan Vasilievich since eighteen hundred and eighty-five.'

'How can that be?'

'They quarrelled in eighteen hundred and eighty-five and since then they have not met or spoken with each other, even on the telephone.'

'My head is spinning! How does the theatre survive?'

'Well, it does, as you can see, and it survives very well. They separated off their own spheres. If Ivan Vasilievich has taken an interest in your play, for instance, then Aristarkh Platonovich will not go anywhere near it, and vice versa. That way there is no ground on which they can clash. It's a very wise system . . .'

'Good Lord! And it's my bad luck that Aristarkh Platonovich is in India. If he were here, I would have appealed to him . . .'

'Hmm,' said Bombardov and glanced out of the window.

'Well, after all, it's impossible to deal with a man who doesn't listen to anybody!'

'Oh, but he does listen. He listens to three people: Gavriil Stepanovich, his aunt Nastasya Ivanovna and Avgusta Avdeevna. Those are the only three people in the entire world who can influence Ivan Vasilievich. If anybody else apart from the three aforementioned individuals should attempt to influence Ivan Vasilievich, the only thing he will achieve is that Ivan Vasilievich will do the opposite of what he wants.'

'But why?'

'He doesn't trust anybody.'

'But that's awful!'

'Every great man has his whims,' Bombardov said in a conciliatory tone.

'Very well. I understand and I regard the situation as hopeless. Since, in order for my play to be performed on the stage, it has to be distorted until it becomes completely meaningless, then I don't want it to be performed! I don't want the public to point its fingers at me when it sees a twentieth-century man, with a revolver in his hands, stab himself with a dagger.'

'It would not have pointed at you, because there would not have been any dagger. Your hero would have shot himself, like any normal man.'

I shut up.

'If you had kept quiet,' Bombardov continued, 'listened to the advice, even agreed to the daggers and to Antonina, then neither of them would ever have existed. There are ways and means of doing everything.'

'What are these means?'

'Misha Panin knows them,' Bombardov replied in a sepulchral voice.

'And so now all is lost?' I asked melancholically.

'Things are certainly rather difficult,' Bombardov replied sadly.

Another week went by and there was no news from the theatre. My wound gradually began to heal and the only thing I found unbearable was visiting the *Shipping Herald* and having to write the feature articles.

But suddenly ... Oh, that accursed word! Even as I depart into eternity I bear within me an insuperable, cowardly fear of that word. I fear it as much as I do the word 'surprise', or the words 'you're wanted on the telephone', 'there's a telegram for you' or 'you're wanted in the office'. I know only too well what follows those words.

And so, suddenly and entirely unexpectedly, Demyan Kuzmich appeared in my doorway, scraped his feet thoroughly and handed me an invitation to come to the theatre the following day at four o'clock.

The following day there was no rain. The following day was a day with a strong autumnal frost. With my heels clattering against the asphalt, I walked to the theatre, feeling rather nervous.

The first thing that caught my attention was a cab horse, as well-fed as a rhinoceros, and a little old man sitting on the coach-box. I don't know why, but somehow I realized immediately that it was Drykin. That made me feel even more nervous. Inside the theatre I was struck by a certain agitation that seemed to affect everything. There was no one in Filya's office and all his visitors, or, rather, the most stubborn of them, were languishing in the yard, shuddering in the cold and occasionally glancing in through the window. Some even tapped on the window, but in vain. I knocked on the door, it opened a little, Bakvalin's eyes appeared in the crack and I heard Filya's voice say:

'Admit him immediately!'

And I was admitted. Those languishing in the yard made an attempt to follow me inside but the door closed. After tumbling down the stairs, I was picked up by Bakvalin and found myself in the office. Filya was not sitting in his usual place, he was in the first room. Filya was also wearing a new tie, as I recall now – with speckles; Filya looked somehow exceptionally clean-shaven.

He greeted me in an especially solemn manner but with a certain hint of sadness. Something was happening in the theatre, and I sensed, as a bull probably senses when he is being led to the slaughter, that it was something in which I – just imagine – played the leading role.

This could be sensed even in the short phrase that Filya directed quietly but commandingly to Bakvalin:

'Take his coat!'

I was astounded by the couriers and the ushers. Not one of them was sitting still, they were all in a state of agitated movement that was quite incomprehensible to the uninitiated. For instance, Demyan Kuzmich overtook me, and went trotting upstairs to the first floor without making a sound. No sooner was he out of sight than Kuskov came dashing out and down the stairs, also moving at a trot, and then also disappeared. In the twilit lower foyer Kliukvin came trudging through and for no apparent reason closed one of the curtains on one of the windows but left the others open, and then disappeared without trace.

Bakvalin went dashing past across the soundless greatcoat fabric and disappeared into the buffet, and Pakin came running out of the buffet and disappeared into the auditorium.

'Come upstairs with me, please,' Filya said to me, politely accompanying me on my way. We walked upstairs. Someone else flew past us soundlessly and went up into the first circle. I began to feel that the shades of the dead were scurrying around me.

As we silently approached the doors of the antechamber I saw Demyan Kuzmich standing at the doors. A small figure in a little jacket tried to dash through to the door, but Demyan Kuzmich gave a quiet squeal and stretched himself across the door in the form of a cross, and the little figure shied away and dissolved into the twilight somewhere on the stairs.

'Let him through!' Filya whispered and disappeared.

Demyan Kuzmich fell against the door, it let me through and then . . . the other door, and I was in the antechamber, where it was no longer twilight. The lamp was lit on Toropetskaya's writing desk. Toropetskaya was not typing but sitting and looking at a newspaper. She nodded to me.

And standing by the doors leading into the boardroom, wearing a green jumper, was Menazhraki, with a diamond cross on her neck and a large bunch of gleaming keys on her lacquered leather belt.

She said: 'This way,' and I found myself in a brightly lit room.

The first thing that caught my attention was the expensive furniture of Karelian birch with gilt decorative details, a gigantic writing desk in the same style and a black Ostrovsky in the corner. The chandelier on the ceiling was lit up and the lamps were blazing brightly on the walls. I suddenly had the feeling that the portraits had emerged from their frames in the portrait gallery and converged on me. I recognized Ivan Vasilievich, sitting on a divan in front of a small round table on which there was a small dish of jam. I recognized Knyazhevich, I recognized several other people from their portraits, including an unusually imposing lady in a scarlet blouse and a brown tailored jacket scattered with buttons like stars, over which a short sable cape was thrown. A little hat sat dashingly on the lady's greying hair, her eyes glinted under black brows, and her fingers, wearing heavy diamond rings, also glinted.

But there were also people in the room who had not been included in the gallery. Standing at the back of the divan was the same doctor who had saved Milochka Pryakhina during her fit and was now again holding a small glass in his hands, and standing by the doors was the buffet manager, with that same expression of woe on his face.

The large round table at the side was covered with an incredibly white tablecloth. Points of light danced in the crystal and the china, they were reflected gloomily in the bottles of 'Narzan' mineral water, there was a glitter of something red, I think red caviar. The large company scattered across the armchairs stirred at my entrance, and bows were made in response to my own.

'Ah! Leo! . . .' Ivan Vasilievich began.

'Sergei Leontievich,' Knyazhevich quickly put in.

'Yes . . . Sergei Leontievich, welcome indeed! Have a seat, please do!' And Ivan Vasilievich shook my hand firmly. 'Will you perhaps order a bite to eat? Perhaps you would like to have lunch or breakfast? Please, do not stand on ceremony! We will wait. Our Ermolai Ivanovich is a magician, you only have to say the word to him and . . . Ermolai Ivanovich, can we find something for lunch?'

In reply to this the magician Ermolai Ivanovich did as follows: he rolled his eyes up under his forehead then returned them to their right place and directed an imploring glance at me.

'Or perhaps drinks of some kind?' said Ivan Vasilievich, continuing to regale me with his offers. 'Some "Narzan"? "Citro"? Cranberry water? Ermolai Ivanovich!' Ivan Vasilievich asked severely. 'Are our reserves of cranberries adequate? Please keep track of that very strictly.'

In reply Ermolai Ivanovich smiled bashfully and hung his head.

'Ermolai Ivanovich, by the way, is a ... hmm ... hmm ... wizard. At the most desperate of times he saved every last person in the entire theatre from starvation with sturgeon. Otherwise everyone would have died, every single one of us. The actors adore him!'

Ermolai Ivanovich did not put on airs at this description of his great achievement, on the contrary, a certain gloomy shadow fell across his face.

In a clear, firm, resounding voice I declared that I had taken both breakfast and lunch and categorically rejected both the 'Narzan' and the cranberries.

'Then perhaps a cake? Ermolai Ivanovich is world famous for his cakes!'

But in an even more resounding and powerful voice (Bombardov subsequently imitated me, based on what those present had told him: 'What a voice they said you had!' – 'What about it?' – 'Hoarse, spiteful, thin ...') I refused the cakes.

'By the way, concerning the cakes,' a man with blond hair, dressed with exceptional elegance, who was sitting beside Ivan Vasilievich suddenly put in, 'I recall that we once got together at Pruchevin's place. And the Grand Duke Maximilian Petrovich came as a surprise ... We made ourselves sick with laughing ... You know Pruchevin, don't you, Ivan Vasilievich? I'll tell you this comic incident later.'

'I know Pruchevin,' replied Ivan Vasilievich, 'he's a tremendous rogue. He stripped his own sister of her last kopeck ... Well now.'

At this point the door admitted another person not included

in the gallery – it was Misha Panin. 'Yes, he shot him . . .'
I thought, looking at Panin's face.

'Ah! My dearest Mikhail Alexeevich!' exclaimed Ivan Vasilievich, extending his arms to the newcomer. 'Most welcome
indeed! Please do take a chair. Allow me to introduce you,' said
Ivan Vasilievich, addressing me. 'This is our precious Mikhail
Alexeevich, who carries out the most important functions for
us. And this is . . .'

'Sergei Leontievich!' Knyazhevich put in merrily.

'Precisely so!'

Saying nothing about the fact that we were already acquainted,
while at the same time not denying this acquaintance, Misha
and I simply shook hands with each other.

'Well now, let us get started!' declared Ivan Vasilievich, and
all eyes were fixed on me, which made me shudder. 'Who wishes
to say something? Ippolit Pavlovich!'

An exceptionally imposing man dressed in great taste and
with curls the colour of a raven's wing set a monocle in his eye
and directed his gaze at me. Then he poured himself some
'Narzan', drank a glass, wiped his mouth with a silk handkerchief, hesitated over whether to drink some more, drank a
second glass and started speaking.

He had a marvellous, gentle, well-trained, earnest voice that
went straight to your heart.

'Your novel, Le . . . Sergei Leontievich? That's right, isn't it?
Your novel is very, very good . . . It has . . . ah . . . how might I
express it,' – at this point the orator squinted at the large
table, where the 'Narzan' bottles were standing, and Ermolai
Ivanovich immediately trotted across to him and handed him a
fresh bottle – 'full of psychological depth, characters drawn
with exceptional truth . . . Er . . . As for the descriptions of
nature, there you have attained, I should say, almost Turgen-
evian heights!' Just at that moment the 'Narzan' fizzed up in
his glass, and the orator drank a third portion and ejected the
monocle from his eye with a single movement of his eyebrow.

'These,' he continued, 'descriptions of southern nature . . . er
. . . starry nights in the Ukraine . . . then the rushing Dnepr . . .
er . . . as Gogol put it . . . er . . . the Dnepr is . . . Marvellous, as

you recall . . . and the scent of acacia . . . In your book all this is done in masterly fashion . . .'

I glanced round at Misha Panin – he was squirming about in his chair like an animal at bay and the look in his eyes was terrifying.

'Particularly impressive . . . er . . . is that description of the grove . . . the leaves of the silvery poplars . . . you recall that?'

'I can still see those scenes of night on the Dnepr, when we went on our tour!' said the contralto lady in sable.

'By the way, about that tour,' the bass sitting beside Ivan Vasilievich responded and laughed. 'There was a most piquant incident with Governor-General Dukasov. You remember him, Ivan Vasilievich?'

'I remember. A quite terrible glutton!' responded Ivan Vasilievich. 'But carry on.'

'Nothing but compliments could possibly be . . . er . . . er . . . expressed concerning your novel . . . but . . . you will forgive me for saying this . . . the stage has its own laws!'

Ivan Vasilievich was eating jam, listening with pleasure to what Ippolit Pavlovich was saying.

'In your play you have not succeeded in conveying the full aroma of your south, of those sultry nights. The roles have turned out psychologically incomplete, and the role of Bakhtin has been particularly affected . . .' At this point for some reason the orator took great offence and even puffed out his lips: 'Pe . . . pe . . . and I . . . er . . . I don't know,' – the orator smacked the edge of his monocle against a notebook, which I recognized as my play – 'it is impossible to play it. I'm sorry,' he concluded, completely offended now. 'I'm sorry!'

At that moment our eyes met, and I believe the other man read angry astonishment in mine.

The point is that there were no acacias in my novel, or any silvery poplars, or any rushing Dnepr or . . . in short, there was none of all that.

'He hasn't read it! He hasn't read my novel!' The thought echoed inside my head. 'And yet he feels quite free to talk about it! That gibberish about the Ukrainian nights . . . What did they invite me here for?'

'Who else wishes to say something?' Ivan Vasilievich enquired cheerfully, looking round at everyone.

A strained silence fell. Nobody expressed a wish to say anything. I heard just one voice from the corner:

'Eh-ho-ho . . .'

I turned to look at the corner and saw a plump, elderly man in a dark-coloured blouse. I remembered his face vaguely from a portrait . . . His eyes had a gentle look and his general expression was one of boredom, long-standing boredom. When I looked at him he averted his eyes.

'You wish to say something, Fyodor Vladimirovich?' Ivan Vasilievich said to him.

'No,' he replied.

The silence acquired a rather strange character.

'Perhaps you would like to say something?' Ivan Vasilievich asked, turning to me.

In a voice that was far from resounding and by no means brisk or even clear, I said:

'As far as I can understand, my play has not been found suitable, and I ask you to return it to me.'

For some reason these words caused agitation. Armchairs shifted, someone leaned down towards me from behind and said:

'No, why put it like that? Come now!'

Ivan Vasilievich looked at the jam and then, in consternation, at the people around him.

'Hmm . . . hmm . . .' – he began drumming his fingers – 'we are saying in a friendly way that to perform your play would mean causing you terrible harm! Quite horrific harm. Especially if Foma Strizh takes it on. You will find life unbearable and you will curse us . . .'

After a pause I said:

'In that case I ask you to return it to me.'

And at that moment I quite distinctly glimpsed malice in Ivan Vasilievich's eyes.

'We have a little contract,' another voice suddenly spoke up, and Gavriil Stepanovich's face appeared from behind the doctor's back.

'But your theatre does not wish to perform it, what do you want it for?'

Then a face with very lively eyes behind a pince-nez moved closer to me and a high, thin tenor voice said:

'Surely you won't take it to Schlieppe's theatre? What will they make of it there? Why, they'll have brisk little officers strutting around the stage! What good is that to anyone?'

'Under the terms of the current statutes and interpretations it cannot be given to Schlieppe's theatre – we have a little contract!' said Gavriil Stepanovich, emerging completely from behind the doctor's back.

'What is going on here? What do they want?' I thought and suddenly, for the first time in my life, I had a terrible, suffocating feeling.

'I'm sorry,' I said in a faint voice, 'I don't understand. You do not wish to perform it, but at the same time you say I can't give it to another theatre. Then what am I to do?'

These words produced a quite remarkable effect. The lady in sable exchanged an insulted glance with the bass on the divan. But Ivan Vasilievich's face was the most terrible of all. The smile evaporated from it, leaving the eyes blazing with fury, glaring straight at me.

'We wish to save you from terrible harm!' said Ivan Vasilievich. 'From the certain danger that lies in wait for you around the corner.'

Silence fell again and it became so oppressive that I could not possibly bear it any longer.

After picking at the upholstery of the armchair with my finger for a moment I stood up and bowed in farewell. Everyone replied with a bow except Ivan Vasilievich, who was looking at me in amazement. I sidled my way through to the door, stumbled, went out, bowed to Toropetskaya, who was glancing at *Izvestiya*[42] with one eye and at me with the other, then to Menazhraki, who acknowledged my bow frostily, and went out.

The theatre was immersed in twilight. White patches had appeared in the tearoom – they were laying the tables for the performance.

The door to the auditorium was open; I loitered for a few

moments and glanced in. The stage was entirely bare, right through to the brick wall at the back. Descending on to it from above was a green arbour entwined with ivy; at one side workers like ants were carrying in thick white columns on to the stage.

A minute later I was already out of the theatre.

Since Bombardov did not have a telephone, that same evening I sent him a telegram with the following message:

'Come to wake. Will go mad without you. Don't understand.'

They did not wish to take this telegram from me and only accepted it after I threatened to complain to the *Shipping Herald*.

The next evening Bombardov and I were sitting at a table set for dinner. The foreman's wife I have already mentioned brought in pancakes.

Bombardov had liked my idea of holding a wake, and he also liked my room, now brought into perfect order.

'I have calmed down now,' I said after my guest had sated his initial hunger, 'and I only want one thing – to know what happened. I am simply dying of curiosity. I have never seen anything so amazing.'

In reply Bombardov praised the pancakes, glanced round the room and said:

'You ought to get married, Sergei Leontievich. Get married to some attractive, affectionate woman or girl.'

'This conversation has already been described by Gogol,' I replied. 'Let us not be repetitious. Tell me, what happened?'

Bombardov shrugged.

'Nothing special happened, Ivan Vasilievich held a consultation with the senior members of the theatre.'

'I see. Who is that woman in sable?'

'Margarita Petrovna Tavricheskaya, one of our theatre's artistes, a member of the group of elders or founders. Famous for the fact that when the late Ostrovsky saw Margarita Petrovna's acting in eighteen hundred and eighty – it was her debut – he said: "Very good."'

After that I learned from my companion that nobody had been present in the room but the founders, who had been summoned to the meeting about my play as a matter of extreme urgency, and that Drykin had only been informed the day before and had spent a long time cleaning the horse and washing the cab with carbolic.

Upon enquiring about the man who had mentioned the Grand Duke Maximilian Petrovich and the gluttonous governor-general, I learned that he was the youngest of all the founders.

I should say that Bombardov's replies were quite distinctly restrained and cautious. Taking note of this, I tried to press my questions home in order to obtain from my guest something more than merely formal, terse replies, such as 'he was born on such-and-such a date, his name and patronymic are such-and-such', to actually get some idea of what those people were like. I felt a truly profound interest in the people who had assembled in the boardroom that day. I assumed that their characters ought to weave together into an explanation of their behaviour at that mysterious meeting.

'So is this Gornostaev (the one who spoke about the governor-general) a good actor?' I asked, pouring Bombardov some wine.

'Aha-a,' Bombardov replied.

'No, "aha-a" won't do. Now, for instance, concerning Margarita Petrovna we know that Ostrovsky said, "Very good." That at least is some sort of a start! But what does "aha-a" mean? Perhaps Gornostaev has done something to make himself famous?'

Bombardov cast a sly, sideways glance at me and mumbled . . .

'What can I tell you about that? Hmm, hmm . . .' And then, after draining his glass, he said: 'Well then, quite recently Gornostaev astounded everybody when something miraculous happened to him . . .' Then he started pouring melted butter on a pancake and went on pouring it for so long that I exclaimed:

'For God's sake, get on with it!'

'Napareuli really is a fine wine,' Bombardov put in anyway, to try my patience, and then continued: 'This little business happened four years ago. In early spring and, as I recall, at that time Gerasim Nikolaevich was especially cheerful and excited. Evidently his cheerfulness was not a good omen! He was making plans of some kind, eager to be off somewhere, he even started looking younger. I should tell you that he loves the theatre passionately. I remember, at the time he kept saying: "Ah, I've fallen behind a bit, I used to keep up with theatrical life in the West; I used to go abroad every year, and naturally, I was abreast of everything going on in the theatre in Germany, and in France! But never mind France, just imagine, I even paid a visit to America in order to study developments in the theatre." "Well then," they told him, "put in an application and go." He just smiled in a gentle sort of way. "Absolutely not," he answered. "Now's not the time to be putting in applications! How could I allow the state to spend its precious hard currency on me? Better let some engineer or industrial manager go!"

'A stout fellow, really! Well then . . .' Bombardov peered through his wine at the light of the lamp and praised the wine again. 'Well then, a month went by and the genuine spring began. And then the tragedy struck. One day Gerasim Niko-laevich came to Avgusta Avdeevna's office, but he didn't say anything. She looked at him and saw that he looked awful, he was as pale as a napkin and there was a mournful look in his eyes. "What's wrong, Gerasim Nikolaevich?" – "Nothing," he replied. "Take no notice." He went across to the window, drummed on the glass with his fingers and began whistling something sad that was terribly familiar. She listened and realized it was Chopin's funeral march. She couldn't bear it, her heart began aching with human sympathy, she pressed him for an answer: "What is it? What's wrong?"

'He turned towards her, smiled crookedly and said:

' "Swear to me that you will not tell anyone!" Naturally, she swore immediately. "I have just been to the doctor, and he discovered that I have sarcoma of the lung." He turned and went out.'

'Yes, that's no joke . . .' I said in a quiet voice, with a terrible feeling in my heart.

'But of course!' Bombardov agreed. 'Well now, Avgusta Avdeevna immediately told Gavriil Stepanovich in strict confidence, he told Ippolit Pavlovich, he told his wife, the wife told Evlampia Petrovna; in short, two hours later even the

apprentices in the tailoring shop knew that Gerasim Nikolaevich's artistic career was over and we might as well order the
wreath straightaway. Three hours later the actors were already
talking in the tearoom about who Gerasim Nikolaevich's roles
would be given to.

'Meanwhile Avgusta Avdeevna got on the phone to Ivan
Vasilievich. After exactly three days Avgusta Avdeevna called
Gerasim Nikolaevich and said: "I'm coming round to see you."
And she did. Gerasim Nikolaevich was lying on the divan in
a Chinese dressing gown, as pale as death itself, but proud
and calm.

'Avgusta Avdeevna is a no-nonsense woman and she slapped
the red passport and the cheque down on the table – bang!

'Gerasim Nikolaevich shuddered and said:

' "This is unkind of all of you. This is not what I wanted!
What point is there in dying in a foreign land?"

'Avgusta Avdeevna is a loyal woman and a genuine secretary!
She ignored the dying man's words and shouted:

' "Faddei!"

'Now, Faddei is Gerasim Nikolaevich's faithful and devoted
servant.

'Faddei instantly appeared.

' "The train is leaving in two hours. A rug for Gerasim Nikolaevich! Underwear. Suitcase. Toiletry bag. The car will be here
in forty minutes."

'The condemned man merely sighed and gestured hopelessly.

'Somewhere, either on the border of Switzerland, or perhaps
not in Switzerland, in short, in the Alps there is . . .' – Bombardov wiped his forehead – 'in short, it's not important. At a
height of three thousand metres above sea level lies the alpine
clinic of the world-famous Professor Kli. People only go to him
in desperate cases. When it's kill or cure. Things can't get
any worse, miracles have sometimes happened. Kli puts such
hopeless cases out on an open veranda, in sight of the snowy
summits, gives them injections of sarcomatine, gets them to
breathe oxygen – and sometimes Kli has managed to put death
off by a year.

'Fifty minutes later they drove Gerasim Nikolaevich past the theatre, at his own request, and Demyan Kuzmich told me afterwards that he saw him raise his hand and bless the theatre, and then the car left for the Belorussian-Baltic Station.

'Then summer was upon us and the rumour spread that Gerasim Nikolaevich had passed away. Well, people tittle-tattled and expressed their sympathies ... But it was summer ... The actors were just about to leave, their tours were just beginning ... So somehow there wasn't really all that much grieving ... They were expecting Gerasim Nikolaevich's body to be brought back at any moment ... Meanwhile the actors went away, the season was over. But I ought to tell you that our Plisov ...'

'He's that pleasant-looking one, with the moustache?' I asked. 'Who's in the gallery?'

'That's the one,' Bombardov confirmed and continued: 'Anyway, he was offered a business trip to Paris to study theatre machinery. Naturally, he got his documents straightaway and off he set. Plisov, I should tell you, is an incredibly hard worker and is literally in love with his stage turntable. People were extremely envious of him. Everybody fancies a visit to Paris ... "What a lucky man!" everyone said. Well, lucky or not, he collected his papers and scooted off to Paris, at exactly the same time that the news arrived of Gerasim Nikolaevich's demise. Plisov is an unusual kind of character, and while he was in Paris he managed not to see even the Eiffel Tower. A real enthusiast. He spent all his time sitting in dungeons under stages, studied everything he needed to, bought stage lights, did an honest job. Finally he had to leave, and then he decided to take a walk round Paris and at least have a quick look at it before coming back home. He walked and walked, rode around in buses, explaining himself mostly by grunting and mooing and finally got as hungry as a wolf. He ended up somewhere way off the beaten track. "I'll just drop into a little restaurant and have a bite to eat," he thought. He saw lights. He could tell he wasn't very near the centre, everything ought to be cheap. He went in, and it really was a moderately priced restaurant. Looking inside, he froze on the spot.

'Sitting at a table, dressed in a smoking jacket, with a flower

in his buttonhole, he saw the late Gerasim Nikolaevich and
two French women sitting with him, both of them positively
splitting their sides with laughter. And standing on the table in
front of them a bottle of champagne in a bucket of ice, and
some kind of fruits.

'Plisov simply staggered back in the doorway. "Impossible!"
he thought. "I'm seeing things. Gerasim Nikolaevich can't
be here, laughing. There's only one place he can be, in the
Novodevichy Cemetery!"[43]

'He stood there, goggling at this individual so terrifyingly
like the dead man, and the individual got up, with an expression
of something like alarm on his face. It even seemed to Plisov
that he was displeased in some way by Plisov's appearance, but
afterwards it turned out that Gerasim Nikolaevich was simply
amazed. And then Gerasim Nikolaevich, for it really was he,
whispered something to his French companions and they
suddenly disappeared.

'Plisov only recovered his wits when Gerasim Nikolaevich
kissed him. And there and then everything was explained. Plisov
could only exclaim: "Well I never," as he listened to Gerasim
Nikolaevich. Well, it really was a miracle.

'When they brought Gerasim Nikolaevich to the Alps he
was in such a state that Kli shook his head and all he said
was: "Hmm . . ." Well, they put Gerasim Nikolaevich on that
veranda. They injected him with that substance. Gave him
oxygen. At first the patient became worse, and so much worse
that, as they admitted afterwards to Gerasim Nikolaevich, Kli
began entertaining the most unpleasant of expectations for the
following day. For his heart had failed. However, the following
day passed successfully. They repeated the injection. The day
after that went even better. And so on – it was unbelievable.
Gerasim Nikolaevich sat up on the couchette and then he said:
"Let me try a little walk." All the assistants, and even Kli, were
wide-eyed. In short, after another day Gerasim Nikolaevich
was walking around the veranda, his cheeks had turned pink,
he had acquired an appetite . . . temperature 36.8, pulse normal,
not a trace of pain left.

'Gerasim Nikolaevich told us that people came to look at

him from the villages in the district, people came from the cities. Kli gave a conference paper, claimed that cases like this only happened once in a thousand years. They wanted to put Gerasim Nikolaevich's portrait in the medical journals, but he flatly refused, saying, "I don't like a lot of fuss!"

'Meanwhile Kli told Gerasim Nikolaevich there was no point in his staying in the Alps and he was sending Gerasim Nikolaevich to Paris so that he could rest after all the shocks he had suffered. So that's how Gerasim Nikolaevich turned out to be in Paris. And the French women, Gerasim Nikolaevich explained, were two young local Parisian doctors who were intending to write an article about him. So there you have it.'

'Yes, that's astonishing,' I remarked. 'But I still don't understand how he managed to get away with it!'

'That's the wonder of it,' replied Bombardov. 'It seems that following the first injection Gerasim Nikolaevich's sarcoma began to disperse and it dispersed completely!'

I flung my hands up in the air.

'You don't say!' I exclaimed. 'But that never happens!'

'It happens once in a thousand years,' Bombardov replied and continued: 'But wait, that's not all. In the autumn Gerasim Nikolaevich came back in a new suit, he was looking well and had a tan – after Paris his Parisian doctors had sent him to the sea. In the tearoom our actors literally hung on Gerasim Nikolaevich's every word as he told them about the ocean, Paris, the alpine doctors and all sorts of other things. Well, the season started as usual, Gerasim Nikolaevich acted, and he acted quite decently, and things dragged on like that until March ... And in March Gerasim Nikolaevich suddenly arrived at a rehearsal of *Lady MacBeth of Mtsensk*[44] with a stick. "What's wrong?" – "It's nothing. I've got this stabbing pain in my waist." Well, it kept stabbing and stabbing away. It should have stabbed for a while and stopped. Ah, but it didn't stop. The longer it went on, the worse it got ... he tried blue light – it didn't help ... Insomnia, he couldn't sleep on his back. He started losing weight before our very eyes. Tried "Pantopon". It didn't help! Well, he went to the doctor, of course. And just imagine ...'

Bombardov paused expertly and the expression in his eyes sent a cold shiver down my spine.

'And just imagine . . . the doctor looked at him, felt him and blinked . . . Gerasim Nikolaevich said to him: "Doctor, don't drag it out, I'm not some stupid woman, I've seen life . . . tell me, is it – that thing?" It was!' Bombardov barked hoarsely and downed his glass in a single gulp. 'The sarcoma had started up again! It had moved down into Gerasim Nikolaevich's right kidney and begun to devour him! Naturally, it was a sensation. Rehearsals be damned, Gerasim Nikolaevich was sent home! Well, this time it was easier. There was hope now. Again the passport and ticket were there in three days, and it was off to the Alps, to Kli. He greeted Gerasim Nikolaevich like a member of the family. Well, of course! Gerasim Nikolaevich's sarcoma had brought the professor worldwide publicity! A day later the pain abated, after two days Gerasim Nikolaevich was walking round the veranda, and after three days he asked Kli if he could play a game of tennis! The things that went on at the clinic defy the imagination. There were patients coming to Kli by the trainload! Gerasim Nikolaevich told us they started putting up a second building close by. Kli, reserved foreigner that he was, kissed Gerasim Nikolaevich three times and sent him off for a rest just as he ought to, only this time to Nice, then to Paris, and then to Sicily.

'And once again Gerasim Nikolaevich came back in the autumn – we had just got back from a tour of the Donbass – looking fresh and well and in good spirits, only he had a different suit: the autumn before it had been chocolate brown, and now it was grey with small checks. For three days he told us about Sicily and how the bourgeois play roulette in Monte Carlo. He said it was a revolting sight. The season came again, and in spring it was the same story again, only in a different place. A relapse, but this time below the left knee. Off to Kli again, then to Madeira and finally, in conclusion – to Paris.

'But now there was no real alarm about the outbreaks of sarcoma. It was clear to everyone that Kli had found the way to save him. It turned out that every year the strength of the sarcoma was reduced by the injections and Kli hoped, he was

even certain, that in another three or four seasons Gerasim
Nikolaevich's body would be able to cope on its own with the
sarcoma's attempts to flare up in one spot or another. And
indeed, the year before last it only caused slight pains in the
maxillary sinus and disappeared immediately at Kli's clinic.
But now Gerasim Nikolaevich is under strict and unremitting
observation and, whether he has any pains or not, in April they
send him off!'

'How wonderful!' I said, sighing for some reason.

Meanwhile our feast was in full swing, as they say. Our heads
were buzzing from the Napareuli, the conversation became
more lively and, most importantly, more frank. 'You are a very
interesting, observant, naughty man,' I thought about Bombardov, 'and I like you enormously, but you are cunning and
secretive, and you have been made that way by your life in the
theatre . . .'

'Don't be like that!' I suddenly appealed to my guest. 'Tell
me, after all, I admit to you that I am miserable . . . Is my play
really that bad?'

'Your play,' said Bombardov, 'is a good play. Full stop.'

'But why, why did all those strange things that frightened me
so much happen in the boardroom? Didn't they like the play?'

'Quite the opposite,' Bombardov said in a firm voice. 'It all
happened because they liked it. They liked it immensely.'

'But Ippolit Pavlovich . . .'

'It was precisely Ippolit Pavlovich who liked it most of all,'
Bombardov said quietly but emphatically, and it seemed to me
that I glimpsed sympathy in his eyes.

'It's enough to drive me mad . . .' I whispered.

'No, don't go mad . . . It's just that you don't know what the
theatre's like. There are complicated machines in the world,
but the theatre is the most complicated of all . . .'

'Tell me! Tell me!' I exclaimed and clutched my head in my
hands.

'They liked the play so much it actually caused a panic,'
Bombardov began. 'That's why things turned out the way they
did. The moment they saw it and the elders heard about it
they immediately even decided who should play which roles.

They gave Bakhtin to Ippolit Pavlovich. They were going to give Petrov to Valentin Konradovich.'

'Who ... Val ... the one who ...'

'That's right ... him.'

'But come on!' I didn't simply shout but yelled. 'After all ...'

'I know, I know ...' said Bombardov, who obviously took my meaning at once. 'Ippolit Pavlovich is sixty-one, Valentin Konradovich is sixty-two ... How old is your oldest character, Bakhtin?'

'Twenty-eight!'

'There, you see. Well now, I simply can't describe what happened as soon as the copies of the play were sent to the elders. Nothing like it had ever happened in the theatre in all the fifty years of its existence. All of them simply took offence.'

'At whom? The casting manager?'

'No. The author.'

There was nothing I could do but gape wide-eyed, which I did, and Bombardov continued:

'The author. Honestly – the way the group of elders reasoned was this: here we are, desperately looking for parts; we, the founders, would like to demonstrate all our skill in a modern play ... and then look what happens! This grey suit turns up and brings us a play with characters who are boys! That means we can't act in it! Did he bring it as a joke? The very youngest of the elders is fifty-seven – that's Gerasim Nikolaevich.'

'I don't have any ambition for my play to be acted by the founders!' I yelled. 'Let the young actors do it!'

'Oh, that's very smart of you!' exclaimed Bombardov, putting on a satanic face. 'Just let Argunin, Galin, Elagin, Blagosvetlov and Strenkovsky walk out and take the bow – bravo! Encore! Hoorah! Just look, good people, how wonderfully we perform! And that means the founders will be left sitting there, smiling in embarrassment – that means, doesn't it, that we're not needed any more? That means we can be packed off to the almshouse? Hee-hee-hee. Smart! Very smart!'

'I get it!' I shouted, trying also to shout in a satanic voice. 'I get it!'

'What is there to get?' snapped Bombardov. 'Didn't Ivan

Vasilievich say that you needed to turn the fiancée into a mother, and then Margarita Pavlovna or Nastasya Ivanovna would play her . . .'

'Nastasya Ivanovna?!'

'You're not a man of the theatre,' Bombardov replied with an insulting smile, but he didn't explain what he was insulting me for.

'Tell me one thing, who did they want to give Anna's part to?'

'Naturally, Ludmila Silvestrovna Pryakhina.'

At that I was simply overcome by fury.

'Wha-at? What on earth? Ludmila Silvestrovna?' I leapt up from the table. 'You must be joking!'

'Why, what's wrong?' Bombardov enquired with gleeful curiosity.

'How old is she?'

'That, I'm afraid, is something that no one knows.'

'Anna is nineteen! Nineteen! Do you understand? But that's not even the most important thing. The most important thing is that she can't act!'

'You mean Anna's part?'

'Not just Anna, she can't do anything at all!'

'Oh, come on.'

'No, you come! An actress who tried to represent the lament of a person who is persecuted and downtrodden, and played it so badly that a cat went crazy and tore a curtain to shreds, cannot act at all.'

'The cat's an idiot,' Bombardov responded, savouring my fury. 'It suffers from fatty degeneration of the heart, myocarditis and neurasthenia. It just sits on the bed for days at a time and never sees anyone, so naturally it was frightened.'

'The cat's a neurasthenic, I agree there!' I shouted. 'But its instincts are sound and it understands the stage very well. It heard a false note! Do you understand, a repulsively false note. It was shocked! What was that Punch and Judy show about, anyway?'

'There was a botch-up,' Bombardov explained.

'What does that word mean?'

'In our language a botch-up is any confusion that occurs on

stage. An actor suddenly gets his lines wrong, or they don't close the curtains in time, or . . .'

'I get it, I get it . . .'

'In this case two people botched things up: Avgusta Avdeevna and Nastasya Ivanovna. The former when she let you in to see Ivan Vasilievich without warning Nastasya Ivanovna that you would be there. The latter when she let Ludmila Silvestrovna make her entrance without checking if there was anyone with Ivan Vasilievich. Although, of course, Avgusta Avdeevna is less to blame – Nastasya Ivanovna had gone to the shop for some mushrooms . . .'

'I get it, I get it,' I said, trying to force out a Mephisophelean laugh, 'I get absolutely the whole thing! So anyway, your Ludmila Silvestrovna can't act.'

'Oh, come on! According to the people of Moscow she acted beautifully in her time . . .'

'Your people of Moscow are liars!' I exclaimed. 'She represents lamenting and grief, and she has fury in her eyes! She jigs about, crying "Indian summer", and her eyes look anxious! She laughs, and anyone listening to her feels shivers down his spine, as if someone's poured "Narzan" down inside his collar! She's no actress!'

'You go too far! For thirty years she has been studying Ivan Vasilievich's famous theory of incarnation . . .'

'I don't know that theory! It seems to me the theory hasn't done her any good!'

'Perhaps you'd like to tell me that Ivan Vasilievich is no actor either?'

'Oh no! No! The moment he showed me Bakhtin stabbing himself I simply gasped: his eyes went dead! He fell on the divan and I saw a man who had stabbed himself to death. As far as it's possible to judge from that short scene, and it is possible, just as it is possible to recognize a great singer from a single phrase that he sings, he is an immense phenomenon on the stage! Only I absolutely cannot understand what he says about the contents of the play.'

'Everything he says is wise.'

'The dagger!'

'You must understand that as soon as you sat down and opened the notebook he had already stopped listening to you. Yes, yes. He was thinking about how to divide out the parts, how to arrange things so as to include the founders, so that they could perform your play without any detriment to themselves ... And you read out some shots or other. I've been working in our theatre for ten years and I've been told that the only time a shot was fired in our theatre was in 1901, and then it was an absolute failure. In a play by that ... there, I've forgotten ... a famous author ... well, it doesn't matter ... in short, two nervous characters in the play argued over an inheritance, they argued and argued until one of them took a pop at the other with a revolver, and then he missed ... Well, while the ordinary rehearsals were still going on a stagehand imitated the shot by clapping his hands, but at the dress rehearsal he fired in the wings for real. Well, Nastasya Ivanovna had quite a turn – she'd never heard a shot before, and Ludmila Silvestrovna had a fit of hysterics. They changed the play so that the character didn't shoot, instead he brandished a watering can and shouted, "I'll kill you, you villain!" and stamped his feet, which, in Ivan Vasilievich's opinion, only improved the play. The author took serious offence at the theatre and didn't speak to the directors for three years, but Ivan Vasilievich stood firm ...'

As the tipsy night went by my outbursts became weaker, and I no longer raised noisy objections with Bombardov but mostly asked questions. Our mouths were on fire after the salty red caviar and salmon and we quenched our thirst with tea. The room was filled with smoke as thick as milk, the frosty air came streaming in through the small open window, but it brought no freshness, only cold.

'Tell me now, tell me,' I asked in a dull, weak voice, 'in a case like this, if the play simply doesn't suit the actors in a theatre, why don't they want me to give it to another theatre? Why do they want it? What for?'

'A fine question! What for? Our theatre's just longing for someone to put on a new play somewhere nearby, especially one that could clearly be a success! Why on earth would they want that? And didn't you write in the contract that you wouldn't give the play to another theatre?'

At this point I saw before my eyes the countless blazing-green headings saying 'The author does not have the right' and the strange phrase 'should there be' and the cunning little paragraph numbers. I recalled the leather study and seemed to catch a whiff of perfume.

'Curse the man!' I croaked.

'Who?'

'Curse the man! Gavriil Stepanovich!'

'A soaring eagle!' exclaimed Bombardov, with his inflamed eyes glittering.

'And he's so quiet, and always talking about the soul!'

'A misconception, raving nonsense, poor observation!' exclaimed Bombardov. His eyes blazed, his cigarette blazed, the smoke billowed out of his nostrils. 'He's an eagle, a condor. He sits up on the cliff and he can see for forty kilometres on all sides. And the moment a little dot appears he goes soaring upwards and suddenly drops like a stone! A pitiful scream, a gasp . . . and he has already soared back up into the heavens, clutching his prey!'

'Why, you're a poet, damn you!' I gasped.

'And you,' Bombardov whispered with a subtle smile, 'are an angry man! Ah, Sergei Leontievich, I predict that things will go hard with you . . .'

I was stung by his words. I didn't think that I was an angry man at all, but I immediately recalled Likospastov's words about the way I lowered at him . . .

'And so,' I said, yawning, 'that means my play will not be shown? That means all is lost?'

Bombardov looked hard at me and said, with a warmth in his voice that was unusual for him:

'Prepare yourself to endure the worst. I won't try to deceive you. It won't be shown. Unless there's a miracle . . .'

Outside the window the foul, misty autumn dawn was approaching. But even though the left-over scraps of food were repulsive and there were heaps of cigarette butts in the saucers, in the midst of all this ugliness, elevated by what was evidently a final upsurge of feeling, I began declaiming a monologue about the golden horse.

I attempted to convey to my listener the glitter of the sparks on the golden horse's crupper, the cold breath and distinctive smell of the stage, the laughter running through the hall . . . But that was not the most important thing. I smashed a saucer in my passion as I strove to convince Bombardov that from the first moment I saw the horse I had immediately understood the stage and all the very smallest of its mysteries. And that meant that for a long, long time, perhaps since I was still a child, or before I was even born, I had been dreaming about it, vaguely yearning for it. And now I had arrived!

'I'm the new man,' I cried. 'I'm the new man! I'm inevitable, I've arrived!'

And then some wheels span in my feverish brain and out popped Ludmila Silvestrovna, howling and waving her lace handkerchief.

'She can't act!' I croaked in furious rage.

'Oh, come on now! You can't say . . .'

'I'll ask you not to contradict me,' I said severely. 'You have grown used to things, but I am the new man, my gaze is keen and fresh! I can see through her . . .'

'Oh, come now!"

'And no th-theory will do any good. But that little man with the snub nose, who plays a petty bureaucrat, he had white hands and a husky voice, but he doesn't need any theory, and the one who plays the murderer in black gloves . . . he doesn't need any theory!'

'Argunin . . .' I heard a hollow voice say behind the curtain of smoke.

'There aren't any theories,' I shrieked, completely overcome by my presumption, and even grinding my teeth, and then I quite unexpectedly noticed a large spot of grease on my jacket, with a piece of onion stuck to it. I looked around in consternation. There was not a trace left of the night. Bombardov put out the lamp, and in the blue twilight the full ugliness of all the objects was revealed.

The night had been eaten up, the night had fled.

## CHAPTER 14

### Mysterious Miracle-Workers

The human memory is arranged in an amazing fashion. All of this seems to have happened so very recently and yet I find it absolutely impossible to reconstitute the sequence of events accurately. Some links have fallen out of the chain! Some things I recall, they just light up right there in front of my eyes, and other things have crumbled away and been scattered, and only dust and a fine rain remain in my memory. Yes, indeed, there is dust. But rain? Fine rain? Well then, the month that followed that drunken night was November. But of course that means rain alternating with sticky snow. Well, you do know Moscow, I presume? So there's no need to describe it. Its streets are an extremely unpleasant place in November. And its institutions are not so pleasant either. But that's not really so very bad, what's worse is when things are bad at home. How, can you tell me, can grease stains be removed from clothing? I tried this way and that, one thing and another. And it's quite remarkable: for instance, you soak it in petrol and the result is wonderful – the stain dissolves, dissolves and disappears. You feel happy, because there is no torment worse than a stain on your clothes. It's sloppy, it's bad, it gets on your nerves. You hang the jacket on a nail, and when you get up in the morning – the stain is back again, only now it has a slight smell of petrol.

The same thing after boiling water, dilute tea, eau de Cologne. It's a real curse! You start getting angry and twitchy, but there's nothing you can do. No, it's clear that anyone who has once put a stain on his clothes is going to walk around with it until the suit itself wears out and is thrown out for ever. It's all the same to me now, but I wish others fewer of these stains.

And so I tried to remove the stain and I failed, and then, I recall, the laces in my shoes kept snapping, I was coughing and I went to the *Herald* every day, suffering from the damp and insomnia, and I read anything I came across and God only knows what. Circumstances had led to my having nobody around me. Likospastov had gone away to the Caucasus for some reason; my friend, the one I stole the revolver from, had been transferred to Leningrad; Bombardov had come down with an inflammation of the kidneys and they'd put him in a clinic. Occasionally I went to visit him, but of course he was in no mood to talk about the theatre. And he understood, of course, that one way or another, after what had happened with *Black Snow*, it was best not to touch on the subject, but his kidneys could be touched on, because there was, after all, some possibility of consolation there. And so we talked about kidneys, we even recalled Kli after a joking fashion, but somehow it wasn't very funny.

Every time I visited him, however, I remembered about the theatre, but I found enough strength of will not to ask him about anything. I swore to myself that I would not think about the theatre, but of course it was an absurd oath. You can't forbid yourself to think. But you can forbid yourself to enquire about the theatre. And I did forbid myself that.

The theatre itself seemed to have died and gave no sign of life. No news arrived from it. I repeat, I had grown distant from people. I went to second-hand bookshops and sometimes squatted on my haunches in the semi-darkness, rifling through the dusty journals, and I remember I saw a wonderful picture . . . a triumphal arch . . .

Meanwhile the rain stopped and without any warning at all a frost set in. The window in my garret was decorated with lacework and as I sat there, breathing on a twenty-kopeck coin and pressing it into the icy surface, I realized that to write plays and not have them performed is intolerable.

However, in the evenings the sounds of a waltz came from under the floor, always the same one (someone was learning it), and that waltz gave rise to pictures in a little box, rather strange and rare pictures. For instance, I imagined that there was an opium-smokers' den under the floor, and something even took shape that in my wild imagination I called 'the third act'. Grey-blue smoke, a woman with an asymmetrical face, some petty dandy poisoned by the smoke and a man with a lemon-yellow face and slanting eyes creeping towards him with a sharpened bowie knife. A blow with the knife, a stream of blood. Non-sense, as you can see! Rubbish. And where could I take a play with a third act like that?

I didn't even write down what I had invented. The question arises, of course, and above all in my own mind, as to why a man who has buried himself in a garret, suffered a major failure and is a melancholic to boot (I realize that, don't worry) did not make a second attempt to take his own life.

Let me admit frankly that the first attempt had produced a certain revulsion for this act of violence. Speaking for myself, that is. But of course that was not the real reason. The time comes for everything. But then, let us not expand on that subject.

As for the world outside, it is not really possible to cut yourself off from it completely; it made itself felt because during the period of time when I was receiving now fifty, now a hundred roubles from Gavriil Stepanovich I had taken out subscriptions to three theatrical journals, as well as *Evening Moscow*.[45]

The various issues of these journals arrived in a more or less timely manner. Looking through the section 'Theatrical News', every so often I would come across news of people I knew.

For instance, on the fifteenth of November I read:

'The well-known writer Izmail Alexandrovich Bondarevsky is finishing his play *The Knives of Montmartre*, based on scenes from émigré life. It is rumoured that the author will offer the play to the Old Theatre.'

On the seventeenth I opened the newspaper and came across the following piece of news:

'The well-known writer E. Agapyonov is working intensively on his comedy *The Brother-in-Law*, a commission from the Theatre of the Unanimous Cohort.'

On the twenty-second the following was printed:

'In conversation with our correspondent, the well-known dramatist Klinker shared some information about the play that he intends to offer to the Independent Theatre. Albert Albertovich stated that his play represents an expansive canvas of the civil war near Kasimov. The play is provisionally entitled *The Assault*.'

And after that it was like a shower of hail: on the twenty-third and the twenty-fourth and the twenty-sixth. Even the third page of the newspaper had a rather muddy picture of a young man with an exceptionally gloomy head who looked as if he were butting someone and the announcement that this was I. S. Prok. A drama. He was finishing the third act.

Onisim Zhvenko. Anbakomov. Four, five acts.

On the second of January I took offence when I saw the words:

'The consultant M. Panin has called a meeting of a group of dramatists at the Independent Theatre. The subject is the composition of a contemporary play for the Independent.'

This notice was headed 'Long overdue!' and it expressed regret, reproaching the Independent Theatre with being the only theatre that had not yet put on a single contemporary play reflecting our own times. 'And yet,' the newspaper said, 'it is the Independent Theatre, and precisely the Independent Theatre, that is more capable than any other of interpreting a play by a contemporary dramatist in a worthy manner, if this interpretation is undertaken by such masters as Ivan Vasilievich and Aristarkh Platonovich.'

There followed justified reproaches addressed to the dramatists who had still not managed to produce a work worthy of the Independent Theatre.

I had acquired the habit of talking to myself.

'Come now,' I muttered, pouting my lips in offence, 'what do you mean, no one has written a play? What about the bridge? And the accordion? The blood on the trampled snow?'

The blizzard whistled outside the window; I imagined that accursed bridge was out there in the blizzard, that the accordion was playing and I could hear the crackle of shots. The tea grew cold in the glass, a face with sideburns gazed up at me from the page of the newspaper. Below it was the text of a telegram sent to the meeting by Aristarkh Platonovich:

In Calcutta in body, in spirit with you.

'Look at the way life rushes along, like water over a dam,' I whispered with a yawn, 'and it's as if I had been buried.'

The night drifts away, and the next day drifts away, they will all drift away, as many of them as I am granted, and there will be nothing left except failure.

Limping and massaging my bad knee, I dragged myself across to the divan, began taking off my jacket, shuddered from the cold, wound the clock.

Many nights passed like that; I remember them, but somehow all bunched together – it was cold for sleeping. The days seem to have been washed out of my memory – I don't remember anything.

Things dragged on like that until the end of January, and then I distinctly remember a dream I had on the night of the twentieth.

A massive hall in a palace, and I seem to be walking across the hall. There are heavy, greasy, gold-coloured candles burning smokily in candlesticks. I am dressed strangely, my legs are clad in tights; in short, I am not in our century but the fifteenth. I walk across the hall and there is a dagger at my belt. The whole charm of the dream was that I was clearly the ruler, and precisely by virtue of this dagger, which the courtiers standing by the doors clearly feared. No wine can intoxicate as that dagger did, and I smiled, no, I laughed in my sleep as I walked soundlessly towards the doors.

The charm of this dream was so great that when I woke I carried on laughing for some time.

And then there was a knock at the door and I went across to it in a blanket, shuffling my tattered slippers, and my female neighbour's hand was thrust in through the crack and handed me an envelope with the letters 'IT' gleaming on it in gold.

I ripped it open – it is lying here in front of me with its jagged tear even now (and I shall take it with me!). In the envelope there was a sheet of paper, also with golden gothic letters, and a message written in the large, thick handwriting of Foma Strizh:

Dear Sergei Leontievich!
To the theatre immediately! I start rehearsals of *Black Snow* at 12 tomorrow.

Yours, *F. Strizh*

I sat down on the divan, smiling crookedly, staring wildly at the sheet of paper and thinking about the dagger, then for some reason about Ludmila Silvestrovna, as I stared at my bare knees.

Meanwhile someone knocked on the door with imperious merriment.

'Yes,' I said.

Bombardov promptly entered the room, pale, with a yellow tinge, looking taller after his illness, and in a voice that had changed after it he said:

'Do you know already? I came round especially.'

And, rising to my feet to face him in all my nakedness and poverty, dragging the old blanket across the floor, I kissed him, dropping the paper.

'How could this have happened?' I asked as I bent down to the floor.

'Even I can't understand it,' my dear guest replied. 'Nobody can understand and they will never know. I think that Panin and Strizh have done it. But how they have done it is a mystery, for it is beyond all human powers. In short, it is a miracle.'

# PART II

## CHAPTER 15[46]

The electrical cable in its cover lay on the floor like a thin grey snake, extending across the entire stalls and stretching away to some unknown place. It was powering the tiny little lamp on the table standing in the middle aisle of the stalls. The lamp gave out exactly enough light to illuminate the sheet of paper on the desk and an inkwell. There was a snub-nosed face drawn on the sheet of paper and lying beside it there was orange peel, still fresh, and an ashtray, full of butts. A carafe of water glinted dully – it was outside the circle of glowing light.

The stalls were immersed in such dense darkness that people entering them from the light began groping their way along, holding on to the backs of the chairs until their eyes became accustomed to it.

The stage curtains were open and the stage was lit weakly from above with a detachable floodlight. There was a kind of little wall standing on the stage, with its back to the audience and the phrase 'Wolves and sheep – 2' written on it. There were also an armchair, a writing desk and two stools. There was a worker in a collarless Russian shirt and a jacket, sitting in the armchair, and a young man in a jacket and trousers, but with a belt round his waist and a sword with an Order of St George knot, sitting on one of the stools.

It was stuffy in the hall; outside May was already well advanced.

It was the interval at a rehearsal, the actors had gone to the buffet for breakfast. But I had stayed. The events of the last few months had taken their toll and I was feeling somehow beaten and battered; I kept wanting to sit down and sit without moving for a long time. But this state was punctuated quite frequently by outbursts of nervous energy, when I wanted to move about, explain, talk and argue. And now I was sitting there in the first state. Under the shade of the lamp the smoke hung in thick layers, it was sucked into the shade and then disappeared up into the air.

My thoughts revolved around only one thing – my play. Ever since the day Foma Strizh had sent me that decisive letter my life had changed beyond recognition. It was as if a man had been reborn, as if even his room had become a different room, although it was still the same one, as if even the people surrounding him had become different and this man had suddenly been granted the right to exist in the city of Moscow, had acquired meaning and even importance.

But these thoughts were anchored to only one thing, to the play. It filled up all of my time – even my dreams, because I dreamed of it already performed with some quite incredible scenery, I dreamed of it removed from the repertoire, I dreamed of it as a failure or an immense success. In the latter case, I remember, it was performed on inclined scaffolding, across which the actors were scattered like plasterers and they played holding lanterns in their hands, constantly bursting into song. Strangely enough, the author was there as well, striding across the fragile beams as freely as a fly across a wall, and down below him there were lime trees and apple trees, for the action of the play was set in a garden filled with an excited audience.

In the case of failure, the most frequent version of my dream had the author walking to the dress rehearsal but he had forgotten to put on his trousers. He took his first few embarrassed steps along the street, hoping somehow that he would manage to slip past unnoticed, even readying an excuse for the passers-by – something about a bath that he had just taken, and that his trousers were supposedly in the wings. But the further he went, the worse things became and the poor author became stuck to the pavement, looking for a newspaper-seller, but there wasn't one; he wanted to buy a coat, but he had no money; he hid in an entry-way, realizing that he was late for the dress rehearsal . . .

'Vanya!' I heard a faint voice say from the stage. 'Give me the yellow.'

In the box at the end of the circle, right beside the gantry of the stage, something lit up, a beam of light fell downwards, expanding as it came, and a bright round yellow spot appeared on the floor of the stage, creeping around and picking out that armchair with the worn upholstery and the chipped gilding on its arms or the tousle-headed prop-hand holding a wooden candlestick.

The closer the interval came to its end, the more movement there was on stage. The huge canvas flats hanging in countless rows up in the sky of the stage suddenly came to life. One of them receded upwards and immediately revealed a row of one-thousand-candle-power lamps that blinded my eyes. Another moved down for some reason, but before it reached the floor it moved back up and away again. Dark shadows appeared in the wings, the yellow beam withdrew and was sucked back into the box. There were men hammering somewhere. A man appeared wearing civilian trousers but with spurs, jingling them as he walked across the stage. Then someone leaned down to the floor of the stage and shouted into it, holding his hand beside his mouth:

'Gnobin! Let's have it!'

And then, almost silently, everything on the stage began moving away to one side. The prop-hand was drawn away, moving off with his candelabra, the armchair and the desk drifted by. Someone ran onstage against the direction of the moving turntable, began jigging about trying to get his balance and when he had, rode away again. The humming grew louder and strange, complex wooden structures appeared, taking the place of the set that had gone. They consisted of steep, unpainted stairways, beams and floors. 'The bridge is coming,' I thought; for some reason I always felt excited as it moved into place.

'Gnobin! Stop!' someone shouted on the stage. 'Gnobin! Go back!'

The bridge halted. Then, with a sudden splash of light into my exhausted eyes from high up under the gridiron, the pot-bellied lamps were exposed and then concealed again and a crudely daubed canvas flat descended and stood on a slant. 'The watchman's hut . . .' I thought, confusing the geometry of the stage, feeling nervous and trying to figure out how all this would look when they built the real bridge instead of a rough mock-up put together out of the first items that came to hand from other plays. Goggle-eyed floodlights lit up in the wings and down below the stage was bathed in a warm, living wave of light. 'He's put on the footlights . . .'

I squinted in the darkness at the figure that was striding decisively towards the director's table.

'Romanus is coming, that means something's going to happen . . .' I thought, shielding my eyes against the lamp with one hand.

And indeed, only a few moments later a forked beard appeared above me and there were the eyes of the conductor, Romanus, glowing in the dark. There was an anniversary badge with the letters 'IT' glittering in Romanus's buttonhole.

'*Se non e vero, e ben trovato,** and perhaps even more than that!' Romanus began as usual, with his eyes rolling and blazing like the eyes of a wolf in the steppe. Romanus was seeking a victim and, not having found one, he sat beside me.

'How do you like it? Eh?' he asked me, screwing up his eyes.

'He'll draw me in now, draw me into conversation . . .' I thought, squirming there beside the lamp.

'No, please, I beg you, do tell me your opinion,' said Romanus, piercing me through and through with his glance. 'It is all the more interesting because you are a writer and cannot be indifferent to the outrages that are committed here.'

'He does that so deftly . . .' I thought, feeling so miserable that my body started to itch.

'Hit the leader of the orchestra, and a woman too, in the back with a trombone?' Romanus asked with passion. 'Oh no, sir! That's not on! In thirty-five years on the stage I've never

---

* If this is not true, then it is well said (Italian)

seen such a thing happen. Does Strizh think that musicians are pigs and they can be herded into a pen? I wonder, how does that look from the writer's point of view?'

I could not remain silent any longer.

'What's happened?'

That was just what Romanus had been waiting for. In a sonorous voice, trying to make sure the workers would hear, Romanus told me that Strizh had shoved the musicians into the side-pocket of the stage, where it was absolutely impossible to play for the following reasons: first, it was cramped; second, it was dark; third, not a single sound could be heard in the hall; and fourth, there was nowhere for him to stand and the musicians could not see him.

'Of course, there are some people,' Romanus declared loudly, 'who have no more idea about music than certain animals . . .'

'Damn you to hell!' I thought.

'. . . have about certain fruits!'[47]

Romanus's efforts were crowned with success; there was the sound of sniggering from the electrical control booth and a head emerged from it.

'Of course, people like that shouldn't be directing plays, they should be selling kvass outside the Novodevichy Cemetery!' Romanus proclaimed.

The sniggering was repeated.

It then emerged that the outrages committed by Strizh had had serious consequences. In the darkness the trombonist had struck the leader of the orchestra, Anna Anufrievna Denzhina, in the back with his trombone so hard that . . .

'The X-ray will show what will come of it!'

Romanus added that the place for breaking people's ribs was not the theatre but the beer hall, where, as it happened, certain people had acquired their artistic education.

The exultant face of an electrician loomed above the opening of the booth, his mouth contorted in laughter.

But Romanus declared that the matter would not end there. He had instructed Anna Anufrievna on what to do. Thank God, we live in the Soviet state, Romanus reminded me, you can't go around breaking the ribs of trade-union members. He had instructed Anna Anufrievna to submit a complaint to the local committee.

'Of course, I can see in your eyes,' Romanus continued, 'that you are not entirely convinced that our renowned chairman of the local committee is quite as conversant with music as Rimsky-Korsakov or Schubert.'

'What a jerk!' I thought.

'Oh, come now!' I said, trying to speak sternly.

'Oh no, let us speak frankly!' exclaimed Romanus, squeezing my hand. 'You are a writer! And you understand perfectly well that Mitya Malokroshechny, even if he were twenty times a chairman, couldn't tell the difference between an oboe and a cello or between a Bach fugue and the *Hallelujah* foxtrot.'

Then Romanus expressed his delight that it was a good thing at least that his closest friend . . .

'. . . and drinking partner! . . .'

The tenor sniggering in the electrical control booth was joined by a hoarse bass. Now there were two heads exulting above the opening.

. . . Anton Kaloshin apparently helped Malokroshechny to understand artistic matters. And that, by the way, was not surprising, since before he worked in the theatre Anton had been in a fire brigade, where he played the trumpet. And if it were not for Anton, Romanus assured me that a certain director would quite easily have confused the overture to *Ruslan and Ludmila*[48] with a perfectly ordinary funeral chant!

'This man is dangerous, I thought,' looking at Romanus, 'seriously dangerous. There is no way to fight him!'

If it were not for Kaloshin, of course, in our theatre they could have forced a musician to play hanging upside down by his feet from the detachable floodlight, since Ivan Vasilievich never appeared there, but even so the theatre would have to pay Anna Anufrievna for her crushed ribs. And Romanus had advised her to pay a visit to the union and find out what view was taken there of matters of which one really could say: '*Se non e vero, e ben trovato*, and perhaps even more than that!'

I heard soft footfalls behind me, liberation was approaching.

There was Andrei Andreevich standing by the table. Andrei

Andreevich was first assistant director in the theatre and he was managing the production of *Black Snow*.

Andrei Andreevich was a stout, solid man with blond hair, about forty years old, with lively eyes that expressed a wealth of experience. He knew his job well, and this job was a difficult one.

In honour of May, Andrei Andreevich was not wearing his usual dark suit and high brown shoes but a blue satin shirt and yellowish canvas slippers. He had approached the table with the folder he always carried under his arm.

Romanus's eyes flared up even more brightly, and before Andrei Andreevich could even arrange the folder under the lamp a scandal had erupted.

It began with Romanus's phrase:

'I categorically protest against the use of violence against musicians and request the things that are going on to be entered in the minutes.'

'What violence?' Andrei Andreevich asked in an official tone of voice, twitching one eyebrow.

'If they put on plays here that are more like operas . . .' Romanus began, then suddenly realized that the author was sitting right there and continued, twisting his face into a smile directed at me: '. . . which is only right, since our author understands the full significance of music in drama! . . . Then . . . I request that the orchestra be given a place where it can play!'

'It has been given a place in the side-pocket,' said Andrei Andreevich, pretending to open his file to deal with some urgent business.

'In the side-pocket? Perhaps the prompter's box might be better? Or the props room?'

'You said it was not possible to play in the hold.'

'In the hold?' Romanus squealed. 'And I say again that it is not. And neither is it possible in the tearoom, for your information.'

'For your information, I know myself that it is not possible to play in the tearoom,' said Andrei Andreevich, and his other eyebrow twitched.

'You know,' Romanus began and, having checked that Strizh

was not yet in the stalls, continued, 'because you are an old hand and you understand art, which cannot be said for a certain director . . .'

'Nonetheless, speak to the director. He checked the sound quality . . .'

'In order to check the sound quality, you have to have some kind of apparatus with which to check it, for instance ears! But if someone has always had cloth . . .'

'I refuse to continue the conversation in this tone,' said Andrei Andreevich and closed his folder.

'What tone? What tone?' Romanus asked, amazed. 'I appeal to the writer, he can confirm my indignation at the way in which our musicians are crippled!'

'Oh, come now . . .' I began, seeing Andrei Andreevich's glance of amazement.

'No, I beg your pardon,' Romanus shouted at Andrei Andreevich. 'If an assistant director whose obligation it is to know the stage like the back of his own hand . . .'

'I'll thank you not to teach me how I ought to know the stage,' said Andrei Andreevich, tearing the lace tie off his folder.

'I have to! I have to!' Romanus hissed with a venomous grin.

'I shall enter what you say in the minutes!' said Andrei Andreevich.

'And I shall be glad if you do!'

'Kindly leave me in peace! You are disrupting the workers at a rehearsal!'

'Be so good as to enter those words too!' Romanus screeched in a falsetto.

'Kindly do not shout!'

'And I ask *you* not to shout!'

'I ask *you* not to shout,' responded Andrei Andreevich, with his eyes glittering, then he suddenly shouted: 'Hey you up there! What are you doing?' and dashed up the steps on to the stage.

Strizh was already hurrying down the aisle, followed by the black silhouettes of the actors.

I remember the beginning of the scandal with Strizh.

Romanus hurried to meet him, took him by the arm and said: 'Foma! I know that you appreciate music and it's not your fault, but I request and demand that your assistant must not be allowed to humiliate the musicians!'

'You up there!' Andrei Andreevich shouted on the stage. 'Where's Bobylev?'

'Bobylev's at lunch,' a faint voice announced from the sky.

The actors surrounded Romanus and Strizh in a closed ring. It was hot, it was May. Hundreds of times these people, whose faces now appeared mysterious in the gloom above the lamp-shade, had daubed themselves with paint, transformed themselves, become excited and become exhausted ... During the season they had grown tired, become nervous and capricious, joked and teased each other. Romanus provided them with immensely enjoyable entertainment.

Tall, blue-eyed Skavronsky rubbed his hands gleefully and muttered:

'Right, right, right ... Come on. God's truth! You tell him all about it, Oscar!'

The result was only what was to be expected.

'Will you please not shout at me!' Strizh suddenly roared, and slammed the play down on the table.

'You're the one who's shouting!' squealed Romanus.

'That's right! God's truth!' Skavronsky said merrily, urging on first Romanus: 'That's right, Oscar! Our ribs are more important to us than these shows!' – and then Strizh: 'Why are actors any worse than musicians? You note that fact, Foma!'

'I'd like some kvass right now,' Elagin said with a yawn, 'not a rehearsal ... When's this squabbling ever going to end?'

The squabbling continued for a while, with loud shouts emerging from the circle enclosing the lamp and the smoke rising upwards.

But I was no longer interested in the squabble. I stood by the footlights, rubbing my sweaty forehead as I watched the artist from the model room, Aurora Gossier, walking round the turn-table with a measuring rod and applying it to the floor. Gossier's face was calm and a little sad, her lips were pursed. Her light hair alternately blazed up, as if it had been set on fire, as she leaned down to the edge of the footlights, and then dimmed so that it looked like ash. And I was thinking how everything that was happening right now, everything that was dragging out so painfully, all of it would be brought to a conclusion . . .

Meanwhile the squabble came to an end.

'Come on now, lads! Get on with it!' shouted Strizh. 'We're wasting time!'

Patrikeev, Vladychinsky and Skravonsky were already walking around onstage between the prop-hands. Romanus also moved out on to the stage. His appearance was not entirely without consequence. He walked up to Vladychinsky and asked him anxiously whether he, Vladychinksy, did not feel that Patrikeev was overdoing the buffoonery far too much, with the result that the audience would laugh at the very moment when Vladychinksy had a most important line: 'And where would you have me go? I am alone, I am ill . . .'

Vladychinsky turned as pale as death, and a moment later the actors and the workers and the prop-men were lined up at the footlights, listening to the old enemies Vladychinsky and Patrikeev arguing. Vladychinsky, an athletically built man who was naturally pale and now even paler in his spite, squeezed his hands into fists and did not look at Patrikeev as he said, trying to make his powerful voice sound terrifying:

'I shall look into this matter! It's high time someone paid some attention to the circus performers who act in clichés and disgrace the name of the theatre!'

The comic actor Patrikeev, who played funny young men on the stage and in real life was exceptionally agile, nimble and solidly built, tried to adopt an air that was simultaneously contemptuous and frightening, which gave his eyes an expression of sadness and his face one of physical pain, as he replied in a hoarse voice:

'Please take care what you say! I am an actor of the Independent Theatre and not a cinema hack, like you!'

Romanus was standing in one of the wings with his eyes glittering in satisfaction as the voices of the two men arguing drowned out Strizh's voice as he shouted from his armchair:

'Stop that this moment! Andrei Andreevich! Sound the alarm bells for Stroev! Where is he? You're ruining my production plan!'

With a practised hand Andrei Andreevich pressed the button on the board at the assistant director's post and somewhere far away behind the wings, and in the buffet, and in the foyer bells began jangling in shrill alarm.

Just at that moment Stroev, who had got carried away while chatting in Toropetskaya's antechamber, was jumping over every second step as he hurried on his way to the auditorium. He emerged on to the stage not from the hall but from the side, through the gates that led on to the stage, made his way across to the assistant director's post and from there to the footlights, with the spurs on his civilian shoes jingling quietly, and stopped, artfully trying to appear as if he had been standing there for a long time.

'Where's Stroev?' howled Strizh. 'Ring for him, ring! I demand an end to this argument!'

'I am ringing!' replied Andrei Andreevich. Then he turned round and caught sight of Stroev. 'I'm sounding the bells for you!' Andrei Andreevich said severely, and the ringing in the theatre immediately stopped.

'For me?' Stroev responded. 'Why would I need the alarm bell? I've been here for ten minutes already, if not a quarter of an hour . . . at the very least . . . *Mama . . . mia . . .*' he coughed to clear his throat.

Andrei Andreevich filled his lungs with air, but he said nothing and merely gave Stroev a meaningful look. He used the air to shout:

'Outsiders please leave the stage! We're starting!'

Everything settled down, the prop-men left, the actors moved to their various places. In the wings Romanus whispered his congratulations to Patrikeev on his courageous and correct objections to Vladychinsky, who ought to have been told what was what a long time ago.

## CHAPTER 16

### *A Successful Marriage*

June was even hotter than May.

I remember that, but in some amazing manner everything else has become blurred in my memory. Certain fragments, however, have been preserved. For instance, I recall Drykin's cab at the entrance to the theatre, with Drykin himself on the coach-box in a blue padded caftan, and the surprised faces of the motorists driving past his cab.

After that I recall a large hall with chairs laid out in it untidily and actors sitting on these chairs. Sitting at a baize-covered table were Ivan Vasilievich, Foma Strizh and I.

I had got to know Ivan Vasilievich better during this period and I can say that I remember the whole time as being very tense. This was the result of my having directed all my efforts towards producing a good impression on Ivan Vasilievich, and that caused me a great deal of trouble.

Every second day I gave my grey suit to Dusya to iron and paid her ten roubles promptly every time.

I found an alley in which there was a fragile little room that seemed to have been built out of cardboard and there I bought twenty starched collars from a sturdy-looking man with two diamond rings on his fingers, and each day as I set out for the theatre I put on a fresh one. I also bought, not in an alley but in a state department store, six shirts, four white, one with lilac stripes and one with blue checks, as well as eight neckties of various colours. From a man who wore no cap regardless of the weather and sat in a corner in the centre of the city beside a counter with bootlaces hanging on it, I bought two jars of light-brown boot cream and cleaned my brown shoes with it in the morning, borrowing a brush from Dusya, and afterwards polishing up my shoes with the hem of my dressing gown.

These incredible, monstrous expenditures led to my writing a little story entitled 'The Flea' in only two nights and, during the time when I was not occupied by rehearsals, carrying this story in my pocket round the offices of the weekly magazines and newspapers, trying to sell it. I began with the *Shipping Herald*, where they liked the story but refused to publish it on the perfectly reasonable grounds that it had nothing whatever to do with rivers or steamships. The tale of how I visited these editorial offices and how they refused me would be a long and tedious one. The only thing I recall is that for some reason I was met with hostility everywhere I went. I particularly remember a certain stout man wearing a pince-nez who not only rejected my work decisively but even read me something like a lecture.

'I can feel the winking in your story,' the stout man said, and I saw that he was looking at me with revulsion.

I must set matters right. The stout man was mistaken. There was no winking in the story, but (I can say this now) it must be admitted that this story was boring and inept and gave its author away completely; this author could not write stories at all, he lacked the talent for it.

Nonetheless, a miracle occurred. After spending three weeks carrying the story around in my pocket and visiting Varvarka Street, Vozdvizhenka Street, the Clear Ponds Boulevard, Strastny Boulevard and even, I recall, Pliushchikha Street I unexpectedly sold my composition on Zlatoustinsky Lane on Myasnitskaya Street, if I am not mistaken, on the fifth floor, to some man with a large birthmark on his cheek.

Having received the money and plugged the appalling breach, I returned to the theatre, without which I could no longer live, as a morphine addict cannot without morphine.

I must admit, with a heavy heart, that all my efforts were in vain and even, to my horror, produced the opposite of the desired effect. With literally every day that passed Ivan Vasilievich liked me less and less.

It would be naive to think that I invested all my anticipation in my brown shoes that reflected the spring sunshine. No! This was a cunning, complex manoeuvre that included, for instance, the device of pronouncing speeches in a voice that was quiet, deep and sincere. This voice was combined with a gaze that was direct, clear and honest, with a gentle smile on my lips (by no means obsequious, but open-hearted). I was ideally coiffeured, shaved so closely that when I passed the back of my hand over my cheek not the slightest roughness could be felt; the opinions I stated were brief, intelligent and astoundingly well-informed, but they got me nowhere. At first Ivan Vasilievich smiled when he met me, then he started smiling less and less often and finally stopped smiling altogether.

Then I began rehearsing at night. I took a little mirror, sat in front of it so that I was reflected in it and began saying:

'Ivan Vasilievich! You see what the problem is: in my opinion it is not possible to use a dagger . . .'

And everything could not possibly have been better. A decorous, modest smile hovered on my lips, my eyes gazed out of the mirror directly and intelligently, my forehead was unwrinkled, my parting was like a white thread running across my black head. All this could not possibly fail to produce a result, and yet everything went from worse to worse. I wore myself out, lost weight and began neglecting my appearance slightly. I even went so far as to put on the same collar twice.

One night I decided to check things – I pronounced my monologue without looking in the mirror, and then cast a furtive, squinting glance into it – and was horrified.

Gazing out at me from the mirror was a face with a wrinkled forehead, bared teeth and eyes that betrayed not only anxiety but also ulterior motive. I clutched my head in my hands, realizing that the mirror had misled and deceived me, and I flung it to the floor. A triangular piece sprang out of it. They say it's a very bad sign if a mirror breaks. Then what can be said of the madman who deliberately breaks his own mirror?

'You fool, you fool,' I exclaimed, and since I was hoarse, it sounded to me as if a crow had cawed in the quiet of the night – so, I was fine just as long as I watched myself in the mirror, but as soon as I took it away my control disappeared and my face was controlled by my thought and . . . ah, damnation!

I have no doubt that if my memoir should fall into anyone's hands it will not produce a very pleasant impression on the reader. He will believe that he is in the company of a cunning, duplicitous individual who attempted for certain self-serving reasons to produce a good impression on Ivan Vasilievich.

Do not be in any haste to judge. I will tell you now what this self-interest consisted of. Ivan Vasilievich strove stubbornly and insistently to banish from the play the very scene in which Bakhtin (Bekhteev) shot himself, in which the moon shone and someone played the accordion. But I knew, I had seen, that in that case the play would cease to exist. And it had to exist, because I knew that it was the truth. The descriptions I had been given of Ivan Vasilievich had been only too clear. And of course, they were not even necessary. I had studied him and understood him during the very first days of our acquaintance and I knew that any struggle against Ivan Vasilievich was impossible. There was only one approach left open to me: to get him to listen to me. Naturally, for that to happen he needed to see an agreeable individual before him. That was why I had been sitting with the mirror. I had been trying to save the shot, I had wanted people to hear the terrible song of the accordion on the bridge as the patch of blood spread across the snow in the moonlight. I had wanted people to see my black snow. That was all that I wanted.

And then the crow cawed again.

'You fool! You failed to understand the most important thing of all! How can you get someone to like you if you don't like him? What are you thinking of? That you can dupe someone? That you can hold something against him and still try to make him feel a liking for you? But that will never work. No matter how much you pose in front of the mirror.'

I didn't like Ivan Vasilievich. I'd taken a dislike to Aunty Nastasya Ivanovna as well and an extreme dislike to Ludmila Silvestrovna. And people can sense that!

Drykin's cab signified that Ivan Vasilievich was coming to the theatre for the rehearsals of *Black Snow*.

Every day at twelve Panin came trotting into the dark stalls, smiling in terror with a pair of galoshes in his hands. He was followed by Avgusta Avdeevna, carrying a check rug. Avgusta Avdeevna was followed by Ludmila Silvestrovna, carrying a thick exercise book and a little lace handkerchief.

In the stalls Ivan Vasilievich put on his galoshes and seated himself at the director's table. Avgusta Avdeevna threw the rug across Ivan Vasilievich's shoulders and on the stage the rehearsal began.

During this rehearsal Ludmila Silvestrovna, having settled not far away from the director's table, made notes of some kind in the exercise book and uttered occasional exclamations of admiration – in a low voice.

The time has now arrived for explanations. The reason for the dislike that I attempted to conceal in such a foolish manner did not lie in the rug, or the galoshes, or even Ludmila Silvestrovna, but in the fact that Ivan Vasilievich, who had been directing plays for fifty-five years, had invented a famous theory, which was generally acknowledged to be brilliant, about how an actor ought to prepare his role.[49]

Not for a moment did I doubt that the theory was genuinely brilliant, but I was driven to despair by the application of the theory in practice.

I would wager my head that if I had brought some fresh person into a rehearsal from anywhere else he would have been utterly astounded.

In my play Patrikeev was playing the role of a petty government official in love with a woman who did not reciprocate his feelings.

The part was a comic one, and Patrikeev himself played with exceptional humour and better with every day that passed. He was so good that I began feeling as if he were not Patrikeev at all but the actual official that I had invented. As if Patrikeev had existed before this bureaucrat did and through some miracle I had discovered him.

From the moment that Drykin's cab appeared outside the theatre and Ivan Vasilievich was wrapped up in his rug the work began, and it began with Patrikeev.

'Now then, let us begin,' said Ivan Vasilievich.

A reverent silence fell in the stalls, and the anxious Patrikeev (his agitation was expressed in the fact that his eyes became tearful) acted out the scene of his declaration of love with the actress.

'Well now,' said Ivan Vasilievich, his eyes glittering through the lenses of his lorgnette, 'that's no good at all.'

I gasped somewhere deep in my soul and felt something snap in my stomach. I could not imagine how the scene could have been played even the tiniest bit better than Patrikeev had played it. 'And if he can manage that,' I thought, glancing respectfully at Ivan Vasilievich, 'then I'll say that he really is a genius.'

'That's no good at all,' repeated Ivan Vasilievich. 'What was that? Some kind of cheap tricks and unadulterated falsehood. What does he feel for this woman?'

'He loves her, Ivan Vasilievich! Ah, how he loves her!' exclaimed Foma Strizh, who had followed the entire scene.

'Well,' responded Ivan Vasilievich, turning once again to Patrikeev. 'Have you thought about what ardent love is?'

In reply Patrikeev wheezed something from the stage, but it was impossible to tell exactly what.

'Ardent love,' continued Ivan Vasilievich, 'is expressed in a man's willingness to do anything for his beloved,' and he ordered: 'Bring me a bicycle!'

Strizh was ecstatic at Ivan Vasilievich's command and he shouted excitedly:

'Hey, prop-men! A bicycle!'

A prop-man rolled an old bicycle with the paint peeling off its frame out on to the stage. Patrikeev looked at it weepily.

'A man in love does everything for his beloved,' Ivan Vasilievich declared loudly, 'eats, drinks, walks, rides . . .'

With bated breath I glanced curiously into Ludmila Silvestrovna's exercise book bound in oilcloth and saw that she was writing in a childish hand: 'A man in love does everything for his beloved . . .'

'. . . and so, please be so good as to take a ride on a bicycle for the girl that you love,' Ivan Vasilievich ordered and ate a mint lozenge.

My eyes were glued to the stage. Patrikeev clambered up on to the machine, the actress playing the part of his beloved sat in an armchair, pressing an immense lacquered handbag against her stomach. Patrikeev pushed on the pedals and set off uncertainly around the armchair, squinting with one eye at the prompter's box, into which he was afraid of falling, and with the other at the actress.

The people in the hall began to smile.

'Quite wrong,' Ivan Vasilievich remarked when Patrikeev stopped. 'Why were you gaping at the prop-man? Are you riding for him?'

Patrikeev set off again, this time squinting with both eyes at the actress, failed to turn and rode off into the wings.

When he was brought back, leading the bicycle by the handle-bars, Ivan Vasilievich declared this ride to be wrong too and Patrikeev set off for a third time, with his head turned towards the actress.

'Terrible!' Ivan Vasilievich said with bitter reproach. 'Your muscles are tense, you don't trust yourself. Let your muscles go, relax them. Your head's unnatural, I don't believe your head.'

Patrikeev rode round with his head lowered, peering out from under his eyebrows.

'An empty ride, you're riding empty, not full of your beloved.'

And Patrikeev started riding again. He rode round once, with one hand on his hip, gazing dashingly at his beloved. Twirling the handlebars with one hand, he turned sharply and rode straight into the actress, marking her skirt with his dirty tyre and making her cry out in fright. Ludmila Silvestrovna also cried out in the stalls. After enquiring if the actress had been hurt and whether she required any medical assistance, and having ascertained that there was no cause for concern, Ivan Vasilievich set Patrikeev off round his circle once again and the actor rode it many times until Ivan Vasilievich finally enquired if he were tired. Patrikeev replied that he was not tired, but Ivan Vasilievich said he could see that Patrikeev was, and the actor was released.

Patrikeev was replaced by a group of guests. I went out to the buffet for a smoke and when I returned I saw that the actress's handbag was lying on the floor and she was sitting with her hands tucked underneath her, as were her three male guests and one female guest, that same Veshnyakova who had been mentioned in the letter from India. They were all trying to pronounce the phrases that were required by the action of the play at that particular point, but were unable to make any progress, because every time Ivan Vasilievich stopped the person who had just said something to explain what was wrong with it. The difficulties of the guests, and also of Patrikeev's beloved, the heroine of the play, were exacerbated by the fact that at every moment they wanted to pull their hands out from under them to make a gesture.

Seeing my astonishment, Strizh explained to me in a whisper that the actors had deliberately been deprived of their hands by Ivan Vasilievich in order to accustom them to putting the meaning into the words and not helping themselves with their hands.

I went home from the rehearsal full of impressions of new and remarkable things and thinking as follows:

'Yes, this is all astonishing. But it is only astonishing because I am an ignoramus in these matters. Every art has its own laws, mysteries and methods. For instance, a savage would think it funny and strange that anyone should scrub his teeth with a brush, filling his mouth with chalk. To the uninitiated it appears strange that instead of proceeding directly to operate on his patient, a doctor first does all sorts of strange things to him, for instance, he takes blood for analysis and so on . . .'

Above all, I was longing to see the conclusion of the business with the bicycle at the next rehearsal, that is, to see if Patrikeev would manage to ride it 'for her'.

However, the next day no one so much as mentioned the bicycle and I saw other, equally astonishing things. This time Patrikeev had to present his beloved with a bouquet. We started with this at twelve and continued until four.

And Patrikeev was not the only one who presented the bouquet, everybody did it in turn: Elagin, who was playing a general, and even Adalbert, who was playing the part of the leader of a gang of bandits. I was extremely astonished by this, but once again Foma reassured me by explaining that Ivan Vasilievich was, as always, acting extremely wisely by teaching everybody some stage technique all at once. Indeed, Ivan Vasilievich accompanied the lesson with interesting and instructive stories about how bouquets should be presented to ladies and how various people had presented them. This was when I learned that the people who had done it best were the aforementioned

Komarovsky-Billancourt (Ludmila Silvestrovna exclaimed, disrupting the flow of the rehearsal: 'Ah yes, yes, Ivan Vasilievich, I can't forget it!') and an Italian baritone whom Ivan Vasilievich had known in Milan in 1889.

Not being acquainted with that baritone, I can only say that the person who presented the bouquet better than anyone else was Ivan Vasilievich himself. He became enthused, walked out on to the stage and showed us about thirteen times how this welcome gift should be given. In fact I began to be convinced that Ivan Vasilievich was a remarkable and genuinely brilliant actor.

The following day I was late for the rehearsal and when I arrived I saw Olga Sergeevna (the actress playing the heroine) and Veshnyakova (a guest) and Elagin and Vladychinsky and Adalbert and several people I did not know all sitting beside each other on chairs on the stage and, at Ivan Vasilievich's command of 'one, two, three', taking invisible wallets out of their pockets, counting invisible money in them and putting them away again.

When this exercise was over (the reason for it, as I realized, was that in this scene Patrikeev counted his money) another exercise began. The whole crowd of people was called up on to the stage by Andrei Andreevich, where they sat in chairs and began writing letters with invisible pens on invisible sheets of paper on invisible tables and sealing them (Patrikeev once again!). The whole point of the trick was that it had to be a love letter.

This exercise was distinguished by a misunderstanding, in that a prop-man was accidentally included among the letter-writers.

Ivan Vasilievich, who was encouraging those who had gone up on the stage and was not very familiar with the new people who had joined the support staff that year, involved a young, curly-headed prop-man who was loitering at the edge of the stage in the writing of the invisible letter.

'And what about you?' Ivan Vasilievich shouted at him. 'Do I have to send you a separate invitation?'

The prop-man sat down on his chair and began writing in

the air and spitting on his fingers like everybody else. In my own opinion he did this no worse than the others, but he smiled as if he were embarrassed and was red in the face.

This provoked a cry from Ivan Vasilievich:

'Who's that merry fellow at the edge? What's his name? Perhaps he wants to join the circus? What sort of tomfoolery is that?'

'He's a prop-man, Ivan Vasilievich. A prop-man!' groaned Foma, and Ivan Vasilievich fell silent and the prop-man was allowed to leave in peace.

And then the days passed in unceasing labours. I saw a great many things. I saw a crowd of actors on the stage, led by Ludmila Silvestrovna (who, as it happens, was not taking part in the play), running around shouting and pressing their faces to invisible windows.

The point was that the same scene with the bouquet and the letter included a part in which my heroine ran over to a window when she saw the glow of a fire through it in the distance.

This provided the pretext for a large exercise. The exercise expanded incredibly and, I must say quite frankly, plunged me into a most gloomy frame of mind.

Ivan Vasilievich, whose theory included, as it happens, the discovery that the text of a play plays no part at all in rehearsals and that the characters in a play should be created by playing to one's own text, ordered everyone to experience the glow of this fire.

The result was that everyone who ran towards the window shouted whatever he thought he ought to shout.

'Ah, my God, my God!' most of them cried.

'Where's the fire? What's happening?' exclaimed Adalbert.

I heard male and female voices shouting:

'Save yourselves! Where's the water? Eliseev's shop's[50] on fire! (God only knows what that was about!) Save us! Save the children! It's an explosion! Call the fire brigade! We're done for!'

Rising above all this uproar was the screeching voice of Ludmila Silvestrovna, who was shouting some absolute nonsense or other:

'O my God! Oh, Almighty God! What will happen to my trunks? And the diamonds, my diamonds!'

With a gaze as dark as a storm cloud I watched as Ludmila Silvestrovna wrung her hands and thought how the only words that my heroine pronounced were:

'Look ... a fire ...' and she pronounced them splendidly. I was not at all interested in waiting until Ludmila Silvestrovna had learned how to experience the glow of this fire, when she was not taking part in the play. Her wild cries about some trunks that had nothing to do with the play annoyed me so much that my face started twitching.

By the end of the third week of exercises with Ivan Vasilievich I was overcome by despair, for which there were three reasons. Firstly, I had made an arithmetical computation that horrified me. We were in our third week of rehearsal and were still rehearsing the same scene. There were seven scenes in the play. So even if we took only three weeks for each scene ...

'Oh, Lord,' I whispered in my sleeplessness, tossing and turning on my divan at home, 'three times seven is twenty-one weeks or five ... yes, five ... or even six months! When will my play appear? The dead season starts in a week, and there won't be any rehearsals until September! Good grief! September, October, November ...'

The night moved swiftly towards dawn. The window was open but there was no coolness in the air. I arrived at rehearsals with a migraine, I turned yellow and haggard. The second reason for my despair was even more serious. I can entrust my secret to this notebook: I had begun to doubt Ivan Vasilievich's theory. Yes! It is a terrible thing to say, but it is true.

Ominous doubts had begun creeping into my heart at the end of the very first week. By the end of the second week I already knew that this theory was clearly not applicable to my play. Not only had Patrikeev not begun to present his bouquet, write his letter and make his declaration of love any better. Oh no! He had become forced and dry and not funny at all. And, most importantly of all, he had caught a head cold out of nowhere.

When I mournfully informed Bombardov about this latter circumstance he laughed and said:

'Well, his cold will soon pass. He is feeling better and yesterday and today he played billiards at the club. When you finish rehearsing this scene his head cold will be gone. Just you wait: others will have colds too. And first of all, I think, Elagin.'

'Ah, damnation!' I exclaimed, beginning to understand.

Bombardov's prophecy proved correct on this occasion also. A day later Elagin disappeared from rehearsals, and Andrei Andreevich made an entry about him in the minutes: 'Released from rehearsal. A head cold.' The same misfortune struck down Adalbert. The same entry in the minutes. After Adalbert it was Veshnyakova. I gritted my teeth, adding another month into my computation, for head colds. But I did not blame Adalbert or Patrikeev. Why, after all, should the leader of the bandits waste his time shouting about a non-existent fire in the fourth scene when he was required for important bandit business in the third scene and then again in the fifth?

And meanwhile Patrikeev supped his beer and played the marker at American pool, and Adalbert rehearsed Schiller's *Bandits*[51] at the club in the Krasnaya Presnya district, where he ran the theatre circle.

Yes, this system was evidently not applicable to my play, in fact it was probably positively harmful. A quarrel between two characters in the fourth act ended with the phrase:

'I'll challenge you to a duel!'

And more than once in the night I threatened to tear my own hands off for having written the accursed phrase three times.

The moment it was uttered Ivan Vasilievich became very lively and ordered rapiers to be brought. I turned pale. And I watched for a long time as Vladychinsky and Blagosvetlov clashed blade against blade, shuddering at the thought that Vladychinsky would put out Blagosvetlov's eye.

Meanwhile Ivan Vasilievich was recounting the story of how Komarovsky-Billancourt fought a sword duel with the son of the mayor of Moscow.

The important thing, however, was not the damned mayor's son but the fact that Ivan Vasilievich began insisting more and more forcefully that I should write a sword-duelling scene into my play.

I reacted to this as if it were a black joke, and you can imagine my feelings when the perfidious and treacherous Strizh told me that he would like the duel scene to be 'drafted' in a week's time. At this point I began to argue but Strizh refused to budge. I was finally reduced to frenzied rage by a note in his director's book: 'There will be a duel here.'

My relations with Strizh were also spoilt.

At night I tossed and turned from side to side in sorrow and indignation. I felt humiliated.

'I don't suppose he would have written any duels in if it were Ostrovsky,' I grumbled, 'and he wouldn't have let Ludmila Silvestrovna yell about her trunks either!'

The dramatist in me was tormented by a petty envy of Ostrovsky. But it all referred, so to speak, to the particular case of my own play. And there was something even more important ... Consumed by my love for the Independent Theatre, pinned to it as I now was like a beetle to a cork, in the evenings I attended the performances there. And then my suspicions finally became absolute certainty. I began reasoning simply: if Ivan Vasilievich's theory were impeccable and through it an actor could be granted the gift of reincarnation, then it was only natural that in every performance every actor should induce an absolute illusion in the viewer. And act so that the viewer would forget that he was watching a stage ...

*(1936–7)*

# Notes

1. *lowly employee ... published*: Bulgakov himself worked for the railwaymen's newspaper *Gudok* (*Siren*) and found it impossible to get his novel *The White Guard* published. See Introduction.

2. *Unto each according to his deeds ...*: A reference to Matthew 16:26–7, where it is promised that Christ will return and reward each of us according to our deeds.

3. *Tsepnoi Bridge*: The Chain Bridge in Kiev was destroyed by the Poles during their brief occupation of the city during the civil war.

4. *Xavier Borisovich Ilchin ... Theatre*: In April 1925, one of the directors of the Moscow Art Theatre's Second Studio sent Bulgakov a note asking him to come to the theatre to discuss 'a number of matters' of possible mutual interest. The director was Boris Ilich Vershilov (1893–1957), the model for Ilchin, who wanted Bulgakov to dramatize his novel *The White Guard*.

5. *an old grand piano ... in this world*: The sense of nostalgia associated with Maksudov's dream reflects the background of *The White Guard*, which draws on the experiences of Bulgakov's own family.

6. *Faust*: From early in his life Bulgakov was very fond of opera and *Faust* (written in 1856–9 by Charles Gounod) was a particular favourite. He could listen to it over and over again.

7. *Ilya Ivanovich Rudolfi*: The character of Rudolfi is based on Isai Lezhnev (1891–1955), publisher of the journal *Russia* (the novel's *Motherland*). See Introduction.

8. *Likospastov*: Based on Bulgakov's friend Yuri Slyozkin (1885–1947), also a writer, whom he met during the civil war and who introduced Bulgakov around Moscow when he first arrived. They fell out after Slyozkin included an unflattering portrait of Bulgakov in his 1925 novel *Stolovaya Gora* (*Table Mountain*).

Slyozkin didn't read *A Dead Man's Memoir* and they rekindled their friendship just before Bulgakov's death.

9.  *Which one ... Lev Nikolaevich*: The Tolstoys alluded to here are Alexei Konstantinovich Tolstoy (1817–75), author of *Prince Serebriany* and numerous verses that were set to music; Pyotr Andreevich Tolstoy (1645–1729), a diplomat and associate of Peter the Great; Ivan Ivanovich Tolstoy (1858–1916), a minister of education, numismatist, archaeologist and vice-president of the Imperial Academy, well known for his reactionary views; Lev Nikolaevich Tolstoy (1828–1910), the author of *War and Peace*. (The author Alexei Tolstoy, a contemporary and acquaintance of Bulgakov (see n. 15), is not included in this list.)

10. *Glavlit*: The Soviet organization responsible for literary censorship.

11. *Daybreak or Dawn*: A reference to two literary journals of the 1920s, *Krasnaya nov* (*Red Virgin Soil*) and *Novy mir* (*New World*).

12. *Rvatsky*: The character of Makar Rvatsky is apparently based on the publisher Zakhar Leontievich Kagansky, who emigrated from Russia with the publication rights to several manuscripts by Russian writers, including Bulgakov. Kagansky published the works but did not pay the authors. See Introduction.

13. *Averchenko*: Arkadii Timofeevich Averchenko (1881–1925), a well-known satirist, dramatist and theatre critic.

14. *New-Year-tree*: In Russia, fir trees are decorated with toys, fruit, etc. in honour of the New Year, not the religious feast of Christmas.

15. *Bondarevsky... Agapyonov*: The character of Izmail Alexandrovich Bondarevsky is based on Alexei Tolstoy (1883–1945), a Russian writer, who emigrated in 1919 to Paris and then moved to Berlin. In 1922, he became the head of the literary supplement to the newspaper *Nakanunie* (*On the Eve*), which was sold in Russia and in which Bulgakov published several stories. Alexei Tolstoy returned to the Soviet Union in 1923. The character of Egor Agapyonov is based on Boris Pilnyak (Boris Andreevich Vogau, 1894–?1937), a Russian author of novels and short stories often critical of the Soviet regime. He also wrote a travelogue of a 1931 visit to the United States. He disappeared in 1937 and it is assumed that he was executed.

16. Chapter 7 was originally entitled 'The Finger of Fate', but this was crossed out in the manuscript.

17. *I realized that I was writing a play*: Bulgakov's own play *The*

Days of the Turbins was based on his novel The White Guard.
It had its premiere at the Moscow Art Theatre in 1926. See
Introduction.

18.  Ivan Vasilievich: The character of Ivan Vasilievich, 'the old man',
     is based on Stanislavsky (Konstantin Sergeevich Alexeev, 1863–
     1938), co-founder with Vladimir Nemirovich-Danchenko of the
     Moscow Art Theatre.

19.  Sarah Bernhardt: A famous French actress (1844–1923).

20.  Molière: Jean-Baptiste Poquelin (1622–73), a great French play-
     wright. From 1658, a protégé of Louis XIV in Paris, he produced
     performances of various kinds for the amusement of the court.
     He is best known for plays exposing social vices through typical
     characters, such as Le Médecin malgré lui (1666), Le Bourgeois
     gentilhomme (1670) and Le Malade imaginaire (1673).

21.  Nero: AD 37–68, Emperor of Rome from the year AD 54. He
     was renowned for his cruelty and his love of the theatre.

22.  Griboedov: Alexander Sergeevich Griboedov (1795–1829), a
     Russian author, whose plays include Woe from Wit, a classic
     text of Russian literature. He was a friend of Pushkin.

23.  Givochini... Shchepkin: Vasily Ignatievich Givochini (1805–74),
     a Russian comic actor; Carlo Goldoni (1707–93), an Italian
     dramatist, author of more than 250 plays and founder of the
     Italian school of comedy; Pierre Beaumarchais (1732–99), a
     French dramatist (Rossini's opera The Barber of Seville and
     Mozart's Marriage of Figaro were based on his plays); Vladimir
     Vasilievich Stasov (1824–1906), a well-known music critic
     and historian; Mikhail Semenovich Shchepkin (1788–1863), a
     famous Russian actor, a former serf.

24.  dinner at Testov's: The Testov trading house owned a string of
     restaurants that were popular with the more well-to-do.

25.  Aristarkh Platonovich: Based on Vladimir Ivanovich Nemirovich-
     Danchenko (1858–1943), a theatre director, writer and teacher.
     He and Stanislavsky jointly founded the Moscow Art Theatre in
     1898.

26.  Ostrovsky: Alexander Nikolaevich Ostrovsky (1823–86), a great
     Russian dramatist, whose works, especially in the early period,
     depicted the life of the Russian merchantry. He founded Mos-
     cow's Maly Theatre.

27.  The Power of Darkness: A play written by Leo Tolstoy in 1886,
     banned by the censor because of its atmosphere of dismal hope-
     lessness. The ban was lifted in 1895.

28.  Karatygin... Euripides: Vasily Andreevich Karatygin (1802–53),

a famous actor of heroic and tragic roles at the Alexandrinsky
Theatre in St Petersburg; Maria Taglioni (1804–84), an Italian
ballerina, who toured many cities in Europe; Catherine the Great
(Catherine II), Empress of Russia (1762–96); Enrico Caruso
(1873–1921), a famous Italian tenor; Feofan Prokopovich
(1681–1736), a Russian churchman and statesman, who was
also a writer; Igor Severyanin (Igor Vasilievich Lotarev, 1887–
1941), a Russian poet popular in the early twentieth century;
Mattia Battistini (1856–1928), a famous Italian baritone; Euripides (480–406 BC), an ancient Greek poet and dramatist.

29. *RSFSR . . . Ukrainian SSR*: The Russian Soviet Federative Socialist Republic was established in November 1917 and adopted
the first Soviet Constitution in July 1918. The Ukrainian Soviet
Socialist Republic was created on 25 December 1917. They both
became part of the Soviet Union on its creation in 1922.

30. *Aeschylus . . . Orleans*: Aeschylus (525–456 BC), one of the three
great Ancient Greek tragedians (with Sophocles and Euripides),
often regarded as the founder of tragedy; *Agamemnon*, one of
his seven surviving plays; Sophocles (495–406 BC), an Ancient
Greek tragedian, seven of whose plays survive complete; Lope
de Vega (Félix Lope de Vega y Carpio, 1562–1635), a Spanish
playwright and poet, author of more than 1,500 plays, of which
425 survive; William Shakespeare (1564–1616), playwright and
poet, regarded as the greatest writer in the English language;
Johann Christoph Friedrich von Schiller (1759–1805), a great
German poet, philosopher, historian and dramatist, who wrote
*The Maid of Orleans* in 1801.

31. *Poliksena Toropetskaya*: Based on Bulgakov's sister-in-law
Olga Sergeevna Bolshanskaya (the sister of his wife Elena Sergeevna Shilovskaya), who worked as Nemirovich-Danchenko's
secretary.

32. *Turgenev*: Ivan Sergeevich Turgenev (1818–83), a major Russian
novelist and playwright, who famously quarrelled with Tolstoy
and was caricatured by Dostoevsky. He spent much of his life
abroad.

33. *Slavyansky Bazaar*: A famous hotel and restaurant in prerevolu-
tionary Moscow.

34. *Pisemsky . . . Leskov*: Alexei Feofilaktovich Pisemsky (1821–81),
a novelist and playwright, who depicted the life of the peasantry;
Dmitry Vasilievich Grigorovich (1822–99), the author of novels
and stories dealing with peasant life; Nikolai Semenovich Leskov
(1831–95), a journalist and writer of stories and novels in which

he made wide use of colloquial and peasant speech (he also used the pseudonym M. Stebnitsky).

35. *Gogol ... Dead Souls*: *Dead Souls* (1842) is an acknowledged masterpiece by Nikolai Vasilievich Gogol (1809–52), a great Russian writer of Ukrainian origin. His later years were marked by tormented religious searching. In February 1852, he burned the incomplete second part of the novel, together with several other manuscripts, and died nine days later.

36. *Stepan Razin*: A play presumably based on the life of Stepan (Stenka) Razin (1630–71), a Cossack leader who led a major rebellion against the authority of the Tsar and his nobles in the south of Russia.

37. *The Dowryless Bride*: An 1878 play by Alexander Ostrovsky.

38. *Don Carlos*: Friedrich Schiller completed his drama *Don Carlos, Infante of Spain* in 1787.

39. *The Fruits of Enlightenment*: A play by Leo Tolstoy, Stanislavsky's first independent theatrical production in 1891. It impressed Vladimir Nemirovich-Danchenko, who later co-founded the Moscow Art Theatre with Stanislavsky. The theatre prepared a production of the play but Narkompros (the People's Commissariat of Enlightenment) banned it in 1922.

40. *Chernomor*: The wicked sorceror who abducts Ludmila in Pushkin's folktale poem *Ruslan and Ludmila* (see n. 48).

41. *Melpomene*: The Muse of Tragedy in Greek mythology.

42. *Isvestiya*: During the Soviet period, *Isvestiya* (*News*) was the official mouthpiece of the government (with the full title *News of the Soviets of People's Deputies of the USSR*). It began life on 13 March 1917 as *News of the Petrograd Soviet of Workers' Deputies*.

43. *Novodevichy Cemetery*: The Novodevichy (New Maidens') Convent stands in a bend of the Moscow River. It was established in 1524 by Grand Prince Vasily III as part of Moscow's defences. Its New Cemetery, founded in 1898, is the final resting place of many important figures in the arts, including Chekhov and Bulgakov.

44. *Lady MacBeth of Mtsensk*: Originally a novel by Nikolai Leskov (1865).

45. *Evening Moscow*: The daily newspaper *Evening Moscow* first appeared on 6 December 1923. It is still published.

46. Chapter 15 originally had the title 'The Dress Rehearsal', but Bulgakov crossed it out.

47. *no more idea ... certain fruits*: A reference to a Russian saying

about 'knowing as much about something as a pig does about oranges'.

48. *Ruslan and Ludmila*: The title of a retelling of a Russian folktale by Pushkin (1820), which was made into an opera with music by Glinka in 1842.

49. *prepare his role*: Stanislavsky's books on acting actually include *An Actor Prepares*, which forms a trilogy with *Building a Character* and *Creating a Role*. His final book on the subject was *The Method of Physical Actions*.

50. *Eliseev's shop*: A famous grocery store on Moscow's Tverskaya Street (known as Gorky Street for much of the Soviet Period).

51. *Bandits*: Schiller published this drama (also known in English as *The Robbers*) in 1781.

**WAR AND PEACE**
**LEO TOLSTOY**

*'Yes! It's all vanity, it's all an illusion, everything except that infinite sky'*

At a glittering society party in St Petersburg in 1805, conversations are dominated by the prospect of war. Terror swiftly engulfs the country as Napoleon's army marches on Russia, and the lives of three young people are changed forever. The stories of quixotic Pierre, cynical Andrey and impetuous Natasha interweave with a huge cast, from aristocrats and peasants, to soldiers and Napoleon himself. In *War and Peace* (1863–9), Tolstoy entwines grand themes – conflict and love, birth and death, free will and fate – with unforgettable scenes of nineteenth-century Russia, to create a magnificent epic of human life in all its imperfection and grandeur.

Anthony Briggs's superb translation combines stirring, accessible prose with fidelity to Tolstoy's original, while Orlando Figes's afterword discusses the novel's vast scope and depiction of Russian identity. This edition also includes appendices, notes, a list of prominent characters and maps.

'A book that you don't just read, you live' Simon Schama

'A masterpiece ... This new translation is excellent' Antony Beevor

Translated with an introduction and notes by Anthony Briggs
With an afterword by Orlando Figes

# PENGUIN CLASSICS

**THE BEAST WITHIN**
**EMILE ZOLA**

*'He was driven by a single overriding need; he must appease the beast that raged within him'*

Roubaud is consumed by a jealous rage when he discovers a sordid secret about his lovely young wife's past. The only way he can rest is by forcing her to help him murder the man involved, but there is a witness – Jacques Lantier, a fellow railway employee. Jacques, meanwhile, must contend with his own terrible impulses, for every time he sees a woman he feels an overwhelming desire to kill. In the company of Roubaud's wife, Séverine, he finds peace briefly, yet his feelings for her soon bring disastrous consequences. The seventeenth novel in the Rougon-Macquart cycle, *The Beast Within* (1890) is one of Zola's most dark and violent works – a tense thriller of political corruption and a graphic exploration of the criminal mind.

Roger Whitehouse's vivid translation is accompanied by an introduction discussing Zola's depiction of the railways, politics and the legal system and the influence of the studies of criminology and the Jack the Ripper murders on his novel. This edition also includes a chronology, suggestions for further reading and notes.

Translated with an introduction and notes by Roger Whitehouse

# PENGUIN CLASSICS

**THE LOST ESTATE (LE GRAND MEAULNES)**
**HENRI ALAIN-FOURNIER**

*'Meaulnes was everywhere, everything was filled with memories of our adolescence, now ended'*

When Meaulnes first arrives at the local school in Sologne, everyone is captivated by his good looks, daring and charisma. But when he disappears for several days, and returns with tales of a strange party at a mysterious house and a beautiful girl hidden within it, Meaulnes has been changed forever. In his restless search for his Lost Estate and the happiness he found there, Meaulnes, observed by his loyal friend François, may risk losing everything he ever had. Poised between youthful admiration and adult resignation, Alain-Fournier's compelling narrator carries the reader through this evocative and often unbearably moving portrayal of desperate friendship and vanished adolescence.

Robin Buss's major new translation sensitively and accurately renders *Le Grand Meaulnes*'s poetically charged, expressive and deceptively simple style, while the introduction by *New Yorker* writer Adam Gopnik discusses the life of Alain-Fournier, who was killed in the First World War after writing this, his only novel.

'I find its depiction of a golden time and place just as poignant now'  Nick Hornby

Translated by Robin Buss
With an introduction by Adam Gopnik

# PENGUIN CLASSICS

**THE SHOOTING PARTY**
ANTON CHEKHOV

'Why did I marry him? Where were my eyes? Where were my brains?'

*The Shooting Party,* Chekhov's only full-length novel, centres on Olga, the pretty young daughter of a drunken forester on a country estate, and her fateful relationships with the men in her life. Adored by Urbenin, the estate manager, whom she marries to escape the poverty of her home, she is also desired by the dissolute Count Karneyev and by Zinovyev, a magistrate, who knows the secret misery of her marriage. And when an attempt is made on Olga's life in the woods, it seems impossible to discover the perpetrator in an impenetrable web of deceit, lust, loathing and double-dealing. One of Chekhov's earliest experiments in fiction, *The Shooting Party* combines the classic elements of a gripping mystery with a story of corruption, concealed love and fatal jealousy.

Ronald Wilks's new translation of this work is the first in thirty years. It brilliantly captures the immediacy of the dialogue that Chekhov was later to develop into his great dramas. This edition also includes suggestions for further reading and explanatory notes.

Translated and edited by Ronald Wilks

# PENGUIN CLASSICS

## RUSSIAN SHORT STORIES FROM PUSCHKIN TO BUIDA

*'Light's all very well, brothers, but it's not easy to live with'*

From the early nineteenth century to the collapse of the Soviet Union and beyond, the short story has occupied a central place in Russian literature. This collection includes not only well-known classics but also modern masterpieces, many of them previously censored. There are stories by acknowledged giants – Gogol, Tolstoy, Chekhov and Solzhenitsyn – and by equally great writers such as Andrey Platonov who have only recently become known to the English-speaking world. Some stories are tragic, but the volume also includes a great deal of comedy – from Pushkin's subtle wit to Kharms's dark absurdism, from Dostoyevsky's graveyard humour to Teffi's subtle evocations of human stupidity and Zoshchenko's satirical vignettes of everyday life in the decade after the 1917 Revolution.

This new collection of translations includes works only recently rediscovered in Russia. The introduction gives a vivid insight into the history of the Russian short story, while the work of every author is preceded by an individual introduction. This edition also includes notes and a chronology.

Edited by Robert Chandler

# PENGUIN CLASSICS

**RESURRECTION**
LEO TOLSTOY

> 'In the very depths of his heart, he knew that he had behaved so meanly,
> so contemptibly, so cruelly'

Serving on a jury at the trial of a prostitute arrested for murder, Prince Nekhlyudov
is horrified to discover that the accused is a woman he had once loved, seduced and
then abandoned when she was a young servant girl. Racked with guilt at realizing
he was the cause of her ruin, he determines to appeal for her release or give up
his own way of life and follow her. Conceived on an epic scale, *Resurrection*
portrays a vast panorama of Russian life, taking us from the underworld of prison
cells and warders to the palaces of countesses. It is also an angry denunciation of
government, the upper classes, the judicial system and the Church, and a highly
personal statement of Tolstoy's belief in human redemption.

Rosemary Edmonds's fine translation is accompanied by an introduction
discussing how *Resurrection* relates to Tolstoy's own spiritual development and
how the scope and depth of the book are even more ambitious than his other works.

Translated with an introduction by Rosemary Edmonds

# THE STORY OF PENGUIN CLASSICS

**Before 1946** ... 'Classics' are mainly the domain of academics and students; readable editions for everyone else are almost unheard of. This all changes when a little-known classicist, E. V. Rieu, presents Penguin founder Allen Lane with the translation of Homer's *Odyssey* that he has been working on in his spare time.

**1946** Penguin Classics debuts with *The Odyssey*, which promptly sells three million copies. Suddenly, classics are no longer for the privileged few.

**1950s** Rieu, now series editor, turns to professional writers for the best modern, readable translations, including Dorothy L. Sayers's *Inferno* and Robert Graves's unexpurgated *Twelve Caesars*.

**1960s** The Classics are given the distinctive black covers that have remained a constant throughout the life of the series. Rieu retires in 1964, hailing the Penguin Classics list as 'the greatest educative force of the twentieth century.'

**1970s** A new generation of translators swells the Penguin Classics ranks, introducing readers of English to classics of world literature from more than twenty languages. The list grows to encompass more history, philosophy, science, religion and politics.

**1980s** The Penguin American Library launches with titles such as *Uncle Tom's Cabin*, and joins forces with Penguin Classics to provide the most comprehensive library of world literature available from any paperback publisher.

**1990s** The launch of Penguin Audiobooks brings the classics to a listening audience for the first time, and in 1999 the worldwide launch of the Penguin Classics website extends their reach to the global online community.

**The 21st Century** Penguin Classics are completely redesigned for the first time in nearly twenty years. This world-famous series now consists of more than 1300 titles, making the widest range of the best books ever written available to millions – and constantly redefining what makes a 'classic'.

The Odyssey continues ...

*The best books ever written*

PENGUIN CLASSICS

SINCE 1946

Find out more at www.penguinclassics.com